Unit
Betty

Praise for
Edward Marston's
Elizabethan mysteries:

The Queen's Head

"Humor and suspense are cleverly interplayed, but the
novel's best feature is the reality with which the people
and the period are brought to life."
—*Booklist*

The Merry Devils

"A believable, satisfying, mystery, colorfully costumed
and staged, with a bawdy, raffish, and utterly amiable
cast."

—*Publishers Weekly*

The Trip to Jerusalem

"The plot moves briskly as a mystery, [and] the detail
gives the book a fascinating array of colors."
—*Chicago Tribune*

Also by Edward Marston
Published by Fawcett Books:

THE QUEEN'S HEAD
THE MERRY DEVILS
THE TRIP TO JERUSALEM

THE NINE GIANTS

Edward Marston

FAWCETT CREST • NEW YORK

A Fawcett Crest Book
Published by Ballantine Books
Copyright © 1991 by Edward Marston

Library of Congress Catalog Card Number: 91-21758

ISBN 0-449-22128-8

This edition published by arrangement with St. Martin's Press, Inc.

Manufactured in the United States of America

First Ballantine Books Edition: November 1993

To Lady Diane Pearson

The love I dedicate to your Ladyship is without end: whereof this Book is but a superfluous Moiety. The warrant I have of your Honourable disposition, not the worth of my untutored Lines makes it assured of acceptance. What I have done is yours, what I have to doe is yours, being part in all I have, devoted yours. Were my worth greater, my duety would shew greater, meane time, as it is, it is bound to your Ladyship; to whom I wish long life is still lengthned with all happinesse.

The famous Mayor by princely governance
With sword of justice thee ruleth prudently
No lord of Paris, Venice or Florence
In dignity and honour goeth to him nigh.
He is exemplar, lode-star and guy
Principal patron and rose original
Above all mayors as master most worthy
London thou art the flower of cities all.

William Dunbar

Chapter One

LAWRENCE FIRETHORN GAZED DOWN IN HORROR AT THE corpse of his young wife and let out a sigh of utter despair that sent tremors through all who heard it. Swaying over the hapless figure of the child-bride who had been plucked from him on his wedding night, he howled like an animal then held up his hands to heaven in supplication. When no comfort came from above, he was seized with an urge to wreak revenge for the savage murder and he pulled out his dagger to slash wildly at the air. The hopelessness of the gesture made him stand quite still and weep fresh tears of remorse. Then, on impulse, with a suddenness that took everyone by surprise, he turned the point of the dagger on himself and used brute power to plunge it deep into his own breast. Firethorn shuddered and fell to one knee. Though fading with each second, he managed to deliver a speech of sixteen lines with poignant clarity. He was down on both knees when he breathed his last.

> Bereft am I of heart and hope, dear bride,
> In your foul death, happiness itself has died.
> Adieu, cruel world! Farewell, abhorred life!
> I quit this void to join my loving wife.

1

Firethorn hit the ground with a thud that echoed through the taut silence. His outstretched fingertips made a last contact with the pale and forlorn hand of his bride. Anguished servants entered and the two bodies were lifted on to biers with reverential care before being carried out to solemn music. The noble Count Orlando and his adored young Countess would share a marriage bed in the family vault. Harrowed by the tragedy and caught up in its full implications, the onlookers did not dare to move or speak. Mute distress enfolded them.

It was broken in an instant by the reappearance of Lawrence Firethorn, leading out his company to take their bow before the full audience that was packed into the yard at the Queen's Head in Gracechurch Street. He was no stricken aristocrat now, no Italian nobleman who had just committed suicide in a fit of unbearable grief. Firethorn was the finest actor in London, pulsing with vitality and bristling with curiosity, coming out to take his place at the centre of the stage and reap his due reward while at the same time scanning the upper gallery for a particular face. Count Orlando was only one in a long line of tragic heroes played by the acknowledged star of Westfield's Men and it was a role in which he never ceased to work his will upon the raw emotions of the audience. They clapped and cheered and stamped their feet to show their approval of the play. *Death and Darkness* had weaved its magic web once more. Firethorn was being feted.

Applause was the life-blood of an actor and each member of the cast felt it coursing through his veins. Firethorn might think that all the adulation was being directed solely at him and he was replying with a bow of almost imperious humility but his fellows could dream their dreams as well. The small, squat figure of Barnaby Gill, standing beside him, believed that the ovation was in recognition of his performance as Quaglino, the ancient retainer, the one comic character in a tragic tale, the single filter of light in the prevailing blackness of the play. Edmund Hoode, tall, spare and with a youthful innocence that belied his age, pretended that the applause was in gratitude both for his affecting performance as the doomed lover of the Countess and for his skill as a playwright. *Death and Darkness* was an early piece from his pen but it had stood the test of time and the close scrutiny of many an audience.

And so it was with the rest of the company, right down to its meanest member, George Dart, the tiny assistant stage-keeper, pressed into service as a soldier, proudly wearing the uniform of Count Orlando's guard and quietly congratulating himself on having got his one deathless line—'My lord, the Duke of Milan waits upon you'—right for the first time in weeks. Though put inconspicuously at the outer limit of the semi-circle of actors, he bowed as deep as any of them, feeding hungrily on the sustained clapping while he could, knowing that he would be back to a more meagre diet of chores, complaints, gibes, outright abuse and occasional blows once he left the stage and returned to his accustomed role as the lowliest of the low. Theatre was indeed sweet fancy.

Nicholas Bracewell watched it all from his position behind the curtains. He was a big, well-groomed, handsome man with fair hair and a full beard. As book holder with the company, he stage-managed every performance with an attention to detail that lifted Westfield's Men above so many of their rivals. No matter how generous it might be, applause never penetrated to his domain behind the scenes and this state of affairs suited Nicholas. He had a commanding presence that was offset by a gift for self-effacement and he courted the shadows more than the sun.

While Lawrence Firethorn and the others lapped up the tumultuous admiration, the book holder was still calmly doing his job, noting from his vantage point that Barnaby Gill had torn his hose, that Edmund Hoode had dropped a stitch in the rear of his doublet and that George Dart had somehow lost a buckle off his shoe. Nicholas had also observed in the course of a hectic two hours that entrances had been missed, lines had gone astray and the musicians had not been at their most harmonious. He would have stern words for the offenders afterwards and would even be courageous enough to tell the volatile Firethorn that, during one of his major speeches, the leading man had mistakenly inserted four lines from another play. Nicholas was a relentless perfectionist.

He had also come to know his employer very well. Even though his view of Firethorn was confined to a bending back and a pair of thrusting buttocks, he could see what was animating Count Orlando. Somewhere in the gallery was a new female face with a roguish charm that had ensnared the actor. Nicholas had spotted the signs earlier when Firethorn was in the tiring-house, working himself up to full pitch, smiling benignly for once on all around him, evincing a confidence that was fringed with nervousness and hogging the mirror even more than usual. The book holder groaned inwardly. It was bad news for the whole company when its actor-manager blundered into yet another romantic entanglement, and it was an extra burden on Nicholas Bracewell because he was invariably used as a reluctant go-between. There was danger in the air.

Lawrence Firethorn confirmed it within a matter of seconds. After taking a last, loving, lingering bow, he blew a kiss to the upper gallery then led his troupe from the stage. As they poured into the tiring-house, they could still hear the tide of approval as it slowly ebbed away. The actors fell into happy chatter and the musicians began to play in their elevated position to cover the noisy departure of their patrons. With his familiar eagerness, Firethorn swooped down on his book holder.

'Nick, dear heart! I have important work for you.'

'There are chores enough to keep me busy, sir.'

'This is a special commission,' said Firethorn. 'It comes direct from Cupid.'

'Can it not wait, Master?' said Nicholas, trying to evade a duty that was about to be thrust upon him. 'I am needed here, as you may well judge.'

Firethorn grabbed him by the arm, pushed him towards the curtain then drew it slightly back to give them a view of the yard. His voice was an urgent hiss.

'Find out who she is!'

'Which lady has caught your attention?'

'That creature of pure joy and beauty.'

'There are several to fit that description,' said Nicholas, surveying the crowd as it dispersed. 'How am I to pick her out from such a throng?'

'Are you blind, man!' howled Firethorn, pointing a finger. 'She is there in the upper gallery.'

'Amid three dozen or more fair maids.'

'Outshining them all with her splendour.'

'I fear I cannot pick her out, Master.'

'The angel wears blue and pink.'

'As do several others.'

'Enough of this, you wretch!'

Firethorn punched him playfully and Nicholas saw that he could not escape his appointed task by a show of confusion. He had seen the young woman at once and the sight of her had rung a warning bell inside his skull. Even in the blaze of colour provided by the gallants and the ladies all around her, she stood out with ease. Her face was small, oval and exquisitely lovely with none of the cosmetic aids on which others had to rely so heavily. She was quite petite with a delicate vivacity apparent even at a cursory glance. Nicholas put her age at no more than twenty. She wore a dress in the Spanish fashion with a round, stiff-laced collar above a blue bodice that was fitted with sleeves of a darker hue. Pink ribbons flowed down both arms. Her skirt ballooned out with a matching explosion of blue and pink. Jewellery added the final touch to a glittering portrait.

'I think you have marked her now,' said Firethorn with a chuckle. 'Is she not divine?'

'Indeed, yes,' agreed Nicholas. 'But you are not the first to make that observation.'

'How so?'

'She is in the company of two young gentlemen.'

'What should I care?'

'Haply, one of them might be her husband.'

'That will not deter me, Nick. Had she fifty or more husbands, I would still pursue her. It only serves to add spice to the chase. I have something that no other man can offer. True genius upon the stage!'

'The lady has seen you at your peak.'

'Count Orlando has conquered her,' said Firethorn grandly. 'I saw it every time I stepped out upon the boards. I drew tears from those pearls that are her eyes. I made her little heart beat out the tune of love.'

Nicholas Bracewell gave the resigned sigh of someone who had heard it all before. The actor had immense talent but it was matched by immense vanity. Firethorn believed that he simply had to perform one of his major roles in front of a woman and she would fling herself into his bed without reservation or delay. What made his latest target more alarming to Nicholas was the fact that she did not conform to the accepted type. Here was no practised coquette, sending hot glances down to stir Firethorn's ardour. The young woman was self-evidently not the kind of court beauty who enjoyed an occasional dalliance to break up the monotony of an idle and powdered existence. For all her undeniable charms and her gorgeous array, there was a wan simplicity about her, a lack of sophistication, the shy awkwardness of someone who was enthralled by the play without quite knowing how to comport herself at a playhouse.

She was unawakened and Lawrence Firethorn had elected himself as the man to open her eyes.

'Find out who she is, Nick.'

'Leave it with me, sir.'

'About it straight.'

'As you wish.'

A stocky man of medium height, Firethorn filled his lungs to expand his chest and got a last, fleeting glimpse of her before she left the gallery. He had reached an irrevocable decision. Still in the attire of an Italian aristocrat, he stroked his dark, pointed beard and gave a Machiavellian smile.

'I must have her!'

Born and brought up in Richmond with its quiet beauty and its abundant royal associations, Anne Hendrik had never regretted her move to Southwark. It was a dirtier, darker and more populous area with lurking danger in its narrow thoroughfares and the threat of disease in its careless filth. But it was also one of the most colourful and cosmopolitan districts of London, a vibrant place that throbbed with excitement and which had become the home of theatres and bear-baiting arenas and other entertainments which could flourish best outside the city boundaries. Anne had chosen to live there when she married Jacob Hendrik, an immigrant hatmaker, who brought his Dutch skill and conscientiousness to his adopted country. Theirs was a happy marriage that produced no children but which gave birth to a steady flow of fashionable headgear for all classes. The Hendrik name became a seal of quality.

When her husband died, Anne inherited a comfortable house and a thriving business in the adjoining premises. A handsome woman in her thirties, she was expected by almost everyone to mourn for a decent interval before taking another man to the altar and there was no shortage of candidates seeking that honour. Anne Hendrik kept them all at bay with a show of independence that was unlikely in a woman in her position. Instead of taking the softer options posed by re-marriage, she picked up the reins of the business and proved that she had more than enough shrewdness and acumen to drive it along. Like her husband before her, she was not afraid to use a judicious crack of the whip over her employees.

'This will not be tolerated much longer,' she said.

'Hans is a good craftsman,' argued her companion.

'Only when he is here.'

'The boy was sent on an errand, Mistress.'

'He should have been back this long while.'

'Give him a little more time.'

'I have done that too often, Preben,' she said. 'I will have to speak more harshly to Master Hans Kippel. If he wishes to remain as an apprentice under my roof, then he must mend his ways.'

'Let *me* talk to him in your stead.'

'You are too fond of the boy to scold him.'

Preben van Loew accepted the truth of the charge and nodded sadly. A dour, emaciated man in his fifties, he was the oldest and best of her employees and he had been a close friend of Jacob Hendrik. Though he specialized in making

7

ostentatious hats for the gentry, the Dutchman was soberly dressed himself and wore only a simple cap upon his bulbous head. Hans Kippel was far and away the most able of the apprentices when he put his mind to it but there was a wayward streak in the youth that made for bad timekeeping and lapses of concentration. Entrusted with the task of delivering some hats in the city itself, he should have been back with the money almost an hour ago. Anne liked him enormously but even her affection was not proof against the nudging suspicion that temptation might have been too much for the lad. The money that he was carrying was worth more than three months' wages and he would not have been the first apprentice to abscond.

Preben van Loew read her mind and rushed to the defence of his young colleague.

'Hans is an honest boy,' he said earnestly.

'Let us hope so.'

'I know his family as well as my own. We grew up together in Amsterdam. You can always put your trust in a Kippel. They will never let you down.'

'Then where is he now?'

'On the road back, Mistress.'

'By way of Amsterdam?'

She had meant it as a joke but she rued it when his face crumpled. Preben van Loew was the mainstay of the business and she did not want to upset him in any way. At the same time, she could not allow an apprentice too much leeway or he would be bound to take advantage. Anne tried to make amends by praising the handiwork of her senior employee who was about to put the last carefully-chosen feather into a tall hat with a curling brim. It was a small masterpiece that would grace the head of a gallant. The Dutchman allowed himself to be mollified then fell into a refrain that she had heard all too often on the lips of her husband.

'They do us wrong to keep us out,' he moaned.

'It is the English way, I fear.'

'Why do they fear the foreigner so?'

'Simply because he is foreign.'

'We make hats as good as theirs but they will not let us

8

join their Guilds. They have the first choice of all the work that is on offer. We have to struggle on down here, outside the city limits, so that we do not offend their noses with our Dutch smell.'

'They are jealous of your skills, Preben.'

'It is unjust, Mistress.'

'Jacob said as much every day,' she recalled. 'He went to them and put his arguments but they were deaf to his entreaties. All they would do was to boast about their history. They told him that the Hatters and the Furriers united with the Haberdashers at the very start of this century. Among those Hatters were the Feltmakers who have been trying to form their own Guild of late.'

'I know, Mistress,' he said gloomily. 'But the move has been opposed. What does it matter to us? None of these precious Guilds will appreciate our quality. They just wish to look after themselves and keep us out.'

'It may change in time, Preben.'

'I will not live to see it.'

'Justice will one day be done.'

'It has no place in business.'

Anne Hendrik was unable to reply. Before she could open her mouth, the door flew open and a scrawny youth in buff jerkin and hose came staggering in. Hans Kippel could not have made a more dramatic entrance. Anne moved across to reproach him and Preben van Loew stepped in to protect him then they both took a closer look at the newcomer. He was in great distress. His clothes were torn, his face was bruised and blood was oozing freely from a deep gash in his temple. Hans Kippel could barely stand. They helped him quickly to a seat.

'Rest yourself here,' said Anne.

'What happened?' asked Preben van Loew.

'I will send for a surgeon directly.'

'Tell us what befell you, Hans.'

The boy was trembling with fear. On the verge of exhaustion, he could barely dredge up strength enough to speak. When the words finally dribbled out, there was a tattered bravery to them.

9

'I saved . . . it. They . . . did not get . . . the money . . .'

With a ghost of a smile, he pitched forward on to the oak floorboards in a dead faint.

Stanford Place stood in a prime position on the east side of Bishopsgate and dwarfed the neighbouring dwellings. It was built in the reign of Edward IV and had now been arresting eyes and exciting envy for well over a century. With a frontage of almost two hundred feet, it had four storeys, each one jettied out above the floor below. Time had wearied the timber framing somewhat and the beams had settled at a slight angle to give the facade a curiously lop-sided look but this only added to the character of the house. It was like a keystone in an arch and the adjacent buildings in Bishopsgate Street leaned against it for support with companionable familiarity.

The establishment ran to a dozen bedchambers, a small banqueting hall, a dining parlour, a drawing room, butler's lodging, servants' quarters, kitchens, a bake house, even a tiny chapel. There were also stables, outhouses and an extensive garden. It was around this last impressive feature of the house that its owner was perambulating in the early evening sunlight. Walter Stanford was a big, bluff man with apparel that suggested considerable wealth and a paunch which hinted at too ready an appetite. Yet though his body had succumbed to middle age, his plumb face still had a boyish quality to it and the large brown eyes sparkled with childlike glee.

'There is always room for improvement, Simon.'

'Yes, Master.'

'No expense must be spared in pursuit of it.'

'That was ever your way, sir.'

'Look to the example of Theobalds,' said Stanford with a lordly wave of his hand. 'When Sir Robert Cecil was gracious enough to invite a party of us there, we were conducted around his garden. Garden, do I say? It was truly a revelation.'

'You have commended it to me before, Master.'

'No praise is too high, Simon. Why, man, it beggars all

description.' Stanford chortled as he hit his stride. 'The garden at Theobalds is encompassed with a ditch full of water, so broad and inviting that a man could row a boat between the shrubs if he had a mind to. There was a great variety of trees and plants with labyrinths to provide sport and decoration. What pleased me most was the *jet d'eau* with its basin of white marble. I must have such a thing here.'

'Order has already been given for it.'

'Then there were columns and pyramids of wood at every turn. After seeing these, we were taken by the gardener into the summerhouse, in the lower part of which, built, as it were, in a semicircle, are the twelve Roman emperors in white marble, and a table of touchstone. The upper part of it is set round with cisterns of lead into which the water is conveyed through pipes, so that fish may be kept in them, and in summertime they are very convenient for bathing. And so it went on, Simon.'

'Indeed, sir.'

As steward of the household, Simon Pendleton was well-acquainted with his master's enthusiasms. Unlike many who make large amounts of money, Walter Stanford was always looking for new ways to spend it and his home provided him with endless opportunities. The steward was a short, slim, unctuous man in his forties with a high forehead and greying beard. Trotting discreetly at the heels of the other, he made a mental note of any new commissions for the garden and there was much to keep him occupied. Every time Stanford paused, he ordered some new trees, shrubs, flowers, or herbs. Whenever a gap presented itself in some quiet corner, he decided to fill it with some statuary or with a pool. Parsimony was unknown to the master of Stanford Place. He was generosity itself when his interest was aroused.

'It must all be ready in time,' he warned.

'I will speak to the gardeners, sir.'

'My hour of triumph comes ever closer, Simon.'

'And much-deserved it is,' said the steward with an obsequious bow. 'Your whole establishment is conscious of the honour that you bestow upon them. It will indeed be a privilege to serve the next Lord Mayor of London.'

11

'It will be the summit of my achievement.'

Stanford was lost for a moment in contemplation of the joys that lay ahead. Like his father before him, he was a Master of the Mercers' Company, the most prestigious Guild in the city, first in order of precedence on all ceremonial occasions, and immortalized by the name of London's revered mayor, Dick Whittington, who had slipped immoveably into the folk-memory of the capital. The great man had also been Master of the Company and it was Stanford's ambition to emulate some of his achievements. He wanted to leave his mark indelibly upon the city.

'He built the largest privy in London,' he mused fondly. 'In the year of our Lord, 1419, Richard Whittington erected a convenience in Vintry Ward with sixty seats for Ladies and for Gentlemen, flushed with piped water. What a legacy to bequeath to old London town!'

Pendleton coughed discreetly and Stanford came out of his reverie. He was about to continue his walk when he saw someone flitting through the apple trees towards him on the tips of her toes. She wore a dress of blue and pink that set off the colour of her eyes and the rosiness of her cheeks. Stanford held his arms wide to welcome her and his steward melted quickly into the undergrowth. The young woman came gambolling excitedly up.

'Matilda!' said Stanford. 'What means this haste?'

'Oh, sir, I have so much to tell you!' she gasped.

'Catch your breath first while I steal a kiss.' He bent over to peck her on the cheek then stood back to admire her. 'You are truly the delight of my life!'

'I have found delights of my own, sir.'

'Where might they be?'

'At the playhouse,' she said. 'We saw Westfield's Men perform this dolorous tragedy at the Queen's Head. It made me weep piteously but it also filled me with such wonder. I beg of you to indulge me. When you are made Lord Mayor of London, let us have a play to mark the occasion.'

'There will be a huge procession, child, a ceremonial parade through the streets of the city. It will lack nothing in pomp and pageant, that I can vouch.'

'But I want a play,' she urged. 'To please me, say that I may have my way in this matter. It was a transport of delight from start to finish. Master Firethorn is the best actor in the whole world and I worship at his feet.' She threw her arms around his neck. 'Do not deny me, sir. I know it is *your* day but I would round it off with a performance of some lively play.'

Walter Stanford gave an indulgent chuckle.

'You shall have your wish, Matilda,' he said.

'Oh, sir! You are worthy husband!'

'And you, a wife among thousands. I strive to satisfy every whim of my gorgeous young bride.'

Nicholas Bracewell paid the penalty for being so reliable and resourceful. The more competent he proved himself in every sphere, the more onerous became his duties. While he made himself indispensable to the company and thereby attained a degree of security that none of the other hired men could aspire to, he found himself coping with additional responsibilities all the time. Nicholas made light of them. Having run his errand for Lawrence Firethorn, he went straight back to his post to supervise the dismantling of the stage and the storing of the costumes and properties. Westfield's men were not due to perform at the Queen's Head until the following week and so their makeshift theatre had to be taken down so that the yard could be returned to its more workaday function as a stabling area for visitors to the inn. The valuable accoutrements of the actor's art had to be carefully gathered up and locked away in a private room that was rented from the landlord.

While marshalling the stagekeepers, Nicholas also had to deal with countless enquiries from members of the company who wanted details of future engagements, repairs made to some hand prop or other, simple praise for their afternoon's work and, most of all, confirmation of when and where they would get their wages. The book holder was also the central repository of complaints and there was never a shortage of these as peevish actors pursued their vendettas or argued their case for a larger role. It was tiring work but Nicholas sailed through it with the quiet smile of a man who revels in his occupation.

When the last complaint had been fielded—George Dart wondering why Count Orlando had boxed him on the ear in the middle of Act Two—Nicholas went on to tackle one of his most daunting tasks. This was his all too regular encounter with Alexander Marwood, the gloomy landlord of the Queen's Head, a man temperamentally unsuited to the presence of actors because he believed, in that joyless wasteland known as his heart, that their avowed purpose in life was to destroy the fabric of his inn, scandalize his patrons and debauch his nubile daughter. That none of these things had so far actually happened did nothing to subdue his restless pessimism or to still his nervous twitch.

Nicholas met this merchant of doom in the taproom and smiled into the cadaverous, ever-mobile face.

'How now, Master Marwood!'

'You do me wrong to vex me so,' said the landlord.

'In what way, sir?'

'Fire, Master Bracewell. Yellow flames of fire. It is not enough that my thatch is at risk from those pipe-smokers who crowd my galleries. Westfield's Men have to bring it on to the stage as well. It was almost *Death and Darkness* indeed for me. Those torches could have set my whole establishment ablaze. Do but consider, I might have lost my inn, my home, my livelihood and my hopes of future happiness.'

'Water was at hand in case of any mishap.'

'Would you burn me to the ground, sir?'

'Indeed not, Master Marwood,' soothed Nicholas. 'We would never destroy that which we hold most dear. Namely, your good opinion which is attested by your contractual dealings with us. In token of which, allow me to pay the rent that is now due. In full, sir.'

He handed over a bag of coins and sought to steal away but the landlord's skeletal fingers clutched at his sleeve to detain him.

'I crave a word with you, Master Bracewell.'

'As many as you wish.'

'It concerns your contract with the Queen's Head.'

14

'We are anxious to renew it.'

'On what terms, though?'

'On those satisfactory to both parties.'

'Aye, there's the rub,' said Marwood, using a hand to push back a strand of greasy hair from his furrowed brow. 'The case is altered, sir.'

'I am sure that we can come to composition.'

'Westfield's Men bring me many woes.'

Alexander Marwood recited them with morbid glee. It was a litany that Nicholas had heard many times and always with the same wringing of hands, the same sighing of sighs and the same uncontrollable facial contortions. Use of the Queen's Head came at a high price. Westfield's Men had to put up with the sustained hysteria of a landlord who was whipped into action by a nagging wife. Ready to reap the financial advantages of having a theatre company in his yard, Marwood also harvested a bumper crop of outrage and apprehension. He was at his most febrile when the contract was due for renewing, hoping to exact more money and greater assurances of good conduct from the acting fraternity. What disturbed Nicholas was that a new note was being sounded.

'We may have to part company, Master Bracewell.'

'You would drive us away to another inn?'

'No other landlord would be foolish enough to have you,' said Marwood fretfully. 'They lack my patience and forbearance. You'll not easily find another home.'

It was a painful truth. Public performance of plays was forbidden within the city boundaries and it was only municipal weakness in enforcing this decree that allowed companies such as Westfield's Men to flourish unscathed. More than once, they aroused aldermanic ire by their choice of repertoire or by the bad influence they were alleged to have on their audiences but they had never actually faced prosecution. Though fearing that every day the hand of authority would descend on his bony shoulder, Alexander Marwood, out of naked self-interest, yet ran the risk of contravening regulations. Other publicans would not be so adventurous, quite apart from the fact that their premises, in most cases, were not at all suitable for the presentation of drama. For some years now, the Queen's Head had furnished Westfield's Men with the illusion of having a permanent base. That illusion could be completely shattered.

'Do not make any hasty decision,' said Nicholas.

'It is one that may be forced upon me, sir.'

'For what reason?'

'The Queen's Head may change hands.'

Nicholas was jolted. 'You are leaving?'

'No, sir, but we may yield up ownership. We have received an offer too generous to ignore. It would give us security in our old age and provide a fit dowry for our daughter, Rose.' He attempted a smile but it came out as a hideous leer. 'There is but one main condition.'

'What might that be?'

'If we sell the inn, the new owner insists that Westfield's Men must go.'

'And who is this stern fellow?'

'Alderman Rowland Ashway.'

Nicholas winced. He knew the man by reputation and liked nothing of what he had heard. Rowland Ashway was not merely one of the most prosperous brewers in London, he was also alderman for the very ward in which the Queen's Head was located. His disapproval of innyard theatre did not spring from any puritanical zeal. It arose from notions of prejudice and profit. Like others who felt they created the wealth of the capital city, Ashway had a deep suspicion of an idle aristocracy that fawned away its time at court and held the whiphand over the growing middle class of which he was a prominent member. To his way of thinking, a theatrical company was an indulgence on the part of a highly privileged minority. In ousting Westfield's Men, he could strike a blow at the epicurean Lord Westfield himself.

It was not only social revenge that activated the brewer. In the final analysis, his account book dictated all his business decisions. If he was buying the Queen's Head, he obviously felt that he could more than compensate in other ways for the revenue he would forgo if he expelled the company. Nicholas was seriously alarmed. The resourceful book holder might be thrown out of work by a ruthless book-keeper.

'This matter must be discussed in full,' he said.

'I give you but advance warning.'

'Speak with Master Firethorn about it.'

'That I will not,' said Marwood. 'I like not his ranting and raving. My ears buzz for a week after I have talked with him. I would rather treat with you, sir. We have always been congenial to each other.'

Nicholas Bracewell had never met a human being less congenial than the twitching publican but he did not want to upset the tricky negotiations that lay ahead by saying so. He thanked Marwood for alerting him to the potential danger. In the circumstances, he did not feel like putting more money into Rowland Ashway's pocket by buying a pint of his celebrated ale. Instead, he nodded his farewell and sauntered across to Edmund Hoode who was hunched over a cup of sack in the corner of the taproom.

The two men were good friends and the playwright always consulted the other during the writing of a new work if any special dramatic effects were required. Nicholas had an instinctive feel for the practicalities of theatre and a way of making even the most difficult effects work. The book holder's willingness to confront any technical problems made Hoode's job as resident poet much easier.

Nicholas had intended to pass on the grim tidings he had just gleaned from the landlord but he saw that his friend already had anxieties enough.

'What, Edmund? All amort?'

'In sooth, I am in the pit of misery, Nick.'

'Why so? Your play was as ever a shining success.'

'Actors must quit the stage when they are done.'

'Your meaning?'

'I detest the role I must play now.'

Nicholas understood at once. Edmund Hoode was going through a fallow period in his personal life. A hopeless romantic, he was always losing his heart and dedicating his verses to some new fancy and, although his love was usually unrequited, the blissful agony of infatuation was reward enough in itself. Without a fresh mistress to make him truly unhappy, he was plunged into despair. It took Nicholas well over an hour to instil some hope into his friend. The questing love of Edmund Hoode and the roving lust of Lawrence Firethorn could be equal tyrannies to him.

It was late evening by the time Nicholas finally left the inn and darkness was pulling its malodorous shroud over the city. Instead of walking back home to Southwark by way of London Bridge, he elected to be rowed across by one of the army of watermen who populated the river. As he headed for the wharf, he had time properly to reflect on what Alexander Marwood had told him. Ejection from the Queen's Head would be a disaster for the company and might even lead to its extinction. How serious the threat really was he had no means of knowing but one thing he did resolve upon. He would not spread panic unnecessarily. Insecurity was rife enough in their blighted profession and he did not wish to add to it in any way. The imminent peril should be concealed for the time being until more details emerged because he did not rule out the possibility of finding a way to solve this horrendous problem. He could best do that by working quietly behind the scenes rather than in an atmosphere of communal frenzy. Meanwhile, therefore, Nicholas would have to keep a very dark and very heavy secret to himself.

The Thames was lapping noisily at the timbers of the wharf when he arrived and the moored craft were thudding rhythmically against each other. Daylight turned the river into a floating village and even at this late hour many of the inhabitants were still promenading over the water. Barges, wherries, hoys, fishing smacks and an occasional tilt-boat could be seen and there was a lone coracle wending its way along. Nicholas did not have to choose his means of transport. His pilot came hopping across to him with gruff deference.

'This way, Master Bracewell. Let me serve you, sir.'

'I will do that gladly, Abel.'

'I have missed you for a se'n-night or more.'

'My legs took me home.'

'Sit in my boat and make the journey in style, sir. There is more music to please your ears.'

Abel Strudwick was an unprepossessing individual, a heavy, round-shouldered man of middle height with unkempt hair and a hirsute beard doing their best to hide an ugly, pock-marked face. Though roughly the same age as his favourite passenger, he looked a decade older. Strudwick had the vices and virtues of his breed. Like all watermen, he had a stentorian voice to hail his customers and a savage turn of phrase with which to assault them if they failed to tip him handsomely. On the credit side, he was an honest, reliable citizen who put the strength of his arms and the warmth of his company at the disposal of anyone who sat in the boat.

What set Abel Strudwick apart from the rest and gave him a special relationship with Nicholas Bracewell was his addiction to what he called music. When the book holder was offered fresh melodies, he knew that the waterman had been busy with his pen, for Strudwick had poetic ambitions. His music came in the form of mundane verse that was always at the mercy of its rhyme-scheme and which flowed from him as readily and roughly as the Thames itself. Nicholas was his preferred audience because he always listened with genuine interest and because his connections with the theatre were a distant promise of some kind of literary recognition.

As they got into the boat, Nicholas felt a sailor's surge of excitement at being afloat again, albeit in a modest craft. Before he came into the theatre, he had sailed with Drake on the circumnavigation of the world and it had made a deep impression on him. The experience gave him another bond with the waterman. Though Strudwick had never been more than ten miles upstream, he saw himself as a great voyager like his friend and it fed his invention.

He declaimed his latest piece of music.

> 'Row on, row on, across the waves,
> Thou monarch of the sea.
> Steer past those rocks, avoid those caves,
> Row on to eternity.'

There was much more to come and Nicholas heard it patiently as he sat in the stern of the boat with his hand trailing gently in the water. Strudwick's methodical rowing was matched by the repetitive banality of his latest verses but his passenger would nevertheless pay him with kind words and encouragement. A warbling poet was milder company than a foul-mouthed waterman.

'A turd in your teeth!'

'How so, Abel?'

'A pox upon your pox-ridden pizzle!'

Strudwick had not lapsed back into his normal mode of speech to berate Nicholas. He was cursing the obstacle which the prow of his boat had struck and which had turned his music to discord. Swearing volubly, he manoeuvred his craft round so that he could see what he was abusing. Nicholas felt it first and it made his blood run cold. His trailing hand met another in the water, five pale, thin, lifeless fingers that touched his own in a clammy greeting. He sat up in the boat and peered into the darkness. Even the roaring Strudwick was frightened into silence.

Caught up in a piece of driftwood was the naked body of a man. There was enough moonlight for them to see that the corpse had met a gruesome death. The head had been battered in and one of the legs was twisted out at an unnatural angle. A dagger was lodged in the throat.

Abel Strudwick was still emptying the contents of a full stomach into the river as Nicholas hauled their sorry cargo aboard.

Chapter Two

ANNE HENDRIK WAS NOT NORMALLY GIVEN TO APprehension. She was a strong-minded woman who had survived all the blows that Fate had dealt her and who always met adversity with resolution. Though her marriage had been sound, it had brought pain and grief to her family who disapproved in frank terms of her choice of husband. London had no love of foreigners and those women who had actually rejected decent English stock in order to marry immigrants were looked upon with disdain, if not outright disgust. Having to cope with the sneers and the cold shoulders had helped to harden Anne in many ways but she was still a sensitive person underneath it all and her emotions could be aroused in a crisis.

The present situation was a case in point. She was very distressed by what had happened to Hans Kippel, her young apprentice, all the more so because the boy had been sent expressly at her command to deliver the order. Anne blamed herself for entrusting such an important duty to such an untried youth. In giving Hans Kippel an extra responsibility, she had exposed him unnecessarily to the dangers of city life. The wounds he got in her service were each a separate reproach to her and she could not bear to look on as they were bathed and bandaged. Preben van Loew tried to assure her that it was not her fault but his words fell on deaf ears. What she needed was the more persuasive, objective, down-to-earth comfort of the man who shared her house with her but he was not there.

The longer she waited, the more convinced she became that he, too, had met with violence on his journey home. As evening became night and night slipped soundlessly into the next day, Anne was almost distraught, pacing the floor of her main room with a candle in her hand and racing to peer through the window every time a footstep was heard on the cobbles outside. The house was not large but she had felt the need for male companionship after her husband's demise and she had taken in a lodger so that she might have the sense of a man about the place once more. It had been a rewarding experiment. The guest had turned out to be not only an exemplary lodger and a loyal friend but—at special moments savoured by both—he had been considerably more. To have lost him at a time when she needed him most would indeed be a cruel stroke of fortune. His movements were uncertain and his hours of work irregular but he should have been back long before now. When there was some unexpected delay, he usually sent word to put her mind at rest.

Where could he be at such a late hour? Bankside was littered with hazards enough in broad daylight. With the cover of darkness, those hazards multiplied a hundredfold. Could he have met the same trouble as Hans Kippel and be lying in his own blood in some fetid lane? Her immediate impulse was to take a lantern and go in search of him but the futility of such a gesture was borne in upon her. It was no use subjecting herself to such grave danger. She was virtually trapped in the house and she had to make the most of it. With a great effort of will, she sat down at the table, put the candle aside, took several deep breaths and told herself to remain calm in the emergency. It worked for a matter of minutes. Worries then flooded back and she was up on her feet again to confront each new horrible possibility that her imagination threw up.

Anne Hendrik was so enmeshed in her concern that she did not hear the key being inserted into the front door. The

22

first she knew of her deliverance was when the solid figure stood before her in the gloom.

Tears came as she flung herself into his arms.

'God be praised!'

'What ails you?'

'Hold me tight, sir. Hold me very tight.'

'So I will, my love.'

'I have been in such dread for your safety.'

'Here I am, unharmed, as you see.'

'Thank the Lord!'

Nicholas Bracewell held her close and kissed the top of her head softly. It was most unlike her to be so on edge and it took him some time to calm her enough to get the full story out of her. Anne sat opposite him at the table and talked of the deep guilt she felt about Hans Kippel. He heard her out before offering his advice.

'You do yourself an injustice, Anne.'

'Do I, sir?'

'The boy is old enough and sensible enough to take on such a duty. It is all part of his apprenticeship. I warrant that he was delighted when you chose him.'

'Indeed, he was. It got him away from here.'

'Out of the dullness of his workplace and into the excitement of the streets,' said Nicholas. 'Hans will have been a little careless, that is all. He will not make the same mistake again.'

'But that is the trouble of it.'

'What is?'

'Hans does not understand the nature of his error.'

'He was off guard for a moment, surely?'

'Maybe, Nick,' she said. 'But he does not remember. Hans took such a blow on the head that it has knocked the memory out of him. All he can recall is that some men attacked him and that he got away. When, where, or why are questions that the lad cannot as yet comprehend.'

'His wounds have been tended?'

'Of course, sir. The surgeon said it is not uncommon to find a lapse of memory in such cases. Hans must be given time to recover. As his body mends, haply his mind will be made whole again.' Anne seized his hands to squeeze them. 'Speak to him, Nick. The boy likes you and looks up to you. Help the poor creature for pity's sake.'

'I will do all that is needful. Trust it well.'

'Your words are a balm to me.'

He leaned forward to embrace her then turned to his own story. When he explained what had detained him, Anne was thrown into disarray once more. The injuries of a young apprentice paled beside the discovery of a dead body in the River Thames. Nicholas Bracewell and Abel Strudwick had taken the corpse back to the wharf from which they had departed. After rousing the watch, they had been required to give sworn statements to a magistrate before being allowed to go. Strudwick had then rowed his friend to Bankside in a grim silence that no music could break. Tragedy had knocked all poetic skills out of him.

Anne was in a state of total dismay.

'Who was the man?' she said.

'We have no means of knowing as yet.'

'But why was he stripped of his clothing?'

'The murderer may have thought his apparel worth the taking,' he said. 'And that argues rich garments which could be sold for gain. I think, however, that there could be another reason behind it. His clothing could have helped to identify him and much care was taken to render the poor soul anonymous. The way that his face was beaten to a pulp, his own kin would not be able to recognize him. He went out of this world in the most damnable way.'

'Could nothing be learned from the corpse, Nick?'

'Only some idea of his age, which I would put around thirty summers. And one thing more, Anne.'

'Well, sir?'

'The body had not long been in the water.'

'How can you be sure of that?'

'By bitter experience,' he said. 'I have seen all too many men who have found a watery grave. *Rigor mortis* sets in after a time and the miserable creatures become bloated in a way too hideous to describe. The person we found tonight was dropped into the river only a short time beforehand.'

'Was any other villainy wreaked upon him?'

'He was stabbed through the neck and one of his legs was horribly broken.' He saw her flinch. 'But these are details enough for you. I would not vex you any more.'

'My joy at seeing you again is blackened by this grim intelligence.' Fresh tears threatened. 'The body in the river could so easily have been yours, Nick.'

'With Abel Strudwick to look after me?' he said with a smile. 'I could not ask for a better guard. A whole armada would not dare to take on Abel when he is afloat. He would give them a broadside with his curses then rake their decks with a fusillade of poems.'

She went back into his arms and hugged him close.

'It has been a long and lonely night for me.'

'I did not stay away from you out of choice, Anne.'

'There is almost too much for me to bear.'

'Let us share the load, my love.'

'That was my hope.'

'Consider it fulfilled.'

'Welcome home, Nick,' she whispered.

They went slowly upstairs to her bedchamber. It was something which they both felt they had deserved.

The change of venue was significant. The meeting was scheduled to take place at Lawrence Firethorn's house in Shoreditch, a rather modest but welcoming abode that gave shelter to the actor's own family and their servants as well as hospitality to the company's four apprentices. What made the establishment function with such relative smoothness was the presiding genius of Margery Firethorn, a redoubtable woman who combined the roles of wife, mother, house-keeper and landlady with consummate ease and who still had enough energy left over to pursue other interests, to maintain a high standard of Christian observance and to terrorize any-one foolhardy enough to stand in her way. Even her husband, fearless in any other way, had been known to quail before her. Indirectly, it was she who had dictated the move to an-other place and Barnaby Gill spotted this at once.

'Lawrence is on heat again!' he moaned.

'Lord save us!' cried Edmund Hoode.

'That is why he dare not have us at his house. In case Margery gets wind of his new *amour*.'

'Who *is* the luckless creature, Barnaby?'

'I know not and care not,' said Gill with studied indifference. 'Women are all one to me and I like not any of the infernal gender. My passions are dedicated to intimacy on a much higher plane.' He puffed at his pipe and blew out rings of smoke. 'What else did our Creator in his munificence make pretty boys for, I ask?'

It was a rhetorical question and Edmund Hoode would in any case not have been drawn into such a discussion. Barnaby Gill's tendencies were well-known and generally tolerated by a company that valued his acting skills and his remarkable comic gifts. Hoode had never plumbed the secret of why his companion—such a gushing fountain of pleasure upon the stage—was so morose and petulant when he left it. The playwright preferred the public clown to the private cynic. They were sitting in a room at the Queen's Head as they waited for Firethorn to arrive. The three men were all sharers with Lord Westfield's Men, ranked players who were named in the royal patent for the company and who took the leading roles in any performance. There were four other sharers but it was this triumvirate that effectively dictated policy and controlled the day-to-day running of the company.

Lawrence Firethorn was the undisputed leader. Even when he burst through the door and gave them an elaborate bow, he was simply asserting his superiority.

'Gentlemen, your servant!'

'You are late as usual, sir,' snapped Gill.

'I was detained by family matters.'

'Your drink awaits you, Lawrence,' said Hoode.

'Thank you, Edmund. I am glad that one of my partners in this enterprise has some concern for me.'

'Oh, *I* have concern in good measure,' said Gill. 'I was a model of concern during yesterday's performance when I feared you might not survive to the end of it.'

'Me, sir?' Firethorn bridled. 'You speak of me?'

26

'Who else, sir? It was Count Orlando who was puffing and panting so in the heat of the day. And it was that same noble Italian who was bocame so flustered that he inserted four lines from *Vincentio's Revenge*.'

'You lie, you dog!' howled Firethorn.

'Indeed, I do. It was six lines.'

'My Count Orlando was simon pure.'

'Give or take an occasional blemish.'

'You dare to scorn my performance!'

'By no means,' said Gill, ready with a final thrust. 'I thought that your Count Orlando was excellent—but not nearly as fine as your Vincentio in the same play!'

'You viper! You maggot! You pie-smoking pilchard!'

'Gentlemen, gentlemen,' soothed Hoode. 'We have come together to do business and not to trade abuse.'

'The man is a scurvy rogue!' yelled Firethorn.

'At least I remember my lines,' retorted the other.

'None are worth listening to, sir.'

'My admirers will be the judge of that.'

'You have but one and that is Master Barnaby Gill.'

'I will not brook insults!'

'Then do not wear such ridiculous attire, sir.'

Gill flared up immediately. The one certain way to bring out his choleric disposition was to criticize his appearance because he took such infinite pains with it. Dressed in a peach-coloured doublet and scarlet hose, he wore a tall hat that was festooned with feathers. Rings on almost every finger completed a dazzling effect. Roused to a fever pitch, he now strutted up and down the room, pausing from time to time to stamp a foot in exasperation. Having routed his enemy, Firethorn reclined in the high-backed chair and took his first sip of the Canary wine that stood ready for him.

Hoode, meanwhile, devoted his energy to calming down the anguished clown, an almost daily task in view of the professional jealousy between Gill and Firethorn. Verbal clashes between them were the norm but they were quickly forgotten when the two actors were on stage together. Both were supreme in their own ways and it was from the dynamic between them that Westfield's Men drew much of their motive force.

Edmund Hoode eventually imposed enough calm for the meeting to begin. As they sat around the table, he reached gratefully for his pint of ale to wash away the memory of yet another needless row between his colleagues who had left him feeling that he had been ground into dust by two whirring millstones. Lawrence Firethorn, poised and peremptory, opened the business of the day.

'We are met to confirm our future engagements,' he said. 'Tomorrow, as you know, we play *Double Deceit* at The Theatre in Shoreditch. It is a well-tried piece but that is no reason for us to be complacent. We will have a testing rehearsal in the morning to add what polish we may. Westfield's Men must be at their best, sirs.'

'I never give less,' said Gill sulkily.

'As to our immediate future . . .'

Firethorn outlined the programme that lay ahead, most of it confined to the Queen's Head which was their home base. One new performing venue did, however, surface.

'We have received an invitation to visit Richmond,' said Firethorn. 'The date lies some weeks hence but it is important to address our minds to it now.'

'Where will we play?' asked Hoode.

'In the yard of an inn.'

'Its name?'

'The Nine Giants.'

'I have never heard of the place,' sneered Gill.

'That is no bar to it,' said Firethorn easily. 'It is a sizeable establishment, by all accounts, and like to give us all that the Queen's Head can offer. The Nine Giants are nine giant oak trees that grace its paddock.'

Gill snorted. 'You ask me to perform amid trees?'

'Yes, Barnaby,' said his tormentor. 'You simply lift your back leg like any common cur and make water. Even *you* may win a laugh by that device.'

'I am against the whole idea,' said the other.

'Your opposition is a waste of bad breath.'

'The Nine Giants does not get my assent.'

'Too late, sir. I have accepted the invitation on behalf of the company.'

'You had no right to do that, Lawrence!'

'Nor any chance to refuse,' said Firethorn, producing the one reason that could silence Gill. 'It was given by Lord Westfield himself. Our noble patron has commanded us to appear in Richmond.'

'To what particular end?' said Hoode.

'As part of the wedding celebrations of a friend.'

'And what will we play?'

'That is what we must decide, Edmund. Lord Westfield has asked for a comedy that touches upon marriage.'

'There is sense in that,' agreed Gill, reviving at once and seeing a chance to steal some glory. 'The ideal choice must be *Cupid's Folly*.'

'The piece grows stale, sir.'

'How can you say that, Lawrence? My performance as Rigormortis is as fresh as a daisy.'

'Daisies are low, dishonest flowers.'

Barnaby Gill banged the table with irritation. His fondness for *Cupid's Folly* was well-founded. A rustic comedy with a farcical impetus, it was the one play in the company's repertoire which gave him a central role that allowed him to dominate throughout. As a result, it was staged whenever they needed to mollify the little actor or to dissuade him for implementing his regular threat to walk out on Westfield's Men. No such exigency obtained here.

'I favour *Marriage and Mischief*,' said Hoode.

'Then you should have wed Margery,' added Firethorn. 'It is an interesting suggestion, Edmund, to be sure, but the play begins to show its age.'

'I stand by *Cupid's Folly*,' said Gill.

'And I by *Marriage and Mischief*,' said Hoode.

'That is why we need a happy compromise.' Firethorn gave a ripe chuckle which showed that the decision had already been made. 'We will favour the nuptials with some sage advice. Let us play *The Wise Widow of Dunstable*.'

It was a compromise indeed and his fellow-sharers came to see much virtue in it. Edmund Hoode, fearing that he might be commissioned to write a new play for the occasion, was ready to settle for a seasoned comedy by another hand, especially as it offered him a telling cameo as the ghost of the widow's departed husband. Barnaby Gill, robbed of the opportunity to star in his favourite play, warmed quickly to the idea of a piece which gave him a prominent role and allowed him to execute no less than four of his famous comic jigs. Inevitably, it was Lawrence Firethorn who would shine in the leading part of Lord Merrymouth but there was light enough for others. *The Wise Woman of Dunstable* satisfied all needs.

They discussed their plans in more detail then the meeting broke up. Barnaby Gill was first to leave. When Edmund Hoode tried to follow him out, he was detained by the actor-manager. The glowing countenance of Lawrence Firethorn said it all and the other braced himself.

'I may have work for you, Edmund.'

'Spare me, sir, I pray you.'

'But I am in love, man.'

'I have long admired your beautiful wife.'

'It is not Margery I speak of!' hissed Firethorn. 'Another arrow has been fired into my heart.'

'Pluck it out in the name of marital bliss.'

'Come, come, Edmund. We are men of the world, I hope. Our passions are too fiery to be sated by a single woman. Each of us must spread his love joyously among the sex.'

Hoode sighed. 'Could I but find her, *I* would be faithful to one dear mistress.'

'Then help me secure mine by way of rehearsal.'

'I will not write verses for you, Lawrence.'

'They would be for *her*, man. For a divinity.'

'Offer up prayers instead.'

'I come to you in the name of friendship, Edmund. Do not let me down in my hour of need. Stand by to help, that is all I ask. Nothing is required from you now.'

'Why cannot you do your wooing alone?'

'And throw away the best chance that I have? Your poems are love potions in themselves, Edmund. No woman can resist your honeyed phrases and your sweet sadness.'

Hoode gave a hollow laugh. In recent months, several women had been proof against the most affecting verse that his pen could produce. It would be ironic if his poetic talent helped to ensnare a new victim for the capacious bed of Lawrence Firethorn.

'Who *is* the doomed lady?' he asked.

'That is the beauty of it, man. Nick Bracewell found out her name for me and it has increased my raptures.'

'How can this be?'

Firethorn shook his head. 'I may not tell you until after my prize is secured. But this I will say, Edmund. The lady in question is not only the most splendid creature in London. She will present me with the sternest challenge that I have ever faced. Your assistance will be the difference betwixt success and failure.'

'Or betwixt failure and disaster.'

'I like your spirit,' said Firethorn, slapping his mournful companion between the shoulder-blades. 'We are yoke-fellows in this business. Mark my words, sir, we will bed this angel between us.'

'Abandon this folly now, Lawrence.'

'It is my mission in life.'

'Draw back while you still have time.'

'Too late, man. Plans have already been set in motion.'

Nicholas Bracewell set out early next morning with his mind still racing. A night in the arms of Anne Hendrik had lifted his spirits but failed to obliterate his abiding anxieties. The first of these concerned the dead body which he had dragged out of the murky waters on the previous night. As he was rowed back across the Thames in the sunlight, he felt once more the touch of the dead man's hand and saw again the mutilated corpse bobbing about before him. The body had been young, firm and well-muscled, sent to its grave before its time with the most grotesque injuries. Nicholas was filled with horror and racked by a sense of waste. The life of some nameless man had been viciously cut short by unknown hands that had worked with malign purpose. Evidently, someone had hated the victim—but who had loved him? Who had borne him and cared for him? What family depended on him? What friends would mourn his absence? Why had he been hacked so cruelly out of existence and sent anonymously to meet his Maker? Over and over again, Nicholas asked himself the question that contained all the others—who *was* he?

One mystery led him on to another. What had really happened to Hans Kippel? He had been given a very incomplete account by Anne Hendrik because she herself did not know the full facts. Something very unpleasant had befallen the apprentice and Nicholas resolved to find out what it was as soon as he was able. He had always liked the boy—despite his lapses—and taken an almost fatherly interest in him. Again, he was upset by Anne's patent agitation and wanted to do all he could to help. It was as important to find Hans Kippel's assailant as it was to identify the body from the Thames.

The boat reached the wharf and he paid the waterman before stepping ashore and making his way towards Gracechurch Street. With his feet on dry land again and his place of work in prospect, he turned to another grim subject. A violent death and a hounded youth had occupied his thoughts this far and those same images still lurked as he considered the walking misery that was Alexander Marwood. The threat of expulsion was indeed real. It was the reputation of Westfield's Men which could meet a violent death if the company was deprived of its home. Sharers and hired men alike would become hounded youths who were driven way from the Queen's Head. Nicholas took a realistic view of possible consequences and shuddered.

Without their base, the company would find it very difficult to survive, certainly in its present form. It might limp along in some attenuated shape for a short while by appearing intermittently at a variety of venues but this could only ever be a temporary expedient. Other companies would move in quickly to pick the bones clean. Outstanding talents such as Lawrence Firethorn, Barnaby Gill and Edmund Hoode would soon be employed elsewhere but lesser mortals would stay out in the cold. Nicholas was confident that he himself would find work somewhere in the theatre but his concern was for his fellows, for the hired men who made up the bulk of the company and who clung to it with the desperate loyalty of those who have tasted the bitterness of neglect. To be thrust once more into unemployment would be a fatal blow to some of them and they might never work again.

Nicholas caught sight of the inn sign outside the Queen's Head and he sighed. Elizabeth Tudor looked as regal and defiant as ever but she might harbour tragedy for some of her subjects. Those least able to defend themselves would be cast adrift in a hostile city. The book holder thought of Thomas Skillen, the old stagekeeper, of Hugh Wegges, the tiremen, of Peter Digby and his consort of musicians. He thought of all the other poor souls to whom Westfield's Men gave a shred of dignity and a semblance of security. One in particular haunted Nicholas.

It was George Dart.

Being a member of a celebrated theatre company was not an unqualified honour. George Dart found that he had to earn his keep and suffer for his art. Even on days when there was no performance, the hard work did not cease and his status as the youngest and smallest of the stagekeepers meant that all the most menial and demanding tasks were assigned to him. It was manifestly unjust and, though that injustice was often reduced by the kindly intercession of Nicholas Bracewell, it could still rankle. George Dart was the company workhorse, the shambling beast of burden on to whom anything and everything could be loaded by uncaring colleagues. In rare moments of introspection, when he could pause to review his lot, he generated such a lather of self-pity that he toyed with the idea of leaving the theatre altogether, a bold move that always evaporated before his eyes when he considered how impossible it would be for him to find employment elsewhere. With all its disadvantages and its insecurities, working with Westfield's Men was the only life he had ever known.

Morning found him attending to one of the jobs that he liked least. He had been sent out early to put up the playbills advertising the performance of *Double Deceit* at the Theatre on the morrow. His first problem was to get the playbills from the printer without having the money to pay for them, assuring the man that Firethorn himself would be around to settle the debt that very day, hoping that the trusting soul was not aware of all the other printers still awaiting payment by Westfield's Men. This time he was lucky and got off lightly with a clip across the ear and a few blood-curdling oaths. Dart left the premises in Paternoster Lane with the playbills under his arm and began the familiar round.

The perils that befall the puny awaited him at every turn. He was jostled by elbows, pushed by hands, tripped by feet, abused by tongues and even chased by a gang of urchins but he continued steadfastly on his way and put up the playbills on every post and fence along the route. The reputation of Westfield's Men went before them and they had built up an appreciable following in a city that was clamouring for lively theatre but that same following needed to be informed of dates and times and places. Though he was involved in unrelieved drudgery, George Dart told himself that he was a vital link between the company and its prospective audience and thereby sought to check his rising sensation of worthlessness.

When the dispiriting work was over, there was one last chore for him. At the command of Lawrence Firethorn himself, he was to deliver the remaining playbill at a house in Bishopsgate. Since it was a continuation of Gracechurch Street, he knew it well but the market was its usual seething mass of humanity and he had to struggle with all his depleted might to make headway. Stanford Place eventually came into sight and he was daunted. Its monstrous size was forbidding and he could hear the barking of dogs from within as he hovered at the threshold. He stepped back involuntarily and was about to turn tail when he remembered the order that had been given to him by Firethorn. Facing his master with the news that he had disobeyed would be worse than hurling his frail body into the midst of a pack of ravening mastiffs. He opted for the lesser punishment and reached out to pull the bell at Stanford Place.

Response was immediate. The barking increased in volume and clawed feet could be heard scrabbling at the other side of the door. When it was opened with a dignified sweep, three dogs let him know that they did not welcome his arrival. They were silenced by a curt command from the slim and supercilious man who was now gazing down his nose at the unsolicited caller. Years as the household steward had given Simon Pendleton an ability to sum up stray visitors in an instant. He felt able to use a tone of complete contempt for the crumpled George Dart.

'Depart from this place at once, boy.'

'But I have business here, sir,' pleaded the other.

'None that need be taken seriously.'

'Do but hear me, master.'

'Away with you and your confounded begging bowl!'

'I ask for nothing,' said Dart hurriedly. 'Except that this be delivered to the mistress of the house.'

Pendleton was taken aback as the handbill was passed over to him. Rolled up into a scroll, it was tied with a piece of pink ribbon to give it a hint of importance. Even though it was covered by the sweaty fingerprints of its bearer, it enforced more serious consideration.

'Who are you?' asked Pendleton.

'A mere messenger, sir.'

'From whom, boy?'

'The lady will understand.'

'I desire further information.'

'My duty has been done,' said Dart gleefully.

And before the dogs could even begin to growl, he swung around and scurried off into the crowd with a speed born of desperation. A typical morning had ended.

Marriage to a much older man was turning out to have many unforeseen advantages and Matilda Stanford enjoyed the process of discovering what they were. When a young woman consents to wed a partner of more mature years, it is usually more of an arranged match than a case of irresistible love and so it was with her. Doting parents had been delighted when so august a figure as the Master of the Mercers' Company took an interest in their daughter and they encouraged that interest as wholeheartedly as they could. While the father worked sedulously on the potential suitor, the mother began to frame the girl's mind to the concept of marriage as social advance and she had slowly broken down all of Matilda's reservations. Now that she had been a wife for five months, the new mistress of Stanford Place was revelling in her good fortune.

Her husband was kind, attentive and ready to please her with touching eagerness. At the same time, Walter Stanford was a wealthy merchant whose continued success depended on the unremitting work he put into his business affairs. His preoccupation with those—and with the many duties of being Lord Mayor Elect—meant that his wife was given ample free time to spread her wings and to learn the power of his purse. Nor was Matilda put under any undue pressure in the marriage bed. He was a patient and considerate man, never enforcing any conjugal rights that she did not willingly concede and treating her with unflagging respect. There was another element in the relationship. Though devoted to his new wife, Walter Stanford was still, to some degree, in mourning for her predecessor, his first wife, Alice, mother of his two children, a charming woman who had been killed before her time in a tragic accident some eighteen months earlier.

What pleased Matilda was the fact that she was not expected to be a complete replacement for someone who had shared her husband's life and bed for well over twenty years. Alice Stanford lay in the past. Matilda was the present and future, a rich prize owing to a rich man, an envied catch, a superb item to display in a household that prided itself above all else on the quality of its decoration. She had no illusions about it. Walter Stanford had married her to fill a gap in nature. She was there primarily to be *seen* as a wife rather than to satisfy his lust or provide him with heirs. It was a situation she came to appreciate.

Romance was signally lacking but there had been none of that in her parents' marriage and that was the model on which she based her judgements. Walter Stanford might not be able to stir her emotions but he could impress her with his wealth, please her with his gallantry and amuse her with the way that he showered gifts upon her. Matilda was indeed unawakened but only because she slept so soundly in such a comfortable existence.

'Where shall we go next?'

'I have not recovered from yesterday's outing yet.'

'London has much more to offer,' he said. 'It is the most exciting city in Europe.'

'I am learning that to be true.'

'Let us sail up the river to Hampton Court.'

'Hold on, sir. Do not hurry me so.'

'Then let us go riding together instead.'

'You are so good to me, William.'

'It is because *you* are so good for father.'

William Stanford was a handsome, upright young man of twenty who had inherited all the best features of his parents. He dressed like a gallant and sought out the pleasures of the day but he also had a shrewd business sense and enjoyed working alongside his father. Shaken by his mother's violent death, he had at first been hostile to the idea of his father's remarriage but Matilda had soon won him over with her beauty and sincerity. She had brought much-needed cheer into the gloom of Stanford Place and, now that she was losing her shyness, she was able to show an effervescence that was delightful. It was William who had taken her to the Queen's Head to watch Westfield's Men in action. He was now anxious to provide further diversions for her.

'Do but wait until Michael returns,' he said.

'When is your cousin due back, sir?'

'At any time now. He has been serving as a soldier in the Low Countries out of sheer bravado.' William gave an affectionate smile. 'You will love Michael. He is the merriest fellow alive and will make you laugh until you beg him to stop lest your sides split.'

'I look forward to meeting him.'

'Michael is the very soul of mirth.'

They were interrupted by a tap on the door. Simon Pendleton oozed into the room with the scroll in his hand and inclined his head in the suspicion of a bow.

'A messenger delivered this for you, mistress.'

'Thank you, sir.'

'He was a ragged creature,' said the steward, handing over the scroll. 'I liked not the look of him and hope that his missive will not cause offence.'

'I do adore surprises,' she said with a giggle and began to untie the ribbon. 'What can it be?'

Pendleton lurked. 'Nothing untoward, I trust.'

'That will be all, Simon,' said William dismissively.

The steward hid his annoyance behind a mask of civility and withdrew soundlessly. Matilda unrolled the playbill and stared at it with sudden ecstasy.

'Dear God, this is wonderful!' she cried.

'May I see?'

'Look, sir. Westfield's Men play again tomorrow.'

'*Double Deceit*,' he noted. 'I have seen the piece before. It is an excellent comedy and well-acted.'

'Let us go to this playhouse to see it, William.'

'But I already have another treat in store for you tomorrow. I purposed to take you to The Curtain to watch Banbury's Men go through their paces.'

'I would see Master Firethorn again.'

'He is a brilliant actor, I grant you,' said William, 'but some people believe that Giles Randolph is even better. He has led Banbury's Men to the heights and plays the title role in the *Tragical History of King John*. Take my advice and give Master Randolph his chance.'

'That I will do at some future time,' she promised. 'For tomorrow, I pray, conduct me to The Theatre. It is my earnest wish.' She held up the playbill. 'It would be churlish to refuse such an invitation.'

William quickly agreed then began to tell her something of the plot of *Double Deceit* but his stepmother was not listening. Matilda's mind was racing. She was young and inexperienced in such matters but she sensed that the playbill had been sent for a purpose. Someone was anxious for her to attend a playhouse in Shoreditch on the following day and that set up all sorts of intriguing possibilities. Matilda Stanford was firmly married and she would be going in the company of her stepson but that did not stop her feeling a surge of joyful expectation such as she had never known before.

A grubby playbill had touched her heart.

Hans Kippel had been told to stay at his lodgings and rest but the force of habit was too strong for the lad. It got him out of his bed and along to his workplace early in the morning. Surprised to see him, Preben van Loew had shown a fatherly care for the apprentice and given him only the simplest tasks but even these were beyond his competence. The boy was clearly suffering the after-effects of his ordeal and could not focus his mind on anything for more than a few minutes. The Dutchman tried to probe him for more details of what had occurred on the previous day but none were forthcoming. A blow to the head had locked all memory of the incident inside the young skull of Hans Kippel.

It was early afternoon when Nicholas Bracewell came back to the house in Bankside. He had spent the morning at The Theatre, finalizing the arrangements for the performance of *Double Deceit* and supervising the transfer of costumes and properties from the Queen's Head. With a little spare time at his disposal, he had hurried home to see if he could coax any further information out of the wounded apprentice. Hans Kippel was pleased to see him and shook his hand warmly but the boy's face then became vacant again. Nicholas sat beside him and spoke low.

'We are all very proud of you, Hans.'

'Why so, sir?'

'Because you are a very brave young man.'

'I do not feel brave, Master Bracewell.'

'How do you feel?'

'Sore afraid. I am lost and know not where to turn.'

'You are among friends here, Hans. Safe and sound.'

'Will you protect me, sir?'

'From what?'

The blank face clouded. 'I cannot tell. My mind has cut me adrift. But I know I have enemies.'

'What enemies? Who are they?'

But Hans Kippel had yielded up all that he could. Not even

the patient questioning of Nicholas Bracewell could draw anything further out of him. The book holder consulted with Preben van Loew who gave it as his opinion that the boy would be far better off in the comfort of his bed. He was patently not fit for work and needed all the rest that he could get. Nicholas agreed only partly with this, arguing that the apprentice would never make a full recovery until his mind had been cleared of the horror that had possessed it. Since that might not happen of its own volition, he suggested an idea that might help. He volunteered to accompany Hans Kippel as they retraced the steps the boy had taken on the previous day, hoping that somewhere along the way his memory would be restored by the sight of something familiar.

Preben van Loew gave his blessing to the enterprise and waved the two of them off at the door. Hans Kippel was a sad figure with his bandaged head and his limp. It had already occurred to Nicholas that it might have been his nationality which told against the youth. His sober attire, open face and general mien marked him out as a Dutch immigrant and thus the natural target for the resentment of many people. In the company of someone as tall and muscular as Nicholas Bracewell, the boy was not likely to be mocked so openly but he might just recognize the point in the journey at which his humiliation took place. They walked slowly on together.

'Look all about you, Hans,' said Nicholas.

'I will do so, sir.'

'Tell me if you see aught that you remember.'

'My mind is still empty.'

'We will try to put something in it.'

The journey came to an abrupt end. One minute Hans Kippel was dragging himself along in a daze, the next, he was staring ahead in terror and refusing to move another step. They had come out of the Bankside labyrinth by St Saviour's Church and were heading towards the bridge. It was one of the finest sights in London, a truly imposing structure that spanned the murky Thames with a series of arches and which housed a miniature city on its broad back. Visitors came from all over Europe to marvel at London Bridge but here was one foreigner who had no sense of wonder. Hans Kippel turned white with fear and let out a scream of intense pain. His trembling finger pointed at the bridge. Before Nicholas could stop him, he turned around and limped away as fast as his injured legs would carry him.

Chapter Three

A BEL STRUDWICK PASSED A TROUBLED NIGHT IN restless contemplation of the incident. Not even the sonorous snoring of the wife who laid beside him could lull him into slumber and this was unusual. As a rule, the waterman enjoyed his sleep to the full, wearied by the physical strains of his working day and by the consumption of ample quantities of bottle ale. He would be dead to the world within minutes and spend a restorative night in dreams of being plucked from the toil of his occupation to become a revered poet. A corpse in the Thames had changed all that. Strudwick had hauled bodies out of the water before now but none had been so gruesome as this one and even his strong stomach had rebelled. Memory turned night into one long, lacerating ordeal.

The next day found him tired and fractious, more ready than ever to burn the ears off his customers with a positive inferno of vituperation. Unlike most watermen, Strudwick plied his trade on his own. The bulk of his fellows took their passengers across the river in six- or eight-oared wherries that enabled them to cope with large parties. Strudwick had only a small rowing boat. He and his son had operated very successfully in it until the latter was press-ganged during the panic that preceded the news of the approach of the Spanish

Armada. The loss of their apprentices to the navy was a source of great pain in the watermen's community but their protests went unheard and unregarded. It was not surprising that they therefore resorted to all kinds of stratagems to protect their young men from such a dire fate.

Strudwick paid a young lad to help him from time to time and to sleep in the boat at night to prevent it from being stolen, but the aspiring poet mostly worked alone. The others mocked him cruelly for his ambitions but none dared do so to his face. In contests of verbal abuse and in wharfside brawls, he was a fearsome opponent who could see off the best. Abel Strudwick's black tongue and bulging biceps created the space in which his verse could thrive unhampered. Drink lubricated his creative powers and it was in a tavern that most of his inspiration came.

So it was that afternoon as he sat in the corner of the taproom at the Jolly Sailor and gave his fertile mind free rein. The verse came haltingly at first, then more fluently and, finally, in a torrent that had him leaping up from his stool. Keen to oblige a regular customer, the landlord had pen and ink at the ready for the waterman and Strudwick pulled out the scrap of parchment that he always carried with him for such precious moments. He scratched away happily for half an hour before he felt it was time to return to work. The Bankside theatres would be emptying soon and there would be passengers for every boatman who was moored on the Surrey side of the river.

As Abel Strudwick came tumbling out of the inn, it was another playhouse that caught his attention. Stuck to a post nearby was something which he felt had been put there by the hand of God. It was a playbill advertising the performance of *Double Deceit* by Westfield's Men on the following day and it crystallized a plan which had been forming in his mind for several months. His days as a fumbling amateur in the world of words were numbered. He wanted to see and hear how a professional pen could write verse in a dramatic vein and get the encouragement to fulfil his vaulting ambition. Nicholas Bracewell was a good friend who had never let him down in the past.

It was time to put that friendship to the test.

Margery Firethorn was kept as busy as ever. In addition to her normal household complements of souls, she had to cater for the three actors who were staying with them in Shoreditch and whom she had packed into the attic room to keep them out of the way of the other inhabitants. She ran a tight ship and nobody was allowed to flout her captaincy. When one of the actors dared to ogle a servant girl, Margery gave him a fierce sermon on self-restraint and warned him that his voice would rise by two octaves if she ever caught him fraternizing again. Since she was carrying the kitchen knife at the time, he understood her meaning all too well and withdrew hastily to the attic to acquaint his fellows with what had passed. All females in the house were treated with excessive respect from that time on and even the she-cats earned more consideration.

Caught up as she was in feeding and caring for her extended family, Margery yet found time to keep an alert eye on her husband. Lawrence Firethorn had swept her off her feet with one of the most sublime performances of his career then borne her off down the aisle before she could even begin to resist. It had been a magical experience that could still flicker in the memory on rare occasions but it was dulled beneath the accumulated debris that a marriage inevitably builds up. One thing she had learned at an early stage: her husband had the defects of his virtues. His overwhelming talent as an actor had indeed seduced her but she was realistic enough to see that it had a powerful effect on other women as well. Temptation was ever-present and Firethorn was not always able to resist it. Without her vigilance, he would be led astray by every red lip and arched eyebrow. She sensed that he was beginning to look elsewhere and decided to fire a warning shot across his bows!

'Good morning to you, sir!'

'Good morning, my dove,' he said expansively. 'The sun is streaming down from the heavens to gild the marital couch.'

'You may well say that from where you lay,' she observed

tartly, 'but I have been up these two hours to make all ready downstairs. Besides,' she added, 'if our marital couch is so special to you, why did you return to it so late last night?'

'Work and worry kept me away.'

'Does she have a name?'

'Margery! How can you even suggest such a thing?'

He sat up in the four-poster with rumpled dignity and scratched at his beard. His wife stood over him with folded arms and snarled her next question.

'Do you love me, sir?'

'I dote on you, my treasure.'

'But do you dote on me *enough*?'

'My devotion is without human limit.'

'That is my complaint, Lawrence,' she said. 'I would that your devotion was limited to *me* but it flies away like a bird on the wing.'

'Only to return with joy. I am your homing pigeon.'

'You are an eagle, sir, who searches out new prey.'

'These suspicions are unfair and unfounded.'

'Prove it!'

He struck a pose. 'My conscience is clear.'

'You do not possess such a thing.'

'Sweetness,' he said. 'What means this discord so early in the day? What crime have I committed?'

'It still lies festering in your brain.'

'That brain is occupied with fond thoughts of you.'

'Only when I stand before you.'

'And lie beneath me, my little pomegranate.'

He spoke with such tender lechery that even her resolve weakened. A big, buxom, bustling woman in a simple working dress, she let herself be flattered by his words and by the admiring glances he now directed at her. With all its faults, the marriage had never lacked excitement or pleasure. Another episode now beckoned.

'You left my side too soon,' he cooed.

'There was much to be done below.'

'Come back to me for a moment of wild madness.'

'It would be madness indeed at this hour.'

'Let me *show* you how much I love you, Margery.'

Her doubts were temporarily wiped away and she moved in close to be gathered into whirling embrace. She was lifted bodily into the bed and let out a girlish laugh as he rolled on top of her but their joy was short-lived. Before he could plant the first whiskery kiss on her eager lips, pandemonium broke out. A pan boiled over in the kitchen and set off an argument between the two servant girls. The children began a noisy fight and the four apprentices went thundering down the stairs for their breakfast. Worst of all, there was a loud knock on the door of the bedchamber and one of the actors put a decisive end to the snatched happiness.

'I must speak with you at once, sir,' he said.

Firethorn's howl of rage deafened all of Shoreditch.

The Theatre was the first purpose-built public playhouse in London. Situated just north of Holywell Lane, at the angle of Curtain Road and New Inn Yard, it was outside the city boundaries and thus free of its niggling regulations yet close enough to attract the large audiences that came streaming out through Bishopsgate to enjoy its facilities and view its productions. It had been constructed in 1576 under the supervision of James Burbage, a determined man who had begun life as a joiner only to renounce his trade in favour of the theatre. Talent and application helped him to become the leading actor with Leicester's Men but he had a fondness for security and a flair for management that led him to erect The Theatre at an estimated cost of some £666. Even though he bickered thereafter with his partner, John Brayne, a litigious grocer who also happened to be his brother-in-law, the importance of his pioneering work could not be denied. The first permanent home for actors gave their art a new lustre and status. They were at last taken seriously.

Animals influenced humans. For it was the bear- and bull-baiting arenas of Bankside which provided the basic principles of construction. The Theatre was a polygonal building made of stout timber and a modicum of ironwork. Where it differed from the animal-baiting houses was in its imaginative detail. The ring itself was covered with brick and stone, thus turning it into a paved yard with efficient drainage. A stage thrust out boldly into the yard, supported by solid posts rather than by the trestles and barrels used at places like the Queen's Head. At the rear of the stage was a tiring-house which gave the company easy access to the playing area. Above the back section of this area was a cover known as the heavens. Held aloft by tall pillars, it was in turn surmounted by a small hut that could be used to house any suspension gear that was needed for a particular play or, indeed, as a tiny acting area in itself.

The last major difference that separated The Theatre from the standard arena was its use of a third gallery. The Bankside baiting-houses were all two-storey buildings that were roughly similar in design. James Burbage did not make his playhouse tower above Shoreditch simply in order to attest its presence. An extra gallery meant an increase in the number of patrons and a corresponding rise in the income that any company could expect. And though the place was an outdoor venue, its cylindrical shape was a form of umbrella against inclement weather and the thatched roofs above the galleries added a great measure of comfort and protection. Much care and thought had gone into the whole venture. It was the brainchild of a true man of the theatre.

Nicholas Bracewell was the first to arrive. His visit to the Queen's Head had only served to deepen his fears that their days at the inn were numbered. With all his appalling faults, Alexander Marwood did actually allow the company to flourish on his premises and the makeshift stage had witnessed some of their finest achievements. If Rowland Ashway acquired the property, he would have no qualms in turning Westfield's Men out into the street. Fresh anxieties surfaced about the likely fate of his fellows. A huge black cloud hung over the future of the company and Nicholas was the only person who knew about it. How long he could keep the fact to himself remained to be seen but it was already causing him profound disquiet.

Thomas Skillen was the next to turn up at The Theatre. The venerable stagekeeper had been with Westfield's Men since their formation but his roots in the drama went much deeper than that. For over forty years now, he had survived in a ruinous profession that had hurled so many people into oblivion, and he had done so by virtue of his quick wits and total reliability. What hope would there be for him if he was driven out of his job now? Advancing age and creaking joints had slowed him down but he could still assert his authority. George Dart found this out when he came running out on to the stage to be given a clip across the ear by the senior man.

'You struck me, Thomas!' he said in alarm.

'Aye, sirrah, I did.'

'For what reason?'

'For none at all, George. The blow was on account.'

'But I have done nothing amiss.'

'You will, sirrah. You will.'

Nicholas stepped in to rescue the injured party and to assign jobs to both men. *Double Deceit* was a highly complicated play which made heavy demands on those behind the scenes. It was an amiable comedy about two pairs of identical twins who get caught up in an escalating series of mistakes and misapprehensions. Inspired by one of the plays of Plautus, it was a glorious romp that never failed to delight its audiences but it called for several scene changes and required an interminable list of properties.

By the time that others began to appear, Thomas Skillen and George Dart had set the stage so that the rehearsal could begin and were attending to a myriad other duties.

Lawrence Firethorn waited until the full company was assembled before he strode out on to the stage with his characteristic swagger. A raised hand compelled silence.

'Gentlemen,' he announced. 'Let me rid your minds of one abiding error. This is not a rehearsal of an old and ailing text whose sparkle has been dimmed by the passage of time. *Double Deceit* is no plodding nag who asks no more of us than to sit back lazily in the saddle and guide her in the right direction. She is a mettlesome filly whom we take out on her first full gallop today. Wear your spurs, my friends, and do not be shy of using them. We must ride hell for leather into glory!'

Younger members of the cast were stirred by his speech

but older hands were more cynical. Barnaby Gill leaned over to whisper to Edmund Hoode.

'As I foretold, *she* is coming to the performance.'

'Who?'

'The latest sacrificial victim for his bed,' said Gill sardonically. 'That is why we would put some ginger into *Double Deceit*. He wants to warm the lady up so that she is glowing strongly when he boards her. Westfield's Men are being used as his pimps.'

'Lawrence does not always meet with success.'

'Nor shall he this time, Edmund. This ignoble plot shall be nipped in the bud. I'll act him off the stage and end the matter there.'

The boast was stillborn. It was easier to perform triple somersaults through the eye of a needle than to out-act Lawrence Firethorn when he turned on his full power. For that is what he did at the rehearsal. There was no holding back, no harbouring of his resources for the afternoon. In the twin roles of Argos of Rome and Argos of Florence, he was a soaring comet who dazzled all around him. Barnaby Gill doubled manfully in the parallel roles of the comic servants, Silvio of Rome and Silvio of Florence, but it took all his energy to keep pace with his two masters, let alone try to overtake either.

It was a bold decision to tackle two roles each and it necessitated great concentration and perfect timing to maintain the illusion for the audience. Argos of Rome and his much-maligned companion, Silvio, were a jaded pair who dressed in mean apparel. Argos of Florence, however, and his chirpy servant, Silvio, were bubbling extroverts with vivid attire. As one pair left the stage, the other would step out on to it almost immediately. Lightning changes of cloak, hat and manner worked wonders.

Firethorn's urgency dragged the rest of the cast along behind it. The major technical problem came in Act Five when the two pairs of twins, separated since birth and totally unaware of each other's existence, finally learn the truth and unite in love and laughter. To effect this climactic moment when all four meet together, two other actors had to stand in as one of the duos. The fleeting appearance as Argos of Rome was made by Owen Elias, a sturdy Welshman whose height and build matched those of Firethorn himself. Dressed in the costume of Silvio of Rome, padded out to give him more substance, was none other than George Dart. The substitute twins were a complete contrast. While the Welshman took the stage with overweening confidence, the assistant stage-keeper crept on to it with all the enthusiasm of a snail crawling into a fiery furnace. The latter was mortified when he knocked over a chair in his nervousness and then accidentally pulled the cloak off Silvio of Florence during an embrace with his putative twin. As the play came to an end, Dart waited in trepidation for the acid comments of Firethorn.

But none came. Delighted with his own account of the two roles, and certain that his company would rise to the occasion in front of a large audience, the actor-manager dismissed them all with a few kind words then swept off into the tiring-house. Nicholas Bracewell was not so uncritical of what he had seen and he had many notes to give to erring performers before they slipped away. He had just administered a gentle reprimand to George Dart when Edmund Hoode sidled up to him.

'Tell me her name, Nick.'

'Who?'

'This enchantress who has bewitched Lawrence.'

'That is his business alone.'

'It is ours as well if it affects his conduct here among his fellows. Why, man, he was grinning at us like some lovesick youth just now. If this lady's magic is so potent, we must lure her into the company and pay her to keep the old bear sweet. It would be money well-spent.'

Nicholas smiled. 'We all would benefit.'

'So who is this paragon?'

'I may not say, Edmund.'

'But it was you who tracked her down.'

'Master Firethorn has sworn me to secrecy.'

'Can you not divulge the name to me?'

'Neither to you nor to any living soul.'

'But I am your friend, Nick.'

'It is my friendship that holds me back,' said the other seriously. 'You would not thank me for breaking my oath. Better it is that you do not know who the lady is.'

Hoode's eyes widened. 'Do I spy danger here?'

'Acute danger.'

'For Lawrence?'

'For all of us.'

Sir Lucas Pugsley, fishmonger, philanthropist and incumbent Lord Mayor of London finished another gargantuan meal and washed it down with a glass of French brandy. His guest was still guzzling away at his lunch and taking frequent swigs of beer from the two-pint tankard that stood before him. The Mayor was dining in private for once and sharing confidences with an old friend. Pugsley was as thin as a rake and as pale as a spectre. No matter how much food he ate—and his appetite was gross—he never seemed to put on any weight. The narrow face with its tight lips, its high cheek-bones and its tiny black eyes resembled nothing so much as the head of a conger eel. Even in his full regalia, he looked as if he were lying on a slab.

Rowland Ashway was a completely different man. His gormandizing had left its mark all too flagrantly upon him. The wealthy brewer had been turned into a human barrel to advertise his way of life. Regular consumption of his own best beer had given the puffed cheeks and the blob of nose such a florid hue that he appeared to be cultivating tomatoes. The two men had a political as well as a personal connection. As Alderman for Bridge Ward Within, the wily Ashway had promoted Pugsley's candidacy for the ultimate civic honour. The fishmonger did not forget such loyalty and it had been rewarded by more than the occasional free meal. Ashway pushed the last mouthful down his throat then emptied his tankard after it. He gave a monstrous belch, laughed merrily and broke wind. It was time for them to sit back in their carved chairs and preen themselves at will.

'My mayoralty has been a triumph,' said Pugsley with easy pomposity. 'I have grown into the role.'

'It fits you like a glove.'

'This city has cause to be grateful to me.'

'Your bounty is in evidence on all sides,' noted the other. 'You have founded schools, built almshouses and donated generously to the Church.'

'Nor have I been slack in my love of country,' said the fishmonger piously. 'Queen Elizabeth herself—God bless her—has been ready to borrow Pugsley money for the defence of the realm. English soldiers are the salt of the earth. I feel honoured that I was able to put uniforms on to their backs and weapons into their hands.'

'A knighthood was a fitting reward, Luke.'

'Sir Lucas, if you please.'

'Sir Lucas.' Ashway fawned obligingly. 'The pity of it is that you cannot remain in place as Lord Mayor.'

'Nothing would please me more, Rowland.'

'We have all been beneficiaries of your term of office and are like to remember it well.'

'There is more still to come. I value friendship above all else and set a true value on it. Aubrey and I were discussing the matter only this morning.'

'Aubrey Kenyon is an upright man,' said the brewer. 'His opinions are to be taken seriously.'

'That is why I always seek them out. My Chamberlain is always the first person I consult on any subject. He is a complete master of the intricacies of municipal affairs and I could not survive for a second without him.'

'You are in safe hands, Sir Lucas.'

'None safer than those of Aubrey Kenyon.'

'Indeed not.' Ashway did some fishing of his own. 'And you say there is something in the wind for me?'

'A small reward for your unfailing loyalty.'

'You are too kind.'

'A trifling matter to a man of your wealth but it may bring some pleasure. You will acquire the control and rent of certain properties in your ward. My Chamberlain advised me on the form of it and he is drawing up the necessary documents.'

'I must thank Master Aubrey Kenyon once again.'

'Where I command, he takes action.'

'Your Chamberlain is truly a paragon.'

'I would trust him like my own brother.' Pugsley took another sip of brandy then appraised his companion. 'Does your business still thrive, Rowland?'

'Assuredly. We go from strength to strength.'

'Feeding off the drunkenness of London!'

'Stout men need strong ale. I simply answer their demand.'

They shared a chuckle then Pugsley fingered his chain with offhand affection. 'I have felt happy and fulfilled as never before in this office,' he said. 'Would that I might stay in it for ever!' A wistful sigh. 'Alas, that is not to be. Election has already been made.'

'*I* did not vote for him, that I swear.'

'Others did.' Pugsley's sadness turned into cold fury. 'It is painful enough to have to retire from office but to be forced to hand over to Walter Stanford is truly galling. I detest the man and all that he represents.'

'You are not alone in that, Sir Lucas.'

'He is unworthy to follow in my footsteps.'

'As for that young wife of his . . .'

'It ought not to be allowed,' said the other in a fit of moral indignation. 'A man should pay for his pleasures in private, not flaunt them before the whole city of London!'

'She is a pretty creature, though, I grant him that.'

'Stanford is bestial!'

'He is not Lord Mayor yet.'

'What do you mean?'

'Many a slip 'twist cup and lip.'

Sir Lucas Pugsley sat upright in his chair and spat out his words like a snake expelling its venom.

'I would do *anything* to stop him!'

Fine weather and high expectation saw large crowds of playgoers surging north out of the city. Many of them converged on The Curtain, the other public playhouse in Shoreditch, a circular structure that stood on land that had once been part of Holywell Priory. Banbury's Men were in residence there and the audience flocked to see Giles Randolph as the evil

King John. His reputation was over-shadowed by that of Lawrence Firethorn who brought even more spectators hurrying through the doors of The Theatre. Once again, Westfield's Men had the critical edge over its hated rivals.

Abel Strudwick had never been to a play before and he was bewildered by the whole experience. Having paid his penny to one of the gatherers, he went through into the yard and stood as close to the stage as he could. He was soon part of a jostling throng with a carnival spirit and he succumbed willingly to the prevailing atmosphere of mirth. His poems were a source of immense pride to him but he had only so far recited them to his wife and to Nicholas Bracewell. The thought of standing up on that scaffold and entertaining a huge crowd with the work of his creative imagination was quite exhilarating. Long before *Double Deceit* began, he had got his penny's worth.

Matilda Stanford was ushered into the second gallery by her stepson. A friend of his had helped to escort her at the Queen's Head but the young man felt able to look after her alone at The Theatre. William Stanford had opted for a black doublet with a wide-shouldered look and for matching hose. Silver flashes relieved the impression of total darkness and silver feathers adorned his hat. His stepmother had chosen a blend of subtle greens in a dress that displayed all her best features to advantage. Her hair and clothing were perfumed and she carried a pomander to ward off any unpleasant smells that might arise in a packed auditorium. The mask which dangled from her other hand could be used to hide the blushes that were already threatening to come as her presence was noted by the gallants who surrounded her. Compliments and comments ambushed her from all sides.

The keenest attention she received, however, was from Argos of Rome. Costumed for his first entrance, Lawrence Firethorn peered through a chink in the curtain at the rear of the stage to pick out his beloved. She looked even more alluring than before, with those blue eyes and red lips lighting up her porcelain skin. Matilda Stanford had true radiance and he prostrated himself before it.

Nicholas Bracewell came quietly up behind him.

'Stand by, sir.'

'She had my invitation, Nick. She is *here*.'

'So is the hour of two.'

'I knew that she would not disappoint me!'

'Stand by, Argos of Rome!'

'This is earthly paradise.'

'We begin!'

The book holder was firmly in control of the whole operation once the performance started and not even the company's star was allowed to forget that. Firethorn moved quickly across to join Barnaby Gill in readiness for their entrance. The signal was given by Nicholas, the trumpet sounded and the Prologue stepped out in a black cloak to receive a virgin ripple of applause and to outline the plot of *Double Deceit* in rhyming couplets. Argos and Silvio then burst on to the stage in a flurry of arms and legs as the master upbraided his servant and beat him black and blue. Firethorn's voice was hoarse with outrage as he listed his complaints and Gill made the audience collapse with laughter at the hilarious way he fell to the ground each time he was struck. The comic timing and the physical dexterity of the two men was breathtaking. They had won everyone over by the time they made their exit then they re-appeared instantly in other guises to win the spectators over even more completely.

Double Deceit had never been played with such panache. There was only one dissentient voice.

'I am wasted in this verminous comedy.'

'Your hour will come, Owen.'

'It is a crime to subdue such talent as mine.'

'Do but wait awhile and it will shine forth.'

'I have waited too long already, Nick.'

'So have many others, I fear.'

'Who cares about those wretches? I am *better*.'

Owen Elias was no shrinking violet. While other hired men took what they could get and were profoundly grateful, he was forever trying to plead his cause. He was without question a far more skilful performer than most of his fellows and his lilting voice was a joy to hear when it was given blank verse to declaim. But his talent as an actor was not matched by his tact as a diplomat. In thrusting himself forward so openly, he jeopardized his already slim chances of advancement. Nicholas liked him immensely for his Celtic charm and forthrightness but he recognized the fatal flaw in his friend. The runaway arrogance made Owen Elias into his own worst enemy.

'Do you see what I mean, Nick?'

'Tell me later, sir.'

'I can do all that Master Firethorn can.'

'You distract me, Owen.'

'They loved me.'

'Stand aside, I pray.'

Nicholas was too busy at his post to listen to the actor at that moment but there was a degree of truth in what the Welshman said. In his brief appearance as Argos of Rome, he not only looked and moved remarkably like Lawrence Firethorn, he even sounded like him. Indeed, the audience was so stunned by the similarity between the two men that they really believed they were looking at a pair of identical twins. It was, literally, a double deceit.

Firethorn was left alone to deliver the Epilogue.

> Comedy, our sages oft advise us,
> May come accoutred in diverse disguises.
> True laughter wears such various attire,
> Colour, cut, fashion and style conspire
> To catch the eye and to create such mirth,
> That heavenly happiness dwells on earth.
> In dressing up our offering today
> We use twice the apparel of another play.
> Behind a cloak hid brooding Argos of Rome,
> His twin of Florence lurked beneath a dome . . .

He was leaving the audience in no doubt about the fact that he had played the two parts. He changed cloaks on the line about the brooding Argos and put on his other hat when he referred to a dome. Then he went on to repeat the process throughout the remainder of the Epilogue, thus confirming his genius as a theatrical chameleon. It was a play in itself and the spectators were spellbound.

Abel Strudwick had been hypnotized by it all for two hours and this final piece of bravura left him totally awe-struck. The furious pace and the freewheeling humour gave him an experience that altered his whole view of himself. He wanted somehow to be part of it all, to shed the onerous burdens of being a waterman and join the marvellous world of theatre. What had aroused most wonder in him was the quality of the verse. *Double Deceit* was written largely in prose but it did contain a number of speeches in rhyming couplets that struck him as superb. Delivered by the masterful Firethorn, their shortcomings were cunningly concealed. Strudwick longed to write such lines for such an actor, even to become a performer himself. It was a more honourable existence than rowing incessantly across the River Thames. Receiving the plaudits of such a delirious auditorium was infinitely better than dragging dead bodies out of dark water.

Matilda Stanford was also entranced by the whole experience. Deeply moved at the Queen's Head, she had been dizzied by the sheer extravagance of today's frolic. A simple playbill had brought her to The Theatre with a curiosity that was soon satisfied. Lawrence Firethorn himself had sent the invitation and he had left her in no doubt of that. Whether he was playing Argos of Rome or Argos of Florence, he found a way to direct certain lines straight at her by way of tribute. Matilda was utterly enraptured. With his scintillating display in the twin roles, the actor-manager had even surpassed his sublime performance as Count Orlando—and *this* was the man who had deigned to notice her. Concluding the Epilogue, he blew her a kiss and bowed in acknowledgement of her smile. Even in the thunder of the curtain call, Firethorn found time to speak to her with his eyes.

A faithful young wife forgot about her husband.

Walter Stanford was indefatigable. He rose early each day and worked late into the night, attending to his business affairs with jovial energy and pushing out the frontiers of his operations all the time. Sunday was his only day of rest and even then stray thoughts of his latest enterprises mingled with his prayers. The Master of the Mercers' Company did not believe in resting on his many laurels. Expansion was his watchword.

Other men would have been daunted by the additional amount of work entailed in being Lord Mayor Elect but Stanford welcomed it. He simply got up even earlier and laboured longer into the darkness. If fatigue ever laid a hand upon him, he never showed it. If obstacles fell across his path, he leapt nimbly over them. If anything even began to depress his spirits, he invoked the memory of his mentor, Dick Whittington, and carried on with restored vigour. It was impossible to compete with Walter Stanford. He was invincible.

That afternoon found him sitting at the table in his study leafing through some contracts pertaining to the coal mines that he owned up in Newcastle. He checked the figures carefully before entering them into a large account book then he turned to consider another part of his burgeoning empire. It did not worry him in the least that his wife was watching a play at The Theatre while he was slaving on at Stanford Place. He worked so that she might enjoy her leisure and he was content with that arrangement. Rocked by the loss of one wife, he could not believe his luck in being given a second chance of happiness and he did not spurn it. His wife and family were all to him and his industry was at their service.

A knock on the door interrupted his concentration. He looked up as Simon Pendleton sidled into the room carrying a long flat box that was tied with string. A faint whiff in the air made Stanford's nose wrinkle.

'I am sorry to intrude, Master,' said the steward.

'What have you brought me?'

'This has just been delivered, sir.'

'By whom?'

'He did not stay to declare himself,' said the other with mild disapproval. 'When I opened the front door, I found this box upon the step. It is addressed to you.'

'What is that strange odour?'

'I am not sure, sir, but it made the dogs sniff their fill.

That is why I brought the box straight to you. They would have torn it open else.'

'Thank you, Simon. Put it on the table.'

'Yes, sir.'

Pendleton laid the box down as if he was glad to part with it then stood back so that its pungency did not invade his nostrils any more. Stanford used a knife to cut through the string then lifted the lid with interest. His eyebrows shot up in amazement when he saw what lay inside. It was almost two feet long and weighed several pounds. The silver scales glittered in the light. He took the item out and held it on the palms of both hands to feel its substance and wonder at its meaning. Gifts from friends or debtors were quite common but he had never received an anonymous present of this nature before. Master and steward stared in complete bafflement.

They were looking at a dead fish.

Chapter Four

NICHOLAS BRACEWELL WAS STILL AT THE THEATRE well after the audience and the cast had departed. With the help of Thomas Skillen and his assistant stagekeepers, he gathered up everything belonging to Westfield's Men and loaded it into a cart. When he had paid the manager for the rental of the playhouse and confirmed details of their next visit to the venue, he drove the cart back towards the city and in through Bishopsgate with his motley crew sitting on the vehicle behind him. As the old horse pulled them on a jolting ride over the cobbles, Nicholas looked up with misgiving at Stanford Place. It was an imposing edifice but perils loitered within for the whole company. George Dart felt it as well. Shrinking away from the house as it appeared on his left, he heard the distant bark of dogs and shivered violently.

They were all glad to reach the Queen's Head where their effects would be stored until required on the following Monday. Willing hands unloaded and locked everything away then extended themselves towards the book holder with open palms. It was the end of the week and their wages were paid. Most of them went straight off to spend some of their money on ale and to toast the end of another long and tiring stint of work. The solitary exception was George Dart who scampered off home to his lodgings in Cheapside to appease his landlady with his rent and to catch up on some of the sleep that he invariably lost in the service of Westfield's Men.

Nicholas went into the taproom to be pounced on by the egregious publican. Alexander Marwood saw the chance to wallow in further misery.

'One of my serving wenches is with child,' he said. 'I blame Westfield's Men.'

'*All* of them?' queried Nicholas.

'Actors are born lechers.'

'Has the lady named the father?'

'She does not need to, Master Bracewell. The finger points at a member of your company.'

'Then the finger is too hasty in its accusation,' said the book holder. 'Lechery is not confined to our profession. Other men are prey to such urges and you have hundreds of red-blooded customers here during any week. Besides, why must you judge the girl so harshly? Perhaps it was love and not lust that was at work here. Haply, she and her swain plan to wed.'

'There is no talk of that,' said Marwood bitterly. '*She* has lost her virtue and *I* have lost a serving wench. Acting and venery go hand in hand. I will not be loath to see Westfield's Men quit my premises.'

'You are unjust, sir. Do not thrust us out before we have been able to argue our case.'

'What case?'

'Consider how well our arrangement has worked in the past. We have all been beneficiaries.'

'I beg leave to doubt that.'

'Come now,' said Nicholas firmly. 'If our contract did not yield advantage, why did you suffer it these three or four years past? When it suited your purpose, you were quick enough to sign the articles of agreement. All that needs to be done now is to make those provisions a little more appealing to you.'

'The offer comes too late, Master Bracewell.'

'What do you mean?'

'I have another suitor at my door.'

Alexander Marwood gave a sickly grin and pointed towards the corpulent figure at the far end of the bar counter. Rowland Ashway was dispensing some flabby charm on Marwood's wife, impressing her with his aldermanic importance and wooing her with smiling promises about the rosy future that lay ahead if she and her husband agreed to let him take over their inn. A stone-faced harridan was being turned into a compliant woman. The landlord marvelled at the transformation; then hurried across in the hopes of gaining some personal advantage from it. Marwood was soon beaming alternately at his wife and at Rowland Ashway, hanging on the words of both with an almost child-like eagerness.

Nicholas Bracewell was shaken by what he saw. There was an easy arrogance about the brewer which showed how confident he was of landing his prize. Evidently, he was offering them blandishments with which Westfield's Men could not hope to compete. It was going to be extremely difficult to fight off the aldermanic challenge but it had to be done somehow. What troubled Nicholas most was that he was likely to be encumbered rather than helped by his fellows. If he broke the news to Lawrence Firethorn and the other sharers, they would react with such violence that any future dealings with Marwood would be greatly imperilled. For the time being, the book holder was on his own. Yet that situation could not last. Sooner or later, he had to take someone into his confidence. It would have to be done in such a way that hysteria did not spread like wildfire through Westfield's Men.

As he glanced around the taproom, Nicholas could see eight or nine members of the company, relaxing after the exigencies of performance and laughing freely, blissfully unaware of the threat that hung over their livelihood. He did not have the heart to smash their fragile dreams with his grim intelligence. Hiding it deep within him, he went across to a table to join two special friends.

Owen Elias was in the middle of a long monologue but his companion was not listening to a word of it. With his round, clean-shaven moon face aglow, Edmund Hoode stared ahead of him at some invisible object of wonder. When the book holder sat opposite them, the fiery Welshman switched his attack to the newcomer.

'I was telling Edmund here even now,' he said with eyes ablaze. 'I would be Ramon to the life.'

'Ramon?'

'Yes, Nick. The Governor of Cyprus.'

'Ah. You talk of *Black Antonio*.'

'We play it on Monday next. I should be Ramon.'

'The part is already cast.'

'I have the better claim to it.'

'That may well be so,' agreed Nicholas reasonably, 'but it is a major role and must of necessity be played by one of the sharers.'

'Even though I have superior talent?'

'Theatre is not always just, Owen.'

'Support me in this. Take up cudgels on my behalf.'

'I have urged your case a dozen times to Master Firethorn. He is a keen judge of acting and recognizes your mettle. But there are other needs to satisfy first.'

'His lice-ridden sharers!'

'It will not help if you abuse your fellows.'

'I am sorry, Nick,' said Elias, lapsing into maudlin vein. 'But it makes my blood boil to see the way that I am held back. In temper and skill, I am the equal of any in the company save Lawrence Firethorn himself yet I languish in the shallows. Take but *Double Deceit*, man. I was partnered with that dolt of a stagekeeper.'

'George Dart does not pretend to be an actor.'

'Others do and get away with murder!'

'Some fall short of greatness, I admit.'

'Help me, Nick,' said the other seriously. 'You are my only hope in this company. Find me the chance to show my genius and they will *beg* me to become a sharer.'

Nicholas doubted it. Owen Elias had many sterling qualities but his relentless self-assertion was a severe handicap. He upset many of his colleagues with his grumbling discontent and would never be accepted by the other sharers, especially as he would show some of them up completely if he were given a sizeable role. Unknown to the Welshman, Nicholas had already saved him from summary dismissal on more than one occasion by pleading on his behalf. The book holder had found an unlikely ally. He had been supported by Barnaby Gill who was highly aware of the potential talent of Owen Elias and who relished the fact that it was akin to that of Lawrence Firethorn. The hired man was no threat at all to Gill but he might steal some of the actor-manager's thunder if he were given the opportunity.

'I grow weary of this damnable life!' said Elias.

'Your hour will come, Owen.'

'Too late, too late. I may not be here to enjoy it.'

He emptied his tankard, hauled himself out of his chair and rolled off towards the exit. His story was typical of so many hired men who toiled in the smaller parts while less able actors scooped the cream. It was one of the many bitter facts of life that had to be accepted by those in the lower ranks of the profession.

Nicholas now turned his attention to Edmund Hoode.

'I am pleased to see you in good spirits.'

'What's that?' Hoode came out of his daydream.

'You have shed your melancholy.'

'No, Nick. It was snatched away from me.'

'By whom?'

'The fairest creature that I ever beheld.'

'That phrase has been on your lips before,' teased the book holder gently.

'This time it finds its mark directly. She has no equal of her sex. I have witnessed perfection.'

'Where did this happen, Edmund?'

'Where else but at The Theatre?'

'During the performance?'

'She condescended to smile down on me.'

'As did the whole assembly. You played your part with great verve and humour.'

'It was dedicated to her,' said Hoode impulsively. 'I noticed her when I had my soliloquy in Act Three. She leaned forward in the middle gallery to hear it all the better. Oh, Nick, I all but swooned! She is celestial!'

It was another phrase which he had sometimes used before

and not always with discrimination. During an earlier period of frustration in his life, his romantic urge had focused itself wildly and inappropriately on Rose Marwood, the landlord's daughter, an attractive wench with the good fortune to resemble neither of her parents. Like so many of Hoode's attachments, it was wholly unwise and brought him only further grief. Deeply fond of his colleague, Nicholas hoped that another disappointment was not in the offing for him.

Edmund Hoode was back in the playhouse again.

'She sat beside an ill-favoured gallant in black and silver,' he recalled. 'Her own apparel was green, so many hues and each so beautifully blended with the others that she drew my eyes to it. As for her face, it makes all others seem foul and ugly. I will not rest until I have wooed her and won her. Nick, sweet friend, I am in love!'

The poet rhapsodized at length and the book holder's discomfort grew steadily. In every detail, the description tallied with the one given to him by another member of the company and that could only set up the possibility of horrendous complications. Edmund Hoode was unquestionably talking about Matilda Stanford. He was intent on pursuing a young woman who had already been targeted by Lawrence Firethorn. The implications were frightening.

'Help me to find out who she is, Nick!'

'How may I do that?'

'Wait until she visits us again.'

'But the lady may never do that.'

'She will,' said Hoode confidently. 'She will.'

The prospect made Nicholas grit his teeth.

The interior of Stanford Place was even more impressive than its facade. Its capacious rooms were elegantly furnished and given over to an ostentatious display of wealth. Large oak cupboards with intricate carvings all over them were loaded to capacity with gold plate that was kept gleaming. Rich tapestries covered walls and hand-worked carpets of exquisite design softened the clatter of the floors. Gilt-framed oil paintings added colour and dignity. Tables, chairs, benches and cushions abounded and there were no less than three backgammon tables. Huge oak chests bore further quantities of gold plate. Four-branched candelabra were everywhere. The sense of prosperity was overwhelming.

Matilda Stanford saw none of it as she ran through the house in her excitement. Her husband was still in his counting house and she raced to knock on its door but a firm voice stopped her just in time.

'The master would not be disturbed.'

'But I have such news for him,' she said.

'He left precise instructions.'

'Do they apply to his wife?'

'I fear they do,' said Simon Pendleton with smug deference. 'The late Mistress Stanford knew better than to interrupt him during the working day.'

'Am I to be denied access to my own husband?'

'I do but offer advice.'

Matilda was quite abashed. The steward's manner was so full of polite reproach that it smothered all her vivacity beneath it. When she gave a resigned shrug and began to move away, Pendleton felt that he had won a trial of strength and that was important to him. He was about to congratulate himself when the door opened and Walter Stanford came out. His face beamed indulgently.

'Come to me, my darling,' he said expansively.

'I am not being a nuisance, sir?'

'What an absurd thought!' He glanced at the steward. 'You do not have to protect me from my own wife, Simon.'

'I did what I considered right and proper, sir.'

'For once, your judgement was at fault.'

A hurt bow. 'I apologize profusely.'

'Even the best horse stumbles.'

Putting an arm around his wife, Stanford took her into the room and closed the door behind him. Pendelton's minor triumph had been turned into defeat. It did nothing to endear him to a woman whose presence in the house he resented on a number of grounds. He stalked away to tend to his wounded dignity.

Walter Stanford, meanwhile, had conducted his wife to a

chair and stood swaying over her with paternal fondness. She started to recover some of her animation.

'Oh, sir, we have had such a merry afternoon.'

'I am delighted to hear it.'

'William took me to another playhouse.'

'I cannot have my son leading you astray,' he said with mock reproof. 'Where will this levity end?'

'It was the most excellent comedy, sir, and we have not stopped laughing since.'

'Tell me about it, Matilda. I could do with some physic to chase away my seriousness. What play was it?'

'*Double Deceit*, performed by Westfield's Men at The Theatre. Such fun, such frolic, such fireworks!'

She tried to outline the plot but got so hopelessly lost that she exploded into giggles. Her husband was a kind listener who was much more amused at her obvious amusement than at anything in the drama itself. When she had finished, she jumped up to seize his hands in hers.

'You have not forgotten your promise, sir?'

'Which one? There have been so many.'

'This comes first. I want a play.'

'You have had two already this week.'

'A play of my own,' she said, dancing on her toes. 'When you become Lord Mayor, we must have a drama written especially for our entertainment. It will set the seal on a truly memorable day. Say you will oblige me, sir.'

'I will honour my promise.'

'And since it is a happy occasion, I would have a sprightly comedy performed. It will crown the whole event for me. I will be in heaven.'

'With me beside you, my love.'

He gave her a fatherly kiss on the forehead and assured her that he had the matter in hand. Her curiosity bubbled but he would say no more on the subject. Walter Stanford wanted to keep an element of mystery about his plans and this threw her into a paroxysm of pleasure. When her second bout of giggles was over, she remembered another person who would enjoy the projected play.

'William has told me about his cousin.'

'Has he?'

'I like the sound of this Michael.'

'He has his good points, certainly.'

'William says that he is so blithe and sunny.'

'Indeed, he is,' conceded Stanford, 'and they are good qualities in a man. But only when they are matched by responsibility and conscientiousness.'

'I hear a note of disapproval in your voice.'

'It is not intended. Michael is very dear to me. He is my sister's pride and joy but he has brought much heartache to his mother.'

'In what way?'

'This merriment of his,' said Stanford. 'It has blighted his young life—except that he is not so young any more. Michael put idle pleasures before honest work and has spent the best part of his inheritance already. Were his father alive, it would never have happened but my sister is a soft, forgiving mother who has no power over her wayward son. Things came to such a pass that she asked me to take Michael to task.'

'What did you say to him?'

'All that was necessary—and in round terms, too, I do assure you. He laughed uproariously but I got my way with him in the end.'

'William told me that he joined the army.'

'That was his final fling,' said her husband. 'He felt that service in the Netherlands would satisfy his spirit of adventure and send him back a more sober man. That is why I have made a place for him.'

'Here?'

'He must learn the rudiments of a real profession.'

'There is not much jollity in business affairs.'

'Michael is resigned to that.'

'Oh!' Her enthusiasm was punctured. 'I knew nothing of this. William spoke so well of his cousin. I was hoping for another cheerful companion to escort me to the playhouse.' She looked up. 'When is he due home?'

'His ship should have docked by now.'

'Has he left the army?'

'So his letters proclaim.'

'Do not take all the merriment out of him, sir.'

Stanford chuckled. 'No man could do that. Michael is a law unto himself. We may check or control him but we can never subdue his spirit entirely. Nor should we wish to do so because it is the essence of the fellow.' He slipped a fond arm around her shoulders. 'Have no fears on his account. Michael will prance gaily through life until the day he dies.'

The corpse lay on its slab beneath a tattered shroud. It kept grisly company. Other naked bodies were stretched out all around it in varying stages of decomposition. The charnel house was a repository of human decay and not even the herbs that were scattered around could sweeten the prevailing stink. A flight of stone steps led down to the vault. As soon as Nicholas Bracewell entered the dank atmosphere, he felt the hand of death brush across his face. It was not a place he would have chosen to visit but he had been drawn there by curiosity. A few coins put into the hands of the keeper gained him entrance.

'Who did you come to see, sir?' asked the man.

'The poor wretch brought in two nights ago.'

'We had four or five delivered to their slabs.'

'This creature was hauled out of the river,' said Nicholas, coughing as the stench really hit him. 'His face was battered, his leg smashed most cruelly and there was a dagger in his throat.'

'I remember him well. Follow me.'

He was a thin, hollow-eyed wraith of a man whose grim occupation had given him a deathly pallor and an easy indifference to the cadavers with whom he spent his day. Moving between his prostrate charges like the curator of a museum, he led Nicholas to the slab in the corner and held up his torch to shed flickering light. With a deft flick of the wrist, he pulled the shroud off the corpse. The book holder blenched. Though the body had been washed and laid out, he recognized it immediately as the one that he had dragged out of the Thames. The facial injuries had been hidden beneath bandaging and the dagger had been extracted from the throat but the right leg was still a tortured mass of flesh and bone.

For the first time, he noticed something else. There was a long, livid scar on the man's chest, a fairly recent wound that was just starting to heal. Nicholas examined the hands.

'What are you doing?' said the keeper suspiciously.

'Looking at his palms, sir. They are quite smooth and the fingernails are well-pared. These are the hands of a gentleman.'

'Not any more. Death treats all as one.'

'This body was strong and upright while it lived.'

'The grave is wide enough for anyone.'

'He would have been able to defend himself.'

'Not any more, sir.'

Nicholas took a last, sad look at the corpse then indicated that it should be covered over again in the name of decency. He headed for the exit with the man shuffling along behind him.

'Will you see anyone else?' said the keeper.

'I have gazed my fill.'

'But we have more interesting sights here.' He plucked at his visitor's sleeve to stop him. 'A young woman was brought in but yesternight. Some punk that was strangled in her bed. She is no more than sixteen with a body as soft and lovely as you could wish. One more coin and I would gladly show you.' He nudged the other. 'If you have money enough, I will let you touch her.'

Nicholas turned away in disgust and stormed out before he gave in to the impulse to hit the man. He vowed to report the incident when he appeared at the Coroner's Court on the following Monday. No matter who they were or what they had been, the dead deserved the utmost respect. He came up into the fresh air and inhaled it gratefully. Light was fading and so he hurried in the direction of the river before it went completely. From the wharf where he had been picked up by Abel Strudwick, he looked out across the water and tried to estimate the point at which they had encountered the body. It was somewhere in mid-stream and he wondered how far it had drifted in order to reach them. He decided that the dead man had been put into the Thames under the cover of darkness but the swift current could still have brought him some distance.

The book holder was no stranger to the wharves and harbours along the Thames. The son of a West Country merchant, he had fallen in love with the sea at an early age and been on numerous voyages with his father. The bold venture of Francis Drake caught his imagination and he sailed around the world with him for three long years. That experience had brought endless disillusion but it had not entirely stilled the call of the sea. When he first came to London, he would often come down to the river to watch the ships putting in and to talk with the sailors about their voyages and their cargoes. This visit was a far less pleasant one.

His eye inevitably fell on the Bridge. It was an extraordinary sight that never palled and Nicholas felt a surge of admiration for those who conceived and built it. Twenty solid piers supported nineteen arches of varying widths. Islands were created around the piers to protect them from the tide race. These starlings, as they were called, were shaped like great flat boats and narrowed the water channels under the arches so much that the tide race was dramatically increased. Nicholas had not been surprised to learn that the Bridge had taken over thirty years to complete and had claimed the lives of some one hundred and fifty workmen. It had stood for some four centuries and more as a tribute to their craftsmanship. Because it was the only structure to span the broad Thames, it became the most important thoroughfare in London and properties along its length were much coveted. The Bridge was also the healthiest part of the city. When the Black Death was decimating the population in every other ward, it could only boast two recorded deaths among those who lived above the swirling waters of the river.

Respect soon changed to foreboding. It was that same Bridge which had put such deep fear into the heart of Hans Kippel that he could not even stand there and behold it. Two of the most appealing parts of London had taken on a different character for Nicholas. The Bridge held the clue to what had happened to a Dutch apprentice and the River Thames knew the secret of the maimed body that it had washed up

71

into the hands of the book holder. He stood there in deep contemplation until evening had washed the last rays of light from the sky.

A boat took him across to Bankside and he walked briskly along the winding lanes on his way home. Another problem now concentrated his mind. Alexander Marwood had lit a raging bonfire of uncertainty. An impending change of ownership at the Queen's Head was a serious threat to the well-being of Westfield's Men. The landlord was a difficult enough man with whom to bargain but Alderman Rowland Ashway would not even talk terms. Nicholas had thought to confide in Edmund Hoode but his friend was too infected with love-sickness to hear any sense. Lawrence Firethorn would need to be told soon and the book holder resolved to call on him the next day. Trying times lay ahead and they could only be made worse by the fact that a fond poet and a lustful actor had chosen as the object of their passion the same unsuspecting young woman. If tragedy was to be averted, Nicholas would have to provide some highly skilful stage-management.

He walked along between rows of tenements then turned into the street where he lived. The house was still some thirty yards away when he sensed danger and it caused him to slow his pace. Someone was lurking beside the front door, seated on the ground and curled up in an attitude of sleep that he did not trust for a second. Those who walked through the darkness of Southwark were used to the skulking presence of thieves and they used all kinds of tricks to lull the unwary off guard. As Nicholas closed in on the house, one hand fondled the dagger at his waist. The figure on the ground was rough and sturdy with a hat pulled down over his face. There was a sense of crude power about him. Ready for any attack, Nicholas extended a foot to push the man over.

'God's blood! I'll cut your rotten liver out!'

A gushing waterfall of vile abuse came from the man's mouth until he recognized who had roused him from his slumbers. He leapt up at once to issue a stream of apologies and to ingratiate himself with bows and shrugs. Abel Strudwick had waited a long time for his hope of a new future. A broad grin split his hideous face in two and gave it an even more alarming quality.

'You may change my whole life, Master Bracewell.'

'May I?'

'Put me upon the stage, sir!'

Sir Lucas Pugsley never tired of admiring himself in his full regalia as Lord Mayor of London. He paraded up and down in front of the long mirror and watched his black and gold gown trail along the floor. Power had turned an ambitious man into a dangerous one who sought means both to retain and enlarge that power. As Alderman Luke Pugsley of the Fishmongers' Company, he was rich, secure and very influential. When he was elevated to the highest civic office, he became like a demi-god and was consumed with his own self-esteem. Over thirty officers belonged to the Lord Mayor's House. They included the Sword-bearer, the Common Crier, the City Marshall and the Coroner for London as well as the Common Hunt, the Water Bailiff and other assorted bailiffs, sergeants and yeomen. There were always three meal-weighers at his beck and call.

The man on whom he relied most was the Chamberlain.

'Will you put on your chain of office, Lord Mayor?'

'Bring it to me, sir.'

'It becomes you so well.'

'I carry it with dignity and good breeding.'

Aubrey Kenyon was tall, well-built and quite stately with greying temples lending an air of distinction to the clear, clean-shaven face. The Chamberlain was responsible for the financial affairs of the city but Kenyon's role had enlarged well beyond that. Like his predecessors, the present Lord Mayor found him a source of comprehensive information about civic life and duty, and befriended him early on. Aubrey Kenyon had no airs and graces. Despite the importance of his position, he was happy to perform more menial tasks for the man whom he served. He stood back to appraise the chain.

'It looks exceeding fine,' he said.

'Its weight reminds me of my civic burdens.'

'You have borne them with lightness.'

'Thank you, Aubrey.' He stroked the gold collar. 'This chain was bequeathed to the mayoralty in 1545 by John Allen who held the office twice. I venture to suggest that nobody has worn it with such pride and with such distinction. Am I not the most conscientious Lord Mayor you have ever encountered? Be honest with me, Aubrey, for I trust your opinion above all others. Have I not been a credit to my office?'

'Indeed, indeed.'

Kenyon bowed his agreement then adjusted the chain slightly to make it completely straight. It consisted of twenty-six gold knots, interspersed with roses and the Tudor portcullis and it set off the gold thread which weighted the gown of stiff silk. Beneath his gown, Pugsley wore the traditional court dress of knee breeches, silk stockings and buckled shoes. Aubrey Kenyon held out the tricorne hat with its flurry of ostrich feathers. When it was placed carefully in position, the Lord Mayor of London was ready to attend yet another civic banquet.

'Is everything in order, Aubrey?'

'We await but your august self, Lord Mayor.'

'My wife?'

'She has been standing by this half-hour.'

'That is a welcome change,' said Pugsley with a quiet snigger. 'When we live at home together, it is always *I* who am kept waiting if we are dining out. I like this new order of precedence. A Lord Mayor of London can even put a woman in her place.'

'Unless she be the Queen of England.'

'Even then, sir. I have spoken honestly with Her Majesty before now and she has respected me for it. My generosity is also well-known to her.'

'As to the whole city.' The Chamberlain pointed towards the door of the apartment. 'Will you descend? The coach has been at the door this long time.'

'There is no hurry,' said Pugsley grandly. 'Though the Guildhall be full, none will dare to start before me. I claim the privilege of my office in arriving late.'

The Chamberlain smiled quietly and crossed to open the

door. Two servants bowed low at the approach of the Lord Mayor. Sir Lucas Pugsley sailed past them and went down the wide staircase to be met by a further display of obeisance in the hall. With his wife on his arm, he left the house and was assisted into the ceremonial coach. The journey to the Guildhall was marred by only one thought. His year of triumph would be over all too soon. Power invaded his brain and gave his resolve a manic intensity.

He had to cling on to office somehow.

Aubrey Kenyon, meanwhile, was pulling a cloak around his shoulders before slipping discreetly out of the house. He walked quickly through the dark lanes until he came to an imposing property in Silver Street near Cripplegate. He was no deferential Chamberlain now but a determined man with an air of self-importance about him. When he knocked at a side-door of the house, he was admitted instantly by a servant and conducted to the main room. His host was waiting anxiously.

'You are a welcome sight, Aubrey!'

'Good even, good sir.'

'We have much to discuss.'

'Time is beginning to run out for us.'

Rowland Ashway dismissed his servant then poured two cups of fine wine. Handing one to his guest, he conducted him to a seat at the long oak table. The portly brewer and the poised Chamberlain were an incongruous pair but they had common interests which tied them indissolubly together.

'How is our mutual friend?' said Ashway.

'Sir Lucas is besotted with his authority. He will not easily yield it up.'

'Nor will we, Aubrey. *You* are the real power behind the Lord Mayor of London and the beauty of it is that Luke is far too addle-brained to notice it.'

'The truth will not escape Walter Stanford.'

'That is why he must never take office. Never, sir!'

The Chamberlain calmly pronounced a death sentence.

'They must find that boy.'

The passage of time had not so far improved the sleeping habits of Hans Kippel. His body had profited from rest but his mind remained a prey to phantoms. The young apprentice was at the mercy of an unknown enemy who would not show his face.

'I will be poor company, Master Bracewell.'

'That is for me to decide.'

'I would not keep you awake.'

'Nor shall you,' said Nicholas with a smile. 'After the day I have endured, I will sleep like a baby.'

'Go upstairs, Hans,' advised Anne Hendrik. 'We have put a truckle bed ready for you.'

'Thank you, Mistress. Good night.'

They exchanged farewells and he went off upstairs. Disturbed nights were taking such a toll of the boy that Nicholas volunteered to share a room with him, hoping that his presence might bring a degree of reassurance. At the same time, he wanted to be on hand in case there was any trickle of information from the memory that had so far been completely dammed up. Anne Hendrik was immensely grateful to her lodger.

'It is kindness indeed, Nick.'

'I hate to see that look of terror upon him.'

'As do I.'

'Besides,' he added, 'Hans may still get the worst end of it. If he does fall asleep, my snoring might yet put him out of his slumbers.'

'You do not snore,' she said fondly.

'How do you know?'

They shared a gentle laugh then he reviewed his day for her. She was fascinated by it all but understandably alarmed at the news about the Queen's Head. If the future of Westfield's Men was in jeopardy, then so was her close relationship with her lodger. He read her concern.

'You will not shake me off so easily, Anne.'

'I hope not, sir.'

'Accompany me through these difficulties.'

'I'll pray in church tomorrow.'

'Add something else while down upon your knees.'

'What do you mean?'

'Abel Strudwick runs mad.'

When he told about how he had been waylaid by the stage-struck waterman, she was torn between laughter and sympathy. Nicholas was placed in a difficult position. He had somehow to deflect his poetic friend without hurting the man's feelings. It was an impossible assignment. As the last of the day dwindled, they parted with a kiss and went off to their separate chambers. When he crept quietly into bed, Nicholas was relieved to hear the steady breathing of Hans Kippel beside him in the dark. The boy was asleep at last. It seemed as if the experiment of bringing him there had worked.

The book holder allowed himself to drift and he was soon lost in a world of floating dreams. How long he stayed there he did not know but when he left there, it was with sudden violence.

'Stop it! No, sirs! Stop it! Stop it!'

Hans Kippel was threshing about in his bed. He sat bolt upright and let out a screech that raised the whole house. He held hands up to defend himself against attack.

'Hold off, sirs! Leave me alone!'

'What is the matter?' said Nicholas, rushing across to him. 'What ails you, lad.'

He put a consoling arm around the apprentice but it provoked the opposite response. Fearing that he was being grabbed by an assailant, Hans Kippel kicked and fought with all his puny might. Anne Hendrik came rushing into the chamber with a candle to hold over the boy. He was neither awake nor asleep but in some kind of trance. His whole body trembled and perspiration came from every pore. His breathing was faster, deeper and much noisier. Demons of the night turned him into a gibbering wreck. It was a disturbing sight and it destroyed all vain hopes that sleep would restore the pitiable creature.

His delirium was worse than ever.

Night was far kinder to Matilda Stanford. She lay beside her husband in the spacious four-poster that graced their bed-chamber and watched moonlight throw ghostly patterns on to the low ceiling. Sleep came imperceptibly and she was led into a land that was full of delight. Sweet songs and lovely images came and went with pulsing beauty and Matilda surrendered to the lackadaisical joy of it all. Greater pleasure yet lay in store for her. A splendid new playhouse appeared before her eyes and she was wafted towards it. When she took up her seat in the topmost gallery, she was part of a large and bubbling audience.

But the play was performed solely for her. Other spectators merely watched from afar. She was engaged from the start. Every gesture was aimed at her, every glance directed her way, every speech laid at her feet in simple homage. Characters came and went with bewildering speed. She saw emperors, kings, soldiers, statesmen, brave knights, bold adventurers and many more besides. Each acted out a story that moved her heart or provoked her laughter, that contained a message for her, that drew her ever closer to the magic of the experience.

And all the parts were played by the same man. He was of solid build and medium height with a fine head and a dark pointed beard. Dazzling apparel changed with each minute as the characters flashed by but his essential quality remained intact throughout. He was Count Orlando about to die, he was Argos of Rome in pensive mood, he was Argos of Florence in hilarious vein, he was here and there to please Matilda in a hundred ways.

Lawrence Firethorn was hers to command.

The next moment she was on the stage beside him, a person in the drama, an anguished young lover greeting the return of her hero from the trials he has undergone on her behalf. She flung herself into his strong arms and lost herself in the power of his embrace. Firethorn's lips touched hers in a kiss of passion that was quite unlike anything she had ever conceived.

It brought her awake in an instant. Matilda Stanford sat up and looked around. It was early morning but her husband had already risen to begin some work before paying his first visit of the day to church. Matilda was stranded alone on the huge, empty beach of their bed. This was the story of their young marriage but it had never caused her any regret before. One dream had altered that. There was a life elsewhere that made her own seem dull and futile. In her own bed, in her own marriage, in one of the finest private houses in London, she was overcome with such a feeling of sadness and loneliness that it made her shudder all over.

Matilda Stanford wept tears of disenchantment. Night had tempered its kindness with a subtle cruelty. She had lost her way. For the first time since she had married Walter Stanford, she realized that she was unhappy.

Chapter Five

MARGERY FIRETHORN CAME INTO HER OWN ON A
Sunday and ruled the roost with a brisk religiosity.
It was not only her husband, children and servants
who were shouted out of bed to attend Matins. The apprentices and the three actors staying at the house in Shoreditch
were also dragged protesting from their rooms to give thanks
to God. Wearing her best dress and a look of prim respectability that she reserved for the Sabbath alone, she lined up
the entire party before they left and admonished them with
six lines that she had been forced to learn in her youth.

When that thou come to Church, thy prayers for to say,
See thou sleep not, nor yet talk not, devoutly look to pray,
Nor cast thine eyes to and fro, as things thou wouldst still
    see
So shall wise men judge you a fool, and wanton for to be.
When thou are in the Temple, see thou do thy Churchly
    works,
Hear thou God's word with diligence, crave pardon for thy
    faults.

Her instructions met with only moderate obedience when
they reached the Parish Church of St Leonard nearby. Pray-

ers were said, attention wandered, tired souls dozed off. During an interminable sermon based on a text from The Acts of the Apostles ('And the disciples were filled with joy, and with the Holy Ghost') Margery was the only occupant of her pew to hear God's word with anything resembling diligence. The actors slept, the apprentices yawned, the servants suffered, the children bickered in silence and Lawrence Firethorn saw only a naked young woman in the pulpit, shorn of her finery and liberated from her escort, beckoning to him to join her atop a Mount Sinai that was set aside for carnal pleasure. That she was also the wife of the Lord Mayor Elect only served to heighten the joyous feeling of sinfulness.

On the journey home, his wife held confession.

'What were you thinking about in church, sir?'

'Sacred matters.'

'I felt that your mind was wandering.'

'It was on higher things, Margery.'

'The Sabbath is a day of rest.'

'Then must you refrain from scolding your husband.'

'Church is an act of faith.'

He sighed. 'How else could we endure that sermon?'

The party brightened as soon as they entered the house. Breakfast was devoured with chomping gratitude and some of them came properly awake for the first time that day. Firethorn adjourned to the small drawing room to receive the visitor that he had invited. Edmund Hoode had put on his best doublet and hose and sported a new hat that cascaded down the side of his head. Amorous thoughts of his lady love painted a beatific smile on his willing features. Firethorn rubbed the smile off at once.

'Stop grinning at me like a raving madman!'

'I am happy, Lawrence.'

'That is what is so unnatural. You were born to be miserable, Edmund. Nature shaped you especially for that purpose. Embrace your destiny and return to the doe-eyed sadness for which your friends adore you.'

'Do not mock me so.'

'Then do not set yourself up for mockery.' He waved his

guest to a chair and sat beside him. 'Let us touch on the business of the day.'

Hoode was wounded. 'I thought you brought me here for the pleasure of my company.'

'And so I did, sir. Now that I have had it, we can turn to more important things.' He glanced around to make sure the door was firmly closed. 'Edmund, dear fellow, I have work for your pen.'

'I have already written two new plays this year.'

'Each one a gem of creation,' flattered the other. 'But no new commission threatens. I wish you merely to compose some verse for me.'

'No, Lawrence.'

'Would you refuse, sir?'

'Yes, Lawrence.'

'This is not my Edmund Hoode that speaks.'

'It is, Lawrence.'

'I am asking you for help. Do not deny me or I will never call you friend again. I am in earnest here.'

'So am I.'

'Write me a sonnet to woo my love.'

'Call in Margery instead and sing her a ballad.'

'Are you a lunatic!' hissed Firethorn. 'What has got into you, sir? I ask but a favour you have done on more than one occasion. Why betray me in this way?'

'Because my verse is reserved for another.'

The actor–manager was livid. Rising to his feet, he released a few expletives then let himself get as angry as he dared without arousing the attention of his wife in the adjoining room. Edmund Hoode was unperturbed. A man whom Firethorn could usually manipulate at will was showing iron resolution for once and would not be moved. There was only one way to bring him to heel.

'Legal process is on my side, Edmund.'

'What do you mean?'

'Your contract with the company.'

'There is nothing in that to make me act as your pandar and fetch in your game with pretty rhymes.'

'Will you push me to violence here!'

'Remember the Sabbath and lead a better life.'

Lawrence Firethorn's rage was about to burst into full flame when he controlled it. What came crackling from his mouth instead were the terms of Edmund Hoode's contract with Westfield's Men, exact in every detail.

'One, that you shall write for no other company.'

'Agreed.'

'Two, that you shall provide three plays a year.'

'I have honoured that clause.'

'Three, that you shall receive five pounds for each new drama performed by Westfield's Men. Four, that you shall publish none of the said plays. Five, that you will receive a weekly wage of nine shillings together with a share of any profit made by the company.'

'All this I accept,' said Hoode. 'Where is my obligation to wear the livery of your wandering eye?'

'I am coming to that.' Firethorn turned the screw with a slow smile. 'Six, that you shall write prologues and epilogues as required. Seven, that you shall add new scenes to revived plays. Eight, that you shall add songs as required. Nine, that you shall write inductions to order. Finis!' The smile became a smirk. 'This is covenanted and agreed between us. Do you concede that?'

'Of course.'

'Then must you bow to my purpose here.'

'How can it be enforced?'

'By those same terms I listed even now, Edmund.'

'No lawyer would support you.'

'I think he might.' Firethorn swooped. 'I require you to write prologues and epilogues. I instruct you to add new material to a revived text. I desire that songs be inserted. Inductions will I command. Shall you follow my meaning now, sir? What I demand for public plays I can use for my personal advantage—and I have a legal contract to hold you to your duty.'

'This is treachery!' spluttered Hoode.

'I think I will start with a song.'

'Can you descend to such foul devices?'

'Only upon compulsion,' said the genial Firethorn. 'Now,

sir, write me a ballad of love to be included in *Cupid's Folly*.
I will sing it before my inamorata.'

'My quill would moult in disgust at such a task!'

'Then cut yourself a new one and pen me a prologue to
Love and Fortune. Let it touch on the themes of the play and
speak tenderly to my lady.'

'You will drain my inspiration dry!' wailed Hoode.

'Do your duty with a gladsome mind.'

'I want to woo my *own* beloved.'

'Watch me, Edmund,' advised Firethorn with avuncular
condescension. 'And I will show you how it is done.'

Consternation broke out at Stanford Place to ruffle the smooth
piety of a Sunday at home. Matilda was listening to her stepson read from the Bible when her husband came striding into
the room. Walter Stanford's affability was for once edged
with concern. Without even apologizing for the interruption,
he held up the letter in his hand.

'I have received disquieting news.'

'From whom?' said Matilda.

'My sister in Windsor. She sends word that Michael has
still not returned home. Yet his ship docked at the harbour
here some three days ago.'

'That is cause for alarm,' she agreed.

'Not if you know Michael,' said her stepson. 'Do not vex
yourselves about him too soon. He has been fighting for his
country in the Netherlands. After the hardship of a soldier's
lot, he will want to celebrate his return by seeking out the
pleasure haunts of the city. That is where we will find him,
have no fear.'

'I like not that thought,' said Stanford solemnly. 'Michael
promised to turn his back on his idle ways.'

'Give him but a few days of licence, father.'

'When he shows no consideration to his mother?'

'All will be mended very soon.'

'Not until I have said my piece to him!' Stanford moved
between anger and apprehension. 'He is so careless and
crack-brained, some ill may have befallen him. If he *has*
been carousing all this while, I'll fill his ears with the hot

pitch of my tongue. Yet what if he has strayed into danger?
I scorn him—yet fear for his safety.'

'Can he not be tracked down?' said Matilda.

'I have already set a search in train, my love.'

'Look that they visit the taverns,' added William.

His father bristled. 'It will be the worse for him if they
find him in such a place. Michael was due to report first to
me before travelling to see his mother in Windsor. I am not
just his uncle now. For my sins, I have elected to be his
employer.'

'Then there is the explanation,' said his son with a fatuous
grin. 'Michael is in hiding from your strict rule.'

'This is not an occasion for levity, sir!'

'Nor yet for wild surmise, Father.'

'My nephew has been missing for three days. Only accident or dissipation can explain his absence and both give
grounds for concern.' He waved the letter. 'There is fresh
intelligence here. Michael saw action as a soldier and received a wound.'

'Merciful heavens!' said Matilda. 'Of what nature?'

'He did not say but it bought him his discharge.'

'This throws fresh light,' said William anxiously.

'Indeed, it does,' reinforced his father. 'If my nephew
carries an injury, why did he not mention it in his letters to
me? How serious is it? Will it disable him from working?
Then there is the darkest fear of all.'

'What's that, sir?' asked his wife.

'A wounded man may not defend himself so well.'

Walter Stanford said no more but the implication was
frightening. A person whose return had been awaited with
such pleasure was unaccountably missing. The even tenor of
their Sunday morning had been totally disrupted.

A troubled William spoke for all three of them.

'In God's good name, Michael—where *are* you?'

The burly figure crouched over the corpse and studied the
great scar that ran the whole width of the pale chest. Having
recovered from one dreadful wound, the man had been sub-
jected to far grosser injuries in the course of his murder. Abel

Strudwick had paid his money to view the body and he now stood over it with almost ghoulish interest. A low murmuring sound came from his lips and cut through the cold silence of the charnel house. The keeper inched closer with his torch and let the flames illumine his visitor's face.

'Did you say something, sir?'

'Only to myself,' grunted Strudwick.

'What are you doing there?'

'Writing a poem.'

Rowland Ashway finished off a plate of eels and a two-pint tankard of ale by way of an appetizer for the huge meal that awaited him at home. He was seated in a private room at the Queen's Head and gazing around its ornate furnishings with proprietary satisfaction. It was the finest room at the inn and was always set aside for Lord Westfield and his cronies whenever they came to see a play performed in the yard outside. The rotund Alderman smacked his lips with good humour. To have penetrated to the inner sanctum of a disdainful aristocrat was in the nature of a victory. It remained only to expel Lord Westfield completely and the triumph would be complete.

Alexander Marwood fluttered around the table like a moth around a flame, anxious to please a potential owner yet keen to drive as hard a bargain as he dared. His twitch was at its most ubiquitous as he moved in close.

'I have been having second thoughts, Master.'

'About what?' said Ashway.

'The sale of the Queen's Head.'

'But it is all agreed in principle.'

'That was before I listened to my wife.'

'A fatal error, sir. Wives should be spoken at and not listened to. They will undo the best plans we may make with their womanly grumbles and their squawking reservations. Ignore the good lady.'

'How, sir?' groaned Marwood. 'It is easier to ignore the sun that shines and the rain that falls. She will give me no sleep in bed at nights.'

'There is but one cure for that!' His crude laugh made the

landlord recoil slightly. 'Have your pleasure with her until she succumbs from fatigue.'

'Oh, sir,' said the other, sounding a wistful note. 'You touch on sore flesh there.' He became businesslike. 'And besides, her major objection mirrors my own.'

'What might that be?'

'Tradition. My family has owned the Queen's Head for generations now. I am loath to see that end.'

'Nor shall it, Master Marwood. You and your sweet wife will run the establishment as before with full security of tenure. To all outward appearance, the inn will remain yours.'

'But ownership will transfer to you.'

'In return for a handsome price.'

'Yes, yes,' said Marwood quickly. 'That is very much at the forefront of our minds. You have been most kind and generous in that respect.'

'So what detains you? Sentiment?'

'It has its place, surely.'

'What else?'

'Fear of signing away my birthright.'

'The contract keeps you here until you die.' Rowland Ashway used podgy hands to pull himself up from the table to confront the landlord. 'Do not see me as a threat here. We are equal partners in this enterprise and both of us can profit from the venture.'

'My wife might need more persuasion.'

'Do it in the watches of the night.'

'That is when I am least in command.'

'What *will* content the lady, then?'

Marwood shrugged and started to flutter once more. At one stroke, the brewer cut through the threatened delay to their negotiations.

'I increase my bid by two hundred pounds.'

'You overwhelm me, sir!'

'It is my final offer, mark you.'

'I understand that.'

'Will it please Mistress Marwood?'

'It may do more than that,' said the other as a ray of hope

found its way into his desperation. 'I'll raise the matter when we retire tonight.'

'It is settled, then.'

Alderman Rowland Ashway sealed the bargain with a flabby handshake then allowed himself to be conducted down to the yard. Even with the additional payment, he would be getting the inn at a very attractive price and he had already made plans for its improvement. Before new features could be added, however, one old one had to be removed without compunction.

'What of Westfield's Men?' said Ashway. 'Have you acquainted them with their fate?'

'I have mentioned it to their book holder.'

'That will rattle their noble patron.'

'It is Master Firethorn who will roar the loudest.'

'Let him. Rowland Ashway is a match for any man.'

'Rowland Ashway! That barrel of rancid lard! Ashway!'

'This is what I have been told.'

'That fat turd of aldermanic pomposity!'

'The same man, sir.'

'That leech, that vile toad, that bloated threat to every chair he sits upon! I could spit at the wretch as soon as look at him. He should be weighted down with blocks of lead then drowned in a tub of his own beer! Rowland Ashway is a monster in half-human form. Does the creature possess a wife?'

'I believe that he does, Master.'

'Then must we pray for her soul. How can the woman endure to be mounted by that elephant, to be pounded to a pulp by that bed-breaker, to be flattened into a wafer by that scurvy, lousy, red-faced bladder of bilge!'

Lawrence Firethorn had not taken the news well. When Nicholas Bracewell called on him that afternoon, the actor had been pleased to see his colleague and took him into the drawing room in the interests of privacy. That privacy had been rescinded now as Firethorn's voice explored octaves of fury that could be heard half a mile away. Nicholas made a vain attempt to pacify him.

'No contract has as yet been signed, sir.'

'Nor shall it be,' vowed the other. 'My God, I'll grab that walking nightmare of a landlord and hang him up by his undeserving feet. The traitor, the lily-livered hound, the one-eyed, two-faced, three-toed back-stabber!'

'I think it might be better if you steered well clear of Master Marwood,' suggested Nicholas. 'To lay rough hands upon him will not advance our cause.'

'I demand revenge!' howled Firethorn.

'The crime has not yet been committed.'

'But it is planned, is it not?'

'We may yet be able to avert disaster.'

'Only by a show of force, Nick. Let me at him.'

'I counsel the use of diplomacy.'

'Diplomacy! With a twitching publican and a bloated brewer? I'd sooner play the diplomat with a pair of sabre-toothed tigers. Let them hatch their plot and they'll have us turned out of the Queen's Head without a word of thanks. Is it not perfidious?'

'That is why I felt you should be warned.'

'Indeed, indeed.'

'So that we may take the appropriate action.'

'Aye, Nick. Tie those two villains together back to back and drop them in the Thames to curdle the water.' He prowled around the room as he considered more gruesome deaths for the miscreants then he stopped in his tracks. 'We'll attack them from above.'

'How so?'

'Lord Westfield will be told.'

'Only as a last resort,' urged Nicholas. 'It would be wrong to alarm his lordship with a problem that we may be able to solve ourselves. He would not thank us for dragging him into a wrangle of this nature.'

'You may be right,' admitted Firethorn. 'We must keep that last card up our sleeve then. Meanwhile, I will vent my spleen upon that lizard of a landlord.'

'Then might our case be ruined altogether.'

'Heavens, Nick, this is an insult I will not bear! Our plays have helped to fill his coffers generously these last few years.

Our art has put his foul establishment on the map of London. We have *made* the Queen's Head. Instead of selling it to Alderman Rowland Ashway, he should be giving it to us in appreciation.'

'Master Marwood is a businessman.'

Firethorn glowered. 'So am I, sir.'

There was a long pause as the actor–manager fought to subdue his temper and take a more objective view of the crisis into which he was now plunged. Behind all the bombast about the primacy of Westfield's Men there lurked a simple truth. The company's survival depended on the income that it could generate and that would shrink alarmingly if they lost their regular home. Lawrence Firethorn stared blankly ahead as cruel practicalities were borne in upon him. His immediate impulse was to launch an attack but it could bring only short-term benefits. In the long run, they relied on one man.

'What must we do, Nick?' he muttered.

'Move with great stealth.'

'Has anyone else been told of this?'

'No, sir,' said Nicholas. 'Nor should they, except for Edmund and Master Gill. If we spread panic now, it will show in our work and damage our reputation.'

'You give sound advice as usual.'

'Leave me to work on Master Marwood.'

'I'd do so with the sharpest sword in Christendom!'

'Then would we lose all. We must deal softly with the man or he will take fright and run. It is only by talking to him that we can keep abreast of any moves that are made by Alderman Ashway.'

Firethorn snorted. 'The whole city is aware of any moves made by that spherical gentleman. Whenever he stirs abroad, the very earth does shake. If he stood by the river and broke wind, he could launch a whole armada.' He gave a crumpled smile. 'Help us, Nick.'

'I will do everything in my power.'

'That comforts me greatly.' His eyes moistened. 'I would not lose the Queen's Head for a queen's ransom. That stage has seen the full panoply of my genius. Those boards are sacrosanct. Tarquin has walked there. So have Pompey and Black Antonio. King Richard the Lionheart and Justice Wildboare have strutted their hour. A few days past, it was the turn of Count Orlando and I have burned dozens of other fine parts into the imagination of my audience.' He looked up. 'I would not have it end like this, dear heart.'

'There has to be a means of escape.'

Lawrence Firethorn's voice faded into a whisper.

'Find it, Nick. Save us from extinction . . .'

Anne Hendrik's anxiety over her apprentice did not ease. The boy was no better on the following day than he had been during a torrid night. Nor could he provide any clue as to what had upset him so dramatically while he slept. Sunday was no day of rest for Hans Kippel. Watched over carefully by Anne and visited by Preben van Loew, he was unable to do more than hold desultory conversation with either. A depression had settled on his young mind. His face was one large puckered frown and his eyes were dull. All the spirit which had made him so boisterous had been knocked out of him by the experience he had undergone. It would clearly take some time yet before the details of that experience began to emerge.

In the hope that prayer might succeed where all else had failed, Anne took him with her to Evensong at the parish church of St Saviour. It was too close to the Bridge for the boy's complete comfort but far enough away for his attention to be diverted from it by his employer. As the Gothic beauty and the sheer bulk of the building rose up before them, she told him an apocryphal story about its past.

'It was once the Priory-church of St Mary Overy,' she explained. 'Do you know how it got its name?'

'No, mistress.'

'From the legend of John Overy, who was the ferryman before ever a bridge was built across the river. Because his ferry was rented by the whole city—small as it must have been in those days—he became exceedingly rich. But there was a problem, Hans.'

'What was it?'

'John Overy was a notorious miser. He hoarded his money and looked for new ways to increase his wealth. Shall I tell you how mean this fellow really was?'

'If you please.'

'He believed that if he pretended to die, his family and servants would fast out of respect and thus save him the expense of a whole day's food for the household.'

'That is meanness indeed.'

'Master Overy put his plan into action,' said Anne. 'But his servants were so overjoyed by his death that they began to feast and make merry. He was so furious that he jumped up out of his bed to scold them. One of the servants, thinking he was the Devil, picked up the butt end of an oar and knocked out his brains.'

'It served him right, Mistress.'

'Many thought likewise, Hans. But his daughter was grief-stricken. She used her inheritance to found a convent and retreated into it. That convent became, in time, the Priory of St Mary Overy so his name lingers on.'

The apprentice had listened with interest and almost smiled at one point in the story. Anne had a fleeting sensation of making real contact with him at last, of breaking through the mental barrier which surrounded him. They went into the massive church and walked along the shiny-smooth flagstones of the nave beneath the high, vaulted ceiling. Breathtaking architecture and artistry enveloped them and it was impossible not to be touched by the scrupulous magnificence of it all.

They filed into a pew. As Anne knelt in prayer, she felt Hans Kippel drop down beside her and start to gabble in Dutch. She could hear the note of alarm in his voice and sense his trembling. Words that she could recognize finally slipped out of the boy.

'Please, God . . . do not let them kill *me* . . .'

The Coroner's Court was held early on Monday morning and among those charged to appear were Nicholas Bracewell and Abel Strudwick. The book holder was the first to give his testimony, speaking under oath and explaining exactly how and when he had found the dead body in the Thames. His friend made more of the opportunity that was offered. The waterman was not content with a simple recital of the facts of the case. He had transformed it into a dramatic event. Standing before the Coroner and the whole court, he responded to the presence of an audience with alacrity.

> The night was dark, the water fast and fierce,
> No moonlight could the inky blackness pierce.
> I rowed full hard, I strove against the flood,
> And Master Bracewell helped me all he could.
> But when we reached the middle of the stream,
> I glimpsed a sight that almost made me scream.
> A naked body floated on the tide
> With mangled limbs and injuries beside.
> What did I do, sirs, at this fateful hour?

They never found out. With stern command, the Coroner ordered him to stop and give his evidence in a more seemly manner. Strudwick was truculent and had to be cowed into obedience by the sternest warnings. When he gave a straightforward account of the incident, it tallied in every respect with that of Nicholas Bracewell. Both were dismissed and hurried out.

The waterman was anxious for some praise at least.

'What did you think of my music?'

'Quite unlike anything I have ever heard, Abel.'

'Will you commend me to Master Firethorn?'

'I shall mention your name.'

'Instruct him in my purpose.'

'I must away. Rehearsal soon begins.'

Nicholas was glad of the chance to break away and race off to Gracechurch Street. Abel Strudwick could be entertaining enough as a versifying waterman. As a prospective member of the theatrical profession, he was a menace. The book holder was going to have to row very carefully with him through choppy waters.

He made up for his late arrival at the Queen's Head by hurling himself into his work. The stage was set up on its trestles, the props, furniture and scenic devices made ready, and the costumes were brought into the room that was used as the tiring-house. *Black Antonio* was another tragedy of revenge with some powerful scenes and some unlikely but effective comedy from the Court Fool. It had been part of their repertoire for some time now and posed no serious problems. The rehearsal was rather flat but without any mishap. Lawrence Firethorn gave them only a touch of the whip before dismissing them from the stage.

Nicholas knew the cause of the general lethargy. The company took its cue from its acknowledged stars and both were jaded. Fear of ejection from the Queen's Head had seeped into the performances of Black Antonio himself and of the Court Fool. They were still in costume as they accosted the book holder.

'Keep that ghoul away from me, Nick,' said Firethorn. 'Or I will slit his ungrateful throat and string up his polecat of a body for all to see.'

'Master Marwood keeps his own counsel, sir.'

'I spurn the ruffian!'

He went out with a swirl of his cloak and left the book holder alone with Barnaby Gill. The latter was no friend of Nicholas but adversity had taken the edge off his animosity. Dressed as the Fool, he advised wisdom.

'Reason closely with the man, sir.'

'I will, Master Gill.'

'Do nothing to provoke this starchy landlord.'

'We may win him around yet.'

'Remind him of the magic of my art. I have reached the heights upon this stage to please the vulgar throng. Master Marwood *owes* it to me to let me continue. Let him know the full quality of my work.'

'It speaks for itself,' said Nicholas tactfully.

'We count on you for our salvation.'

Barnaby Gill gave his arm an affectionate squeeze, an uncharacteristic gesture that showed how upset he was by the shadow hanging over them. As Gill sloped off to the tiring-house, another voice sought the book holder's ear.

'We must talk alone, Nick,' said Edmund Hoode.

'When I have finished here. Meet me in the taproom.'

'It is the worst blow I have ever suffered.'

'We are all still reeling from its force.'

'How can I endure it?'

'Try to put it out of your mind.'

'It sits there like an ogre that will not shift.'

'Master Marwood may be converted to commonsense.'

'What use is that?' said Hoode peevishly. 'I want Lawrence Firethorn converted to an eunuch. It is the only way to solve my plight. He compels me to write songs of love to his new doxy when I have a mistress of my own to woo. Come to my aid, Nick. I perish.'

It was hectic. In the short time between rehearsal and performance, Nicholas attended to all his duties, ate a meagre lunch, sympathized with Hoode's predicament, fought off another sally from Owen Elias ('Ramon was a disgrace to the theatre this morning. Let me take over'), managed an exchange of pleasantries with Alexander Marwood then went back to his post to watch the stage being swept and strewn with green rushes. When the audience swarmed in to take up their places in the yard or their seats in the galleries, everything was apparently under control.

The sense of order did not last. *Black Antonio* had never been given such a lacklustre performance. Lawrence Firethorn was strangely muted, Barnaby Gill was curiously dull and Edmund Hoode, who usually sparkled in the role of a duplicitous younger brother, was frankly appalling. The disease was infectious and the whole company was soon in its grip. They played without conviction and the mistakes began to multiply. But for the book holder's consoling authority behind the scenes, *Black Antonio* might have become a fiasco. As it was, the audience felt so cheated by what it saw that it began to hoot and jeer with gathering displeasure. Only a minor recovery in the Fifth Act saved the actors from being booed ignominiously off the stage. Westfield's Men had never taken their bows with such indifference.

Lawrence Firethorn came hurtling into the tiring-house to berate everyone in sight for their incompetence only to be told by Edmund Hoode that he himself was the chief offender. The row that developed between them was not only due to the insecurity they now felt at the Queen's Head. There was a deeper reason and Nicholas had noted it from the beginning of the performance. Both men had gone out to act to one person in the packed audience.

Matilda Stanford was not there.

Not even the first hints of calamity could keep Walter Stanford away from home. Though he was still deeply concerned about the fate of his nephew, Michael, he did not interrupt his normal schedule to join in the search. That was now being led by his son who had so far come back empty-handed. Lieutenant Michael Delahaye had indeed disembarked on the previous Thursday but he was only one of hundreds of soldiers who had poured off the ship and into the welcoming bosom of London. Nothing further had been gleaned, not even a description of the wound he had collected in the Netherlands. Medical records had not been kept by the army and Michael was, in any case, no longer a member of it. Discharged into civilian life once again, he had contrived to vanish into thin air.

Walter Stanford put it all to the back of his mind as he walked purposefully into the Royal Exchange on Cornhill. Modelled on the Antwerp Bourse, it was the largest building project undertaken in the city during the Tudor dynasty. Eighty houses had been demolished to clear the site. The Exchange was the work of Thomas Gresham, mercer and financial agent to the Crown, who put some of his vast wealth towards the cost. Enmity between England and Spain had led to trading difficulties with Flanders and created a dire need for a bourse in London. Thomas Gresham obliged and it was duly opened in 1570 by Queen Elizabeth. Its value to the merchant community was inestimable and nobody was more aware of this than Walter Stanford. As he looked around, he was struck yet again by the boldness of the concept.

The Exchange was a long, four-storeyed building that was constructed around a huge courtyard. Its belltower was surmounted by a giant grasshopper which was the emblem of

the Gresham crest. Covered walks faced out on to the courtyard and statues of English kings stood in the niches above
them. It was an inspiring sight at any time but especially so
when it was filled with merchants who stood in groups ac-
cording to their specialized trading interests. Over the years,
the Exchange had also become the haunt of idlers who hung
about the gates to mock, jostle, beg, sell their wares or offer
their bodies but even this did not detract from the bustling
dignity that still prevailed.

Walter Stanford mingled happily and struck many deals
that Monday morning. Well-known and much-respected, his
position as Lord Mayor Elect made him a popular target and
he was courted on every side. Productive hours soon scudded
by but it was not only profit that interested him. A gnarled
face in the crowd reminded him of a promise to his young
wife.

'Good day to you, Gilbert.'

'Well-met, sir.'

'Are you not too old for this madhouse?'

'I will come to the Exchange until I drop, Walter.'

Gilbert Pike was by far the most ancient of the wardens of
the Mercers' Company. Thin, silver-haired and decrepit, he
was bent almost double and hobbled along with the aid of a
stick. But his mind was still as razor-sharp as it had always
been and he could more than hold his own in any business
deal. There was also another facet to the old man's skills
and Walter Stanford drew him aside to gain some advantage
from it.

'I need your kind help, Gilbert.'

'Speak on and it is yours.'

'My young wife must be pleased.'

Pike cackled merrily. 'Do not call on me for that!'

'Matilda is adamant. When I become Lord Mayor, she
would have a play performed in my honour.'

'Then she is a woman after my own heart,' said the other
with croaking enthusiasm. 'The Mercers' Company put on
many pageants in times past. I wrote many of them myself
and took the leading part.'

'That is why I came to you, Gilbert. Nobody is so well-versed in the drama. Would it be possible to stage another piece to brighten up my banquet?'

'It would be an honour!' said Pike eagerly. 'What is more, I have the very play to hand. *The Nine Worthies*.'

'Is that not an antiquated piece?'

'Not in my version, sir.'

'Who are these nine worthies?'

'Three Paynims, three Jews and three Christian men.'

'Explain.'

'Hector of Troy, Alexander the Great and Julius Caesar; then come Joshua, David and Judas Maccabeus; last are Arthur, Charlemagne and Godefroi de Bouillon.'

'I see no comedy there,' said Stanford. 'Matilda orders laughter. Have you no more lively piece?'

'*The Nine Worthies* is my finest invention.'

'I'm sure it is, Gilbert, but it does not suit our purpose here. Unless . . .' An idea took root in his mind and blossomed spontaneously. 'Unless we change these nine fellows to fit our purpose and advance our Guild.'

'How say you?'

'Supposing those same gentlemen wore the livery of the Mercers' Company? Do you follow my inspiration here? Instead of Hector and the rest, we choose nine persons who have brought our guild most honour as Lord Mayors of London. I like it well. Richard Whittington must be our first worthy, of that there is no question.'

Gilbert Pike took a few minutes to understand and adapt to the notion but he welcomed it with a toothless grin and clapped his claw-like hands. Other names sprang from him for consideration.

'Richard Gardener, Lionel Duckett and John Stockton. Ralph Dodmer should be there and even Geoffrey Boleyn that was a hatter first and then a mercer. John Allen must be there, who presented the mayoral collar. Then there is Ralph Dodmer and Richard Malorye and many more besides.' The gums came into view again. 'Nor must we forget the worthiest man of our own day.'

'Who is that, Gilbert?'

'Who else but you, sir?' The old man was warming to the

idea rapidly. 'Walter Stanford. You shall be the ninth in the line. It will be a fitting climax.'

'And a wonderful surprise for Matilda,' agreed the other. 'But can this play have humour in it, too? May not these nine honourable men make us laugh as well?'

'They will provide drama and mirth, sir.'

'This is truly excellent, Gilbert!'

'And my title remains—*The Nine Worthies*.'

'No,' said Stanford. 'It would serve to confuse. That title is too familiar. We must find a new one.'

'But it describes the play so well,' argued the old man. 'Are these men not worthy? And are there not nine of them in number? Each one a giant of the company? What is the objection to my title?'

'You have just given me a better one.'

'Have I, sir?'

'Yes, Gilbert. *That* is what the play will be called.'

'What?'

'The Nine Giants!'

Chapter Six

EVEN AFTER THE BEST PART OF A YEAR IN OFFICE, SIR Lucas Pugsley was still thrilled at the privileges showered upon him as Lord Mayor of London. The city had always jealously guarded its independence even though this often led to friction with the court and the Parliament at Westminster. Within the city walls, the Lord Mayor ranked above everyone except the Sovereign herself, including princes of the Blood Royal. No fishmonger could ask for more than that. Among his many titles, Pugsley was head of the City Corporation, its chief magistrate, and the chairman of its two governing bodies, the Court of Alderman and the Court of Common Council. Perquisites flourished on all sides but there was one that brought him special delight. He was entitled to any sturgeon caught below London Bridge.

Two features of the office conspired to deter many a possible contender. A year as Lord Mayor was extremely costly since it took you away from your business affairs and involved a great deal of incidental expense. To avoid all this, there had been cases in the past of aldermen bribing their way out of election, paying hundreds of pounds to avoid an honour that would take even heavier toll of their purse. Those rich enough to afford the luxury could yet be halted by another drawback. Being a Lord Mayor committed you to an enormous amount of work. Civic duties were endless and banquets were too frequent and too lavish for many stomachs.

Sir Lucas Pugsley made light of both handicaps. He was wealthy enough to take the job and hungry enough to do it without loss of appetite. Though it took him away from his own business, it was a profitable investment since it gave him an insight into every area of activity in the city. He had considerable patronage at his disposal and could bestow lucrative offices on friends and relations. The head of the city also got the profits from the sale of appointments which were his to make, and received income from rent farms and market leases. Pugsley was an archetypal Lord Mayor. What made him able to savour his public role was the immense assistance he got in private.

The Chamberlain was a rock at all times.

'I have brought the judicial accounts, Lord Mayor.'

'Thank you, Aubrey.'

'Here also is some correspondence from Amsterdam.'

'I have been awaiting that.'

'You have to deliver a speech this evening.'

'Lord save us! I had quite forgot.'

'That is why I took the liberty of drafting it out for you, Lord Mayor. Three foreign ambassadors dine at your house this night. A speech of welcome is in order. You are too busy to give much time to it yourself.' He handed the documents over. 'I hope that my humble scribblings find favour.'

'Indeed, they do, man. You are my saviour, Aubrey!'

'I try to be of service.'

As Chamberlain to the city of London, he had wide-ranging duties with regard to finance but his omnicompetence raised him above his calling. Like many before him, Pugsley used the man's advice and expertise at every turn and confided in him things that he kept from almost everyone. That was another reassuring trait of Aubrey Kenyon. He was the very soul of discretion.

They were in the palatial room that Pugsley used as his office. He was seated at the long oak table with documents piled high in front of him. Without the aid of his Chamberlain, he could never hope to find his way through them. Power made him capricious.

'Do I have appointments this afternoon?'

'Five in total, Lord Mayor.'

'I am in no mood to receive anyone. Cancel them.'

Kenyon bowed. 'I have already done so.'

'You know my mind better than I,' said Pugsley with a chuckle. 'You have learned to read me like a book, sir.'

'Then I hope I have read aright.'

'What do you mean?'

'I dismissed only four of your five visitors.'

'And the fifth?'

'He waits outside. I did not think you would wish him to be turned away like the others.'

'Who is the fellow?'

'Alderman Rowland Ashway.'

'Once more, you share my thinking, sir. Rowland Ashway must never be sent away from this door. It is largely because of him that I sit this side of it.' He got up from his chair. 'Admit him at once.'

'I will, Lord Mayor.'

Kenyon bowed, left the room quietly then returned almost at once with the waddling Ashway. With another formal bow, the Chamberlain left them alone to trade warm greetings and even warmer gossip. The old friends were soon chatting away happily about the pleasures of high office. Sir Lucas Pugsley let self-importance get the better of him.

'Nothing can compare with this feeling, Rowland.'

'I trust it well.'

'It is a gift from the gods.'

'And from your admirers on the aldermanic roll.'

'Think, man! A fishmonger who has the Queen's ear.'

'We are two of a kind,' said Ashway complacently.

'In what regard?'

'You have the Queen's ear. *I* have the Queen's Head.'

Nicholas Bracewell bided his time until the landlord came out into the courtyard to speak to one of his ostlers. As Alexander Marwood broke away, the book holder intercepted him. It was early evening at the Queen's Head and the disgruntled audience had long since departed. Westfield's Men had sullied their glowing reputation.

'Good even, good sir,' said Marwood. 'You gave a paltry account of yourselves here today.'

'Some blame must fall on you, I fear.'

'I am no actor, Master Bracewell.'

'Indeed you are not,' said Nicholas. 'Had you been so, you would know the lurching misery of those without a regular wage or a regular home. The Queen's Head has been a beacon in our darkness, sir. Take but that away and you plunge us into blackest night.'

'I must do the best for myself and my family.'

'Granted sir. But we are part of that family now and feel cut off. When you threaten to exile us, you lower our spirits and our performance. The result was plain for all to see this afternoon.'

'Do not put this guilt upon me.'

'I appeal only to your finer feelings.'

Marwood's twitch had been quiescent until now, lying dormant while it considered which part of his grotesque face to visit next. It reappeared below his left eye and made him wink with alarming rapidity. Nicholas pursued him for more information.

'Has anything been settled with Alderman Ashway?'

'In broad outline.'

'Our contract still has some weeks to run.'

'It will not be renewed, Master Bracewell.'

'Despite the mutual advantage it has brought?'

'All things must come to an end, sir.'

'Would you surrender ownership so easily?'

His question made the landlord smart and shifted the nervous twitch to his pursed lips which now opened and shut with fish-like regularity. Evidently, he had some misgivings about the new dispensation. Nicholas tried to apply some gentle pressure.

'The proud name of Marwood has favoured this inn for over a century. That is a fine achievement.'

'I know my family history, Master Bracewell.'

'Then have some thought for your forbears. Would any of them have yielded up their inheritance like this?'

'No, sir,' agreed Marwood. 'Nor would they have given shelter to a troupe of bothersome actors. My father would not have let Westfield's Men across the threshold.'

'Would he turn away the custom of our noble patron?'

'He liked not plays and players.'

'You have been a kinder host.'

'It is time to show kindness to myself.'

'By giving away all that you hold most dear?'

'Only at a price.'

Nicholas shrugged. 'That is your privilege, sir. But I wonder that you have not looked more fully into this.'

'More fully?'

'Alderman Ashway is an ambitious man. The Queen's Head will not be the only inn he has gobbled up. Look to the Antelope and to the White Hart in Cheapside.'

'What of them?'

'Talk to the landlords,' said the other. 'See if they are happy that they sold out to the good brewer. You will find them weighed down with regret, I think.'

'That is their fault,' insisted Marwood. 'I have wrested better terms for myself. You cannot frighten me in that way, Master Bracewell. The Antelope is a scurvy hostelry and the White Hart draws in low company. I'll not compare the Queen's Head with them.'

'They all serve Ashway's Beer.'

'You have drunk your share without complaint.'

Nicholas was making no headway. Foreseeing the attack, Marwood had shored up his defences with care. The twitch might travel to and fro across his battlements but his wall would not be breached. Another form of entry had to be found. The book holder searched with care.

'How does your wife face the impending loss?'

'That is a private matter, sir.'

'Mistress Marwood has her doubts, then?'

'She will see sense in time.'

'Would you sign a contract without her approval?'

The landlord fell into a stony silence but his twitch betrayed him completely. It broke out in four different areas simultaneously so that a swarm of butterflies seemed to have settled on his face. As he watched the fibrillating flesh, Nicholas Bracewell saw that there might be a shaft of hope for them after all. The future of Westfield's Men rested on a woman.

Matilda Stanford was in reflective mood as she strolled along the winding paths in the garden. Early autumn was offering floral abundance and bending fruit trees, all wrapped in a heady mixture of sweet fragrances and brought alive by bright sunshine and birdsong. Stanford Place was blessed with one of the largest and most luxuriant gardens in the area, and its blend of privacy and tranquillity was exactly what she needed at that moment. The front of the house looked out on the daily turbulence of Bishopsgate Street but its rear gazed down upon an altogether different world. In the heart of the busiest city in Europe was this haven of pure peace. Matilda had loved it from the start but she came to appreciate it far more now. What had once been a pure delight was today a means of escape. In the twisting walks of the garden, she could find true solitude to relieve the sharpness of her melancholy.

Ever since she had realized she was unhappy, it had been more and more of an effort to pretend otherwise and she was almost glad of the crisis about her husband's missing nephew, Michael, because it relieved her of the need to be so wifely and vivacious. In sharing the general concern, she could conceal her own feelings of loss and disappointment. In worrying about Lieutenant Michael Delahaye, she was expressing a deeper anxiety about someone else who had gone astray. Matilda Stanford was also missing and the search for her was fruitless.

There were moments of joy but they lay in the fond contemplation of one who was forever beyond her reach. Lawrence Firethorn was unattainable. Though he had sent her a playbill and signalled his admiration during the performance of *Double Deceit*, that was as far as the relationship could realistically go. She was a married woman with no freedom of movement and he was a roving actor. There was no way that she could return the interest he had shown in her even though the desire to do so grew stronger by the hour. Michael's disappearance was a mortal blow to her fleeting hopes. A man who might have accompanied her to the Queen's Head was making sure that she had no means of going there. It was William Stanford who was leading the hunt and thereby depriving his stepmother of her means of attending a play.

As she looked ahead, her spirits sank even more. Her husband was a wonderful man in so many ways but he did not give her anything of the stimulation she received from a ranting actor upon a makeshift stage. When Walter Stanford became Lord Mayor of London, her situation could only get far worse as she was dragged along behind him into an endless round of social events. She would see even less of him and experience more inner torment. A marriage which had brought her such pleasure was now turning into a comfortable ordeal. She was stifled.

The lifeline was brought by Simon Pendleton.

'Hold there, Mistress.'

'What's that?'

'Another missive has arrived for you.'

'Who delivered it?'

'That same miserable creature as before,' said the steward, wrinkling his nose with polite contempt. 'I have brought it to your hand.'

'Thank you, Simon.'

'Will there be anything else, Mistress?'

'Not at this time.'

He bowed and glided off into the undergrowth with practised ease. Though Matilda could not bring herself to like the man, she was profoundly grateful to him at the moment because he had fetched the thing she most desired. It was a playbill, rolled up as before and tied with a pink ribbon. As her nervous fingers released it, the scroll unwound and a sealed letter dropped to the ground. Matilda snatched it up immediately. A glance at the playbill told her that Westfield's Men were due to stage *Love and Fortune* at the Queen's Head on the following day but it was the letter that produced the real elation.

As she tore it open, she found herself reading a sonnet in praise of her beauty that itemized her charms with such playful delicacy that she almost swooned. It was unsigned but the sender—presumably the poet—was no less a person than Lawrence Firethorn himself. All her doubts were cast aside. Hers was no wild infatuation for a man beyond her grasp. It was a shared passion that drew them ineluctably together. A second message lay in the choice of play. *Love and Fortune* could be no accidental selection. It reinforced the sentiments of the sonnet and was an invitation to romance.

She read the poem again, weighing each word on the scales of her mind to extract maximum pleasure from it. That she could have inspired such a mellifluous flight of language was dizzying enough on its own. For it to have come from the hand of the man on whom she doted made the whole thing quite intoxicating. Walter Stanford could not be faulted as a loyal husband who treated his wife with respect. But he had no pretty rhymes in his soul.

Tears of joy formed. During her dark night of disenchantment, she had come to see that she was not happy in her marriage. During her walk in the afternoon sun, she made a discovery of equal import and adjusted her own view of herself yet again. In a garden in London, standing beneath a juniper tree, seeing the colour clearly, inhaling the sweet odours, hearing the melodious birdsong, Matilda Stanford had another revelation. Her heart was no longer bound by the vows made on her wedding day because it had not truly been engaged in the ceremony. Fourteen lines of poetry and a cheap playbill taught her something that sent a thrill through her entire being.

She was in love for the first time in her life.

The charnel house had a new keeper. Nicholas Bracewell's formal complaint to the Coroner's Court had led to the dismissal of the man who treated the dead bodies in his charge with such grotesque lack of respect. His hollow-cheeked successor was no more companionable but he had a greater sense of decency and decorum. Conducting the small party to the slab in the corner, he took hold of the tattered shroud and looked up for a signal from the watchman. The latter deferred to the two visitors he had brought into the grim vault. Walter Stanford exchanged a glance with his son and both braced themselves. A nod was then given to the keeper who drew back the shroud with clumsy reverence, unveiling only the head and trunk of the corpse so that the repulsive injuries to the leg remained hidden away.

'Lord help us!' exclaimed Stanford.

'God rest his soul!' said his son.

Both were thunderstruck by what they saw and fought to control their stomachs. Neither of them needed to view a crippled leg to confirm the identity of the battered body. Walter Stanford was looking at the nephew who was due to renounce a hedonistic existence and commit himself to a more responsible life. His son was staring at a beloved cousin whose merriment was its own justification. Grief dazed them both completely. The watchman gestured to the keeper and the shroud was pulled back over the corpse to check the hostile smell of death. There was a long, bruised silence as the visitors were given time to compose themselves. The watchman then spoke.

'Well, sirs?' he said.

'That is him,' whispered Stanford.

'You have no doubt?'

'None at all,' added William.

'Would you like to view him again?'

Walter Stanford winced and held up a large palm.

'We have seen enough,' he said. 'My son and I know our own kin. That is Michael Delahaye.'

It was Anne Hendrik's idea. After what she felt was the relative success of taking Hans Kippel to church, she believed he might now be ready for a more important outing, especially if it could be presented to the boy as something else. Nicholas Bracewell agreed to her plan. Since Westfield's Men were not playing that Tuesday, he managed to find an hour in the middle of the afternoon when he could slip back home to Bankside to join in the expedition. The intention was to help the apprentice to confront his fear of the Bridge. This could not be done by simply taking him there and forcing him to cross it. Anne told him that all three of them were going to visit the market in Cheapside. With two adults at his side, he felt as if he were part of a family setting out on a small adventure. Apprehensions did not surface.

After prior discussion, Nicholas and Anne tried to keep his mind engaged by feeding him with snippets of information about some of the buildings and churches that they passed on the way. Their casual tone did not alter when the Bridge came in sight and the gatehouse loomed up ahead of them. Hans Kippel gulped when he saw the heads of executed traitors crudely exhibited on poles but he did not check his stride. The barbarous custom had always upset and fascinated the boy.

'Thirty-two,' he said.

'What's that, Hans?' asked Anne.

'Thirty-two heads today. I have not seen so many.'

'Have pity on their souls,' said Nicholas.

'Who were they, sir?'

'Misguided men.'

'Did they deserve such treatment?'

'No, Hans. They have paid for their crime already.'

'What was it, Master Bracewell?'

By the time that Nicholas had explained, they were passing through the gate and beneath the sightless eyes of the severed heads. Another feature of the Bridge now rose up to dominate and impress.

'That is Nonesuch House,' said Anne.

'I have admired it often, Mistress.'

'Did you know that it was Dutch?'

'There is no mistaking it,' he said with a proud smile. 'I have seen other houses like it in Amsterdam.'

Nonesuch House was well-named. No-other-such-house or building stood in the whole of London. Built entirely out of wood, it was a huge, rambling structure that was heavily encrusted with ornament and crowned with carved gables and onion-shaped cupolas. The woodwork was painted with such vivid colours that a remarkable house became quite dazzling in every sense. Nonesuch House was one of the wonders of London and it added immeasurably to the awe-inspiring impact of the Bridge.

Nicholas Bracewell supplied more details for him.

'The foundation stone was laid in 1577,' he said. 'The house was built in Holland and shipped over, section by section, to be reassembled here. Just think, Hans. That building made the same journey as you.'

'Will I be reassembled?' he said plaintively.

'We'll put you together again somehow, lad.'

'It has no nails,' continued Anne. 'That is the real miracle of it. The whole house is held together with wooden pegs. What you see there is Dutch perfection.'

'Like the hats of Jacob Hendrik.'

Nicholas coaxed another smile from the boy and a wink of satisfaction from Anne. Their scheme had so far worked. Instead of rebelling at the very sight of the Bridge, the boy was walking steadily across it. Their afternoon stroll was not unimpeded. As ever, the Bridge was liberally over-populated. Houses and shops stretched every inch of its length and leaned over toward each other with such amiable curiosity that they could almost shake hands. The narrow road was made even narrower by the swirling crowds that moved along it in both directions and horse-drawn traffic had to carve its own rough passage through the human wall. Beautiful to behold from a distance, the Bridge was a dangerous place to cross and rolling wheels all too often brought disfigurement and even death.

It was impossible for the three of them to walk abreast. Holding each by the hand, Nicholas led the way and shouldered a path through the press. There were almost forty shops selling their wares. They included a cutler, a glover, a pouch-maker, a goldsmith, a pinner and a painter but many of the tiny establishments sold articles of apparel. Lavishly decorated, the shops faced inwards and advertised their presence with swinging signs. The merchandise was invariably made on the premises and sold by apprentices from a wooden board which was hinged to the open-fronted shop to form a counter. Behind the boards, shrill-throated youths called for attention.

Hans Kippel edged through it all with bemused interest. While Nicholas had one eye on him, Anne kept up her commentary to relax the boy.

'Do you know the tale of William Hewet?' she said.

'No, Mistress.'

'He was Lord Mayor of London over thirty years ago. A clothworker,' she explained, pointing a finger, 'who owned that house you see up ahead. Note how the windows hang out over the water. William Hewet's daughter fell from one of them straight into the Thames.'

'What happened, Mistress?'

'One of the apprentices dived in after her and dragged her to safety. His name was Edward Osborne. The girl grew up to be a beauty who was much-courted but the father turned them away. "Osborne save her, Osborne shall have her," he said. And so it was, Hans. He married her and inherited the business. Edward Osborne then became Lord Mayor of London himself.'

'Apprentices may yet thrive, then?' said the boy.

'Indeed,' said Nicholas. 'But one detail of the story was missing. The lovely daughter was named Anne.'

He smiled at her by way of compliment and she gave a gracious nod of acknowledgement. In that instant when their attention wandered from the boy, he lost all curiosity in the history of the Bridge. Hans Kippel came to a halt and stared at a house that was boxed in between two shops. Memories came back to test him and to make him gibber soundlessly. He took a few steps towards the house and touched it with his hand as if to make sure that it was the right place. The identification was complete. Mad panic gripped him once again and he turned to race back in the direction of Southwark.

But his way was blocked. A large cart was trundling towards him and it took no account of his youth or his urgency. Before he could get out of the way, the boy was knocked flying by the careless brutality of the vehicle. Nicholas rushed to pick him up in his arms and to search for injury while Anne unbraided the carter roundly. She then joined the little crowd who had gathered around the semi-conscious apprentice. No bones seemed to have been broken and no blood showed but he was severely winded. Nicholas and Anne tended him with concern.

But the keenest interest was shown by someone else. As the sagging body of Hans Kippel was borne away, a pair of dark, malignant eyes stared out from the upstairs window of the house which had alarmed the apprentice so much.

The boy had been found.

Edmund Hoode suffered the pangs of rank injustice. As he toyed with his pint of sack at the Queen's Head, he came to appreciate just how selfish and sadistic Lawrence Firethorn could be. It was unforgivable. After months of emotional stagnation, the poet had finally found someone to rescue him from his plight and supply a focus for the creative energy of his romantic inclinations. His new love had been blighted before it could blossom. Firethorn was exploiting a cruel contractual advantage over him. Instead of releasing his passion in verses dedicated to his own love, Hoode was simply helping to satisfy the actor-manager's libidinous desires. Despair made him groan aloud and turn to Barnaby Gill who was seated beside him on the oak settle.

'Truly, I am out of love with this life.'

'That was ever your theme,' said Gill cynically.

'This time I am in earnest, Barnaby. I would sue to be rid of this wretched existence.'

'Chance may contrive that for you.'

'How say you?'

'Westfield's Men are threatened with execution, sir. If Alderman Rowland Ashway takes possession here, ours will be the first heads on the block.'

'I would welcome the axe.'

'Well, I would not, Edmund,' said the other peevishly. 'Blood would ruin my new doublet and ruff. And I would not have my career cut off by the whim of a brewer. If Marwood sells the inn, I must think the unthinkable.'

'Retire from the stage?'

'My admirers would never countenance that. No, sir, I would need to put survival first and join Banbury's Men.' He saw Hoode's shock and sailed over it. 'Yes, it might be an act of betrayal but my art must take precedence. If West-field's Men cannot sustain me, I must look to the highest bidder and that must be Giles Randolph. He has coveted my services this long time.'

'What about Lawrence?'

'What about him?' challenged Gill.

Hoode pondered. 'You are right, sir. We owe him no loyalty after the way he has treated us. I'll not let him stroke the bodies of his mistresses with my conceits. Do you know his latest demand?'

'A new prologue for *Love and Fortune*?'

'Even so. It is to contain an intimate message.'

'His intimate messages are all contained in his codpiece,' sneered Gill. 'I wonder that he does not teach it to speak for itself. It cannot declaim lines any worse than he and it holds the major organ of his ambition.'

'I'll not endure it longer, Barnaby!'

'Write sixteen lines for Master Codpiece.'

'Lawrence must relent.'

'Not until Margery bites off his pizzle.'

'He'll use me this way no longer.'

'Free yourself from womankind and learn true love.'

'I'll tell him straight.'

Fortified by the sack and by the conversation, Edmund Hoode leapt up from the table and went in search of his colleague. Firethorn had gone to give instructions about some new costumes to Hugh Wegges, their tireman, who worked with needle and thread in the room where the company's equipment was stored. Hoode strode purposefully in that direction but he soon slowed down. A strident voice began to fill the innyard.

Now here upon this field of Agincourt
Let each man take his oath to fight with me
And give these French a taste of English steel,
With bravest arrows cutting down their knights,
With stoutest hearts o'ercoming any odds
That angry France can muster 'gainst our will.
March onwards, lads, into the ranks of death,
Until we vanquish, no man pause for breath!

113

The voice of Lawrence Firethorn thrilled the ear as it reverberated around the empty yard to fill the place with sound and frighten the stabled horses. Edmund Hoode knew the lines well because he had written them himself for *King Henry the Fifth*, a stirring saga of military heroism. Firethorn had always been superb in the role but this time he added some Welsh cadences by way of tribute to the king's birthplace of Monmouth. Stoked up with rage to confront the actor–manager, Hoode yet spared a moment to admire his art afresh. No man could equal Firethorn even when he was just showing off his talent as now. That did not excuse his treatment of his resident poet and it was with seething indignation that Hoode swept out into the yard to tackle the barrel-chested figure who stood right in the middle of it.

'Lawrence!' he said. 'I demand to speak to you!'

'Speak to *me* instead, sir.'

The man turned around with an arrogant smile that stunned Hoode completely. It was not Firethorn at all. The extempore performance had been given by Owen Elias.

Walter Stanford and his son were grief-stricken when they returned home. Michael's death was a shattering blow in itself but the nature of his exit made it unbearably worse. Someone so young and full of promise had been cut down savagely in his prime. Stanford resolved that he would not rest until the murderer had been found and made to pay the full penalty of the law. Vengeful as he was, he did not let his feelings warp his behaviour. In an effort to protect his wife from the full horror, he gave her only an attenuated account of what they had seen. Matilda was devastated by the news. Even though she had never met Michael Delahaye, she had heard enough about him to form some very favourable impressions. Sharing the loss with her husband and stepson, she reserved most sympathy for her sister-in-law.

'What of dear Winifred?' she asked.

'She must be told at once,' said Stanford. 'William and I

will ride to Windsor today to break the sad tidings to her. It will be the ruination of poor Win.'

'Let me come with you,' she offered. 'I may be of help at this trying time.'

'Your kindness is appreciated, my love, but this is a task for me alone. I need to frame Win's mind to accept what has happened. It will be a long and arduous business and too distressing for you to witness.'

'Have funeral arrangements been made?'

'They are set in motion,' he said. 'When Michael's body is released, it will be brought to Windsor for burial in the family vault. It is then that I will call upon you for your comfort and company.'

'Take both for granted, Walter.'

'You are a solace to me.'

He gave her a perfunctory embrace then held back tears as he thought about the body on the slab. It had been hauled out of the Thames without a shred of clothing to give it decency in its last moments. A thought struck him with sudden force.

'I see the meaning of it now,' he said.

'Of what, sir.'

'That present I received, Matilda.'

'Present?'

'The salmon.'

'What did it signify?'

'That Michael slept with the fishes.'

Sir Lucas Pugsley chewed happily on a crisp mouthful of whitebait. Being the Lord Mayor of London obliged him to entertain on a regular basis but only a small number of guests were dining at his house that evening. One of them was the massive figure of Rowland Ashway who was tucking into his meal with voracious appetite. Placed at the right hand of his friend, he was able to have private conference with a lowered voice.

'Has that contract been allocated, Sir Lucas?'

'What contract?'

'We spoke of it even yesterday.'

'Ah, that,' said the Lord Mayor airily, 'Have no fears on that score, Rowland. You will get your just desserts. I have instructed Aubrey Kenyon to handle the matter.'

'That contents me. Master Kenyon is most reliable.'

'He is the chiefest part of my regalia. I wear him about my neck like the mayoral collar. My year in office would not have been the same without Aubrey.'

'Haply, he will notice the change as well.'

'Change?'

'When you hand over to Walter Stanford.'

'Perish the thought!' snarled Pugsley.

'Master Kenyon must feel the same. You and he have worked hand in glove. He will not have the same kind indulgence from that damnable mercer.'

General laughter interrupted their chat and they were forced to join in the hilarity. It was over half an hour before a lull allowed them another murmured debate. Rowland Ashway was remarkably well-informed.

'Have you heard of Stanford's latest plot?'

'What idiocy has he invented now?'

The Nine Giants.

'Nine, sir. We have but two giants in London.'

'That I know. Gogmagog and Corinaeus.'

'From where do the other seven hail?'

'The Mercers' Company,' said Ashway. 'They are to perform a play at the Lord Mayor's banquet to celebrate the triumph of their master. It is called *The Nine Giants* and shows us nine worthies from the ranks of that guild.'

Pugsley grunted. 'They do not *have* nine worthies.'

'Dick Whittington is first in number.'

'And the last, Rowland. They have none to follow him. If the mercers would stage a play, let them be honest and call it *The Nine Dwarves*. They have plenty of those in their company. Walter Stanford is bold indeed.'

'You have not heard the deepest cut.'

'Tell me, sir.'

'He himself will be the ninth giant.'

Sir Lucas Pugsley choked on his meat and had to swill down the obstruction with some Rhenish wine. All his hatred and jealousy swelled up to enlarge his eyes and turn his face purple.

'*I* should remain as Lord Mayor,' he growled.

'No question but that you should. But the law stands in your way. It is decreed that no retiring mayor can serve another term of office until seven years has passed.'

'That law might yet be revoked.'

'By whom?'

'By force of circumstance.'

'Speak more openly, Sir Lucas.'

'This is not the time or place,' muttered Pugsley. 'All I will tell you is this. If Walter Stanford were to fall at the very last hurdle—if something serious were to disable his mayoralty—might not your fellow-aldermen turn to me to help them in their plight?'

Sir Lucas Pugsley began to laugh. Rowland Ashway enlarged the sound with his throaty chuckle. Others found the hilarity infectious and joined in at will. The whole table was soon rocking with mirth even though most of those around it had no idea at what they were laughing. Such was the power of the Lord Mayor of London.

They moved with great stealth through the dark streets of Bankside. One of them was tall, muscular and well-groomed with a patch over his right eye. The other was shorter and more thickset, a bull of a man with rough hands and rough ways. They each carried a bundle of rags that had been soaked in oil to advance their purpose. When they came to the house, they checked all the adjoining lanes to make sure that they were not seen. Revellers delayed their work by blundering out of a nearby tavern and rolling past them in full voice. Only when the sound died away did the two men set about their nefarious business.

The rags were stuffed tight up against the front door of the dwelling then set alight. The accomplices waited until the flames began to get a hold on the timber then they took to their heels and fled into the night. Disaster crackled merrily behind them.

Anne Hendrik's house was on fire.

Chapter Seven

NICHOLAS BRACEWELL WAS THE FIRST TO BECOME aware of the danger. He had developed a sixth sense where fire was concerned because it was such a constant threat to his livelihood. Sparks from careless pipe-smokers had more than once ignited thatch at the Queen's Head and the other venues used by Westfield's Men, and though most of their performances took place in the afternoon, some continued on beyond the fall of darkness and had to be lit by torches or by baskets of burning tarred rope. Extreme care was needed at all times and Nicholas was particularly vigilant. Even in his sleep, his nostrils maintained a watch and so it was that night. As soon as the first whiff of smoke was encountered, he came awake in a flash and leapt up naked.

His bedchamber was at the front of the house and he saw the fierce glow through the window. Instinct took over. After shaking Hans Kippel out of his slumbers, he pulled on his breeches and raised the alarm in the rest of the house. With no means of escape through the front door, he quickly hustled Anne Hendrik, the two servants and the boy into the little garden at the rear then dashed back to tackle the blaze itself. It had now got a firm hold and long tongues of flame were licking their way into the room. Acrid smoke was starting to billow. The triumphant crackle grew louder.

Nicholas moved with great speed. Having once been caught in a blaze in the hold of a ship, he knew that fumes could be as deadly as fire itself. He therefore dipped a shirt in one of the leather buckets of water that stood in the kitchen, then wound it around his neck and mouth. With a bucket in each hand, he hurried back into the drawing room and looked anxiously around. On the wall was one of Anne's most cherished possessions. It was a beautiful tapestry, depicting the town of Ghent, and given to her as a wedding present by Jacob Hendrik who had commissioned it especially for her in Flanders. She would not willingly have parted with it for anything but sentiment had to give way to survival. Nicholas hurled the water over the tapestry then hastily brought two more buckets from the kitchen to repeat the drenching process.

Tearing down the tapestry, he threw it over the floor to douse the smouldering boards then used it to beat out the flames that were coming in through the door. He was soon given support. Anne Hendrik left her servants to look after the quaking apprentice and came back in to help to save her house. She dipped a broom in the last bucket of water then used it to attack the flames as strenuously as she could manage. Smoke invaded her throat and made her cough. Nicholas rent his sodden shirt in two and gave her a piece to cover her mouth and nostrils. The two of them continued the struggle to save the property.

Noise had now reached deafening proportions. The whole street, then the whole neighbourhood, was roused. Panic was readily abroad. Fire was feared almost as much as the plague and its effects were just as devastating. Like the rest of the city, Bankside was predominantly an area of thatched, timber-built dwellings held together with flimsy lath and plaster. Efforts had been made for well over a century to force people to tile their roofs instead of using reed or straw but the ordinances had scant effect. The only precautions that most householders took were to keep buckets of water on hand or, in far fewer cases, to have firehooks hanging at the ready so that they could be used in an emergency to pull down burning wood or thatch. Organized fire-fighting was virtually unknown and pumps were very rudimentary. In any conflagration, people reacted with unashamed self-interest and looked to their own premises. So it was here.

Nicholas and Anne fought the fire from within while their yelling neighbours did their best to stop it from spreading to their tenements. Because the street was so narrow, the houses opposite were as much at risk as those adjoining and their occupants, too, were contributing freely to the communal hysteria. Water was thrown over thatch and timber to keep the fire at bay. Implements of all kinds were used to beat at the flames. As a ferocious glare lit up the night sky, pandemonium ruled. Children screamed, women howled in fear, men bawled unheard orders at each other. Dogs barked, cats shrieked and wild-eyed horses were led neighing from their stables to clatter on the cobbles and add to the gathering confusion. Everyone was soon involved. One old lady in a house directly opposite even opened the upstairs window to hurl the contents of her chamberpot over the small inferno.

Prompt action slowly won the battle. Having subdued the worst of the flames inside the house, Nicholas was able to kick down the charred remains of the door and get into the street. With a clearer view of the danger, he was able to swish the now steaming tapestry against the front of the building. When a few altruists threw buckets and barrels of water at the house, he was grateful for the soaking that he himself got. It enabled him to withstand the fierce heat and get ever closer to its centre. The tapestry eventually secured victory. Torn beyond belief and blackened beyond recognition, it put out the seat of the fire. Nicholas dropped it wearily to the ground and stamped on it with bare feet to stop it smouldering.

Relief spread as rapidly as the fire itself and a ragged cheer went up. People who had been plucked from their beds by the threat of death now saw some cause for celebration. Those terrified neighbours further along the street who had evacuated their homes completely now began to take their furniture and belongings back inside. New friendships grew out of common adversity. Ear-splitting fear was now replaced by gregarious murmur. The crowd began to disperse until the next emergency.

Anne Hendrik stood panting beside her lodger and tried to regain her breath. She was suffering from the effects of inhaling the smoke, but Nicholas Bracewell was in a far worse state. His breeches were scorched, his feet burned and his chest a mass of black streaks. Sparks had even had the temerity to singe his beard. His umbered face was running with sweat and crumpled by fatigue but he found the strength to slip an arm around her waist. She leaned against him for support and looked up at the ravaged frontage of her house.

'Thank you!' she gasped.

'I could not let my lodging go up in smoke.'

'You saved our lives, Nick.'

'God was at our side.'

'How could the fire have started?' she said between bouts of coughing. 'Some careless passer-by?'

'This was no accident, Anne. I see design at work.'

'To what end?'

'Someone here was meant to sleep for ever.'

Anne blanched. 'An attempt on our lives? Why, sir? Who would want to kill us?'

'We may not have been the targets,' said Nicholas as he thought it through. 'It is possible that the fire was lit for someone else—Hans Kippel.'

It was the first night since her marriage that Matilda Stanford had spent entirely alone. With her husband away in Windsor, she had the bed and bedchamber exclusively to herself and she revelled in the new freedom. At the same time, however, she felt even more isolated. The news about Michael Delahaye had been horrific and she was genuinely distressed but it did not touch her heart directly. She had never known the dashing soldier and could not share the desperate loss felt by others. Suffused with real sympathy, she was also distanced from her husband and her stepson as they mourned the death of a loved one and became embroiled in sorrowful duties. Michael had been very much inside the charmed circle of the family. For all her readiness to join in, Matilda remained firmly on the outside.

What kept her awake was not the thought of a dead body pulled from the clutches of the Thames. It was something quite remote from that and it brought its due measure of guilt and recrimination. Indeed, so troubled did she feel that she got up in the middle of the night and went down to the little chapel to pray for guidance and to see if divine intercession could direct her mind to more seemly matters. Even on her knees, she remained unable to sustain more than a passing sigh for the fate of Michael Delahaye. It was another man who occupied her thoughts, not a rotting corpse in a charnel house but a person of almost super-human vitality, a master of his art, a romantic figure, an imp of magic, a symbol of hope.

Lawrence Firethorn even infiltrated her prayers. Instead of asking for a blessing on a departed soul, she begged for the opportunity to meet her self-appointed lover. Happiness no longer lay beside a wheezing mercer in a four-poster bed. True joy resided at the Queen's Head in the formidable person of an actor-manager. In thinking about him at all, she was repudiating the vows taken during holy matrimony. In speculating about the way that their love might be consummated, she was committing a heinous sin. Doing both of these things while kneeling on a hassock before her Maker was nothing short of vile blasphemy but her Christian conscience did no more than bring a blush of shame to her cheeks. Matilda Stanford made a decision that could have dire consequences for her and for her whole marriage.

She would accept the invitation to the play.

First light found Nicholas Bracewell out in the street to assess the damage to the house and to begin running repairs. Word was sent to Nathan Curtis, master carpenter with Westfield's Men, who lived not far away in St Olave's Street, and he hastened across with tools and materials. The front of the house would need to be partially rebuilt and completely replastered but the two men patched it up between them and gave its occupants a much-needed feeling of security and reassurance. Curtis was rewarded with a hearty breakfast and a surge of gratitude but he would accept none of the money that Anne Hendrik offered. As a friend and colleague of the book holder, he was only too glad to be able to repay some of the kindness and consideration that Nicholas Bracewell had always shown him. He shambled off home with the warm feeling that he had done his good deed for the day.

Hans Kippel had been kept ignorant of his role as the intended victim of the arson. Shocked by the grisly experience on the Bridge, he had withdrawn into himself again and could not explain the rashness of his conduct. In the wake of the fire, he was even more alarmed and they did not add to his afflictions by subjecting him to any interrogation. Instead, Nicholas Bracewell set out for the Bridge and walked to the little house which had provoked such an intense reaction from the boy.

There was no answer when he knocked the door but he felt that someone was at home and he persisted with his banging. In the shop next door, an apprentice was letting down the board as a counter and laying out a display of haberdashery for the early customers. Nicholas turned to the lad for information.

'Who lives in this house?'

'I do not know, sir.'

'But they are near neighbours of yours.'

'They moved in but recently.'

'Tenants, then? A family?'

'Two men are all that I have seen.'

'Can you describe them, lad?'

'Oh, sir,' said the boy. 'I have no time for idle wonder. My master would beat me if I did not attend to the shop out here. It is so busy on the Bridge that I see hundreds of faces by the hour. I cannot pick out two of them just to please a stranger.'

'Is there nothing you can tell me?' said Nicholas.

The boy broke off to serve his first customer of the day, explaining that a much greater range of wares lay inside the shop. When the woman had made her purchase and moved on with her husband, the apprentice turned back to Nicholas and gave a gesture of helplessness.

'I can offer nought but this, sir.'

'Well?'

'One of them wears a patch over his eye.'

'That is small but useful intelligence.'

'And all that I can furnish.'

'Save this,' said Nicholas. 'Who *owns* the house?'

'That I do know, sir.'

'His name?'

'Sir Lucas Pugsley.'

The Lord Mayor of London awoke to another day of self-congratulation. After breakfast with his family, he spent time with the Common Clerk who handled all secretarial matters for him, then he devoted an hour to the Recorder. The City Marshal was next, a dignified man of military bearing, whose skill as a horseman—so vital to someone whose job was to ride ahead of the Lord Mayor during all processions to clear the way—had been learned in a dozen foreign campaigns. Among other things, the Marshal headed the Watch and Ward of the city, rounding up rogues and vagabonds as well as making sure that lepers were ejected outside the walls. Sir Lucas Pugsley loved to feed off the respect and homage of a man who wore such a resplendent uniform and plumed helmet. It increased the fishmonger's feeling of real power.

Aubrey Kenyon was the next visitor, cutting a swathe through the dense thickets of the working day with his usual calm efficiency. When they had discussed financial affairs at length, the Chamberlain turned to an area that would normally have been outside his remit had not the Lord Mayor encouraged him to offer opinions on almost every subject of discussion that arose. Kenyon's sage counsel was its own best advertisement.

'Have you taken note of next week, Lord Mayor?'

'Indeed, sir,' said the other pompously. 'I am to have another audience with Her Majesty at the Royal Palace. The Queen seeks my advice once more.'

'I was referring to another event.'

'Next week?'

'On Thursday. It is a public holiday.'

'Ah.'

'You should be forewarned, Lord Mayor.'

Pugsley nodded importantly. The preservation of peace and the maintenance of law and order were his responsibility and they were arduous duties in a city that was notorious for its unruly behaviour. Crimes and misdeameanors flourished on a daily basis and there were parts of London, feared by the authorities, that hid whole fraternities of thieves, whores, tricksters, beggars and masterless men. Cripples, vagrants and discharged soldiers swelled the ranks of those who lived by criminal means. These denizens of the seedy underworld were a perpetual nuisance but the law-abiding could also present serious problems. Public holidays were seized on by many as occasions for riot and excess when the anonymity of the crowd shielded miscreants from punishment at the same time as it fired them on to grosser breaches of the peace. For hundreds of years, the mayoralty had learned to rue the days when the city was at play.

Aubrey Kenyon had strong views on the matter.

'Wild and licentious behaviour must be quashed.'

'So it shall be, sir.'

'Apprentices so soon get out of hand.'

'I know it well,' said Pugsley with a nostalgic smirk. 'I was one myself, Aubrey, and felt that stirring of the blood on every high day and holiday. The pranks that we lads got up to!' He corrected himself at once. 'But it is a tradition much mocked and abused of late. Harmless pleasure can so easily turn to an affray—and I will not permit that in *my* city.'

'Take steps to ward it off then.'

'You have my word that it shall be done.' His beady eyes lit up. 'I take my cue from Geoffrey Boleyn.'

'He was a brave Mayor indeed, sir.'

'In 1458, the King in his wisdom ordered a council of reconciliation in St Paul's between the rival nobility. During the month it took them to arrive, Mayor Boleyn patrolled the streets by day in full armour and he kept three thousand armed men ready by night.' Pugsley's chest expanded. '*I* would ride out at the head of my constables if you think that it is needful.'

'There are other precautions we may take,' said Kenyon tactfully. 'Your bravery does you credit but you do not have to expose yourself to danger.'

'What are these precautions, Aubrey?'

'Appoint sufficient men to keep watch on the city.'

'It shall be done.'

'Look to the selling of ale that it should not be given to those too young to hold it like a gentleman. Discourage large crowds from gathering. Arrest known trouble-makers early in the day before they can work up the apprentices.' Aubrey Kenyon reserved his deepest contempt for another area of social life. 'Subdue what entertainment we can, especially the theatres.'

'Theatres?'

'That is where corruption breeds,' said the Chamberlain. 'If it were left to me, I would close down every playhouse in London.'

Abel Strudwick was ruthless in pursuit of the new career that he now felt awaited him. He was rowing away from a Bankside wharf with two passengers in the stern of his boat when he saw Nicholas Bracewell and Hans Kippel in search of transport. The waterman lost all interest in his current fare and swung the prow of the boat around to head back towards the wharf. His passengers complained bitterly but they were no match for Strudwick. His combination of brawn and bellicosity had them scampering out of the boat and he welcomed Nicholas and the boy instead. All three were soon threading their way through the flotilla of craft that was afloat that day. The waterman was impatient.

'Have you acquainted Master Firethorn with my ambitions?' he asked with hirsute eagerness.

'I mean to speak to him today,' said Nicholas.

'Tell him of my quality.'

'It will not go unremarked, Abel.'

'I would strut upon the scaffold with him.'

'That may not be so easy a wish to fulfil.'

'But I have the trick of it,' said the other. 'Let me come out on to the stage before the play begins to woo the audience with my sweet music.'

Nicholas gave a noncommittal nod. Hans Kippel, at first alarmed by Strudwick's grinning ugliness, now took an interest in him.

'Are you a musician, sir?' he said.

'Yes, lad. Would you hear me play?'

'What is your instrument?'

'Lie back in the boat and you shall hear it.'

Before Nicholas could stop him, the poet recited a long narrative about his visit to the Queen's Head and its extraordinary effect on his life. The verse had the same rocking-horse rhythm as usual and it was imprisoned hopelessly in its rhyme-scheme. A pun of resounding awfulness brought the saga to a grinding conclusion.

> Upon a road did Saul see his new light.
> My Damascus was a theatre bright.
> A water poet, I am the stuff of fable,
> Let Strudwick do all that he is able.

Nicholas manufactured a smile of approval but Hans Kippel was truly impressed. The boy was amazed to hear such fine words coming from such a foul source and he clapped his hands. Abel Strudwick beamed as if he had been given an ovation by a huge audience and he sealed an instant friendship with the Dutch apprentice. The fact was not lost on Nicholas who saw its value at once. He had only brought the boy with him in order to ensure his safety. If Hans Kippel was in danger of attack, he had to be watched over carefully at all times. Taking him away from Southwark had the extra advantage of shifting any threat away from Anne Hendrik. As it was, Nicholas had given Preben van Loew and the other workmen stern orders to be vigilant on her behalf but he did not feel she was now at risk. Unknown to himself, the boy was the target. Friendship with Abel Strudwick meant that there was another safe refuge in the event of an emergency.

They landed, paid their fare and took their leave. The boat-

127

man's tuneless music had served another turn. So mesmerized was Hans Kippel that he did not look once towards the Bridge which held such terrors for him. He was in an inquisitive mood and they picked their way through the busy market in Gracechurch Street.

'What is the name of the play, Master Bracewell?'

'*Love and Fortune.*'

'And shall I be able to watch it?'

'Only during the rehearsal, Hans.'

'I have never been to a theatre before,' said the boy. 'Preben van Loew was not happy that I should come to this one today. I was brought up strictly in Amsterdam and such things are frowned upon. Will it cause me harm?'

'I do not think so.'

'Old Preben believes that it will.'

'Do not pay too much heed to him.'

Nicholas smiled fondly as he remembered an occasion when the Protestant rectitude of the Dutch hatmaker was put to the test by Westfield's Men. Preben van Loew had been asked to escort Anne Hendrik to a performance of the controversial piece, *The Merry Devils*, and he had been embarrassed to find just how much he enjoyed it. The book holder was confident that Hans Kippel would get equal pleasure out of the present offering. With a paternal arm around the boy's shoulders, he guided him in through the main entrance of the Queen's Head.

The apprentice was an incongruous figure amid the flamboyance of the actors and he came in for some good-natured ribbing. George Dart warmed to him at once because he recognized a kindred spirit in the waif-like youth with his pale face and his wide-eyed wonder. Nicholas introduced his companion to everyone then left him with Richard Honeydew, the youngest and most talented of the four apprentices, a bright, alert, soft-skinned boy with a mop of fair hair and a friendly grin. While the book holder was busy setting the rehearsal up, the little actor took the visitor under his wing. Inevitably, there was especial interest shown from one quarter.

'Welcome to our humble show, Master Kippel.'

'Thank you, sir.'

'Barnaby Gill, at your service.' He gave a mock bow and appraised the newcomer. 'Is not that jerkin a trifle warm for you in this weather?'

'There is a cold breeze blowing, sir.'

'That will not hurt you. Come, let me help you off with it. I promise you will feel more comfortable.'

Hans Kippel did not get the chance to find out. Before the actor could even touch the boy, Nicholas came over to interpose himself between them. Having rescued the lad from an attempt on his young life, he was not going to let him fall into the dubious clutches of Barnaby Gill. One glance from the book holder made the actor back off at once. Neither Hans Kippel nor Richard Honeydew fully understood what had happened in that moment. Their innocence remained intact.

The voice of authority boomed out across the yard.

'Gentlemen, we tarry!' yelled Firethorn.

'All is ready, sir,' said Nicholas.

'Then let us show our mettle.'

With no more ado, the rehearsal began. *Love and Fortune* was a romantic comedy about the dangers of committing the heart too soon and too completely. It featured three sets of lovers and its use of mistaken identity was both deft and effective. Westfield's Men put real spirit into it and the play romped along at speed. Lawrence Firethorn crackled hilariously in the leading role, ably supported by Edmund Hoode as a lovelorn gallant and by Barnaby Gill as an ageing cuckold. The small but demanding part of Lorenzo was played with Celtic ebullience by Owen Elias who tackled the speeches as if he were auditioning for much greater theatrical honours. After their patent failure with *Black Antonio*, the company was determined to vindicate its reputation in the most positive manner. The rehearsal had edge.

Hans Kippel loved every moment of it. Seated on an empty firkin in the middle of the yard, he was the lone spectator of a comedy that made him laugh so loud and so much for two whole hours that he kept falling off his perch. The pace of the action bewildered him but that did not dull his appreciation of the play itself or of the many splendid performances. Without quite knowing why, he was happy for the first time in a week. The only things that puzzled him were the absence of Richard Honeydew and the other boy apprentices, and the sudden appearance of four beautiful young women on the stage. When the most affecting of these creatures—a demure maid in a high-waisted dress of pink taffeta—spoke to him, Hans Kippel felt his cheeks burn with modesty.

'Did you like the entertainment?' she said.

'Yes, yes.'

'Be honest with me, Hans.'

'I liked it exceedingly, good mistress.'

'And did you recognize us all?'

'Well . . .'

The visitor's confusion was total. Richard Honeydew cut through it by taking off his auburn wig to reveal the telltale mop of fair hair. Hans Kippel jumped up with a shock that quickly turned to amusement as he realized how completely he had been fooled by the excellence of the playing. The four apprentices had been so convincing in their female roles that he had never suspected for a moment that they might be anything but young ladies themselves. As he looked at his new friend now, then saw the lantern-jawed John Tallis ease off the shoulders of his dress to expose a padded bust, he beat out a tattoo of joy on the firkin. This was the funniest thing of all and it put some of the old zest back into the Dutch boy.

Nicholas Bracewell watched with approval from the back of the stage. The decision to bring Hans Kippel to the Queen's Head had been a sound one. It had not only guaranteed his safety, it gave a lift to his spirits that nothing else had been able to do. The antics of *Love and Fortune* might be able to unlock the demons that were chained up in his mind.

Demons of another kind prompted Lawrence Firethorn.

'Nick, dear heart!' he sighed.

'I am here, sir.'

'Have you spoken with that creeping insect yet?'

'Master Marwood will not be moved.'

'Then shall he feel the end of my sword up his mean-spirited arse. That will move him, I vow!'

'We must do nothing rash,' said Nicholas.

'He'll not disown us without a fight.'

'Let me use subtler weapons.'

'They have no power to kill.'

'Yet might they preserve our place here, Master.'

'Can you be certain of that, Nick?'

The book holder shook his head and replied honestly.

'No, sir. The portents are bad.'

Alderman Rowland Ashway surveyed the inn yard through the window of an upstairs room. With the fidgeting landlord at his shoulder, he pronounced the death sentence.

'I want them out of here at once,' he said.

'Their contract still has weeks to run, sir.'

The alderman was peremptory. 'My attorneys will find a way out of that. Good lawyers will sniff out a loophole in any document. When you have signed the Queen's Head over to me, we'll have Westfield's Men out on the street before they draw breath to protest.'

'Hold fast,' said Alexander Marwood. 'Do they not deserve a fair warning?'

'Notice of eviction is all that they will get.'

'I have scruples.'

'There is no such thing in business affairs.'

Ashway's easy brutality made the landlord pause to consider his own position. If the alderman dealt with his enemies so callously, how would he handle Marwood himself if the two of them ever fell out? Cunning lawyers who could revoke a legal contract with Westfield's Men could do as much with any document of sale. Security of tenure might turn out to rest on the whim of Rowland Ashway.

'I need more time to think this over,' said Marwood.

'You have had weeks already, sir.'

'Fresh doubts arise.'

'Smother them at birth.'

'I must make safe our future.'

'That is my major concern here,' said the other with adipose affability. 'The Queen's Head is nothing without the name of Marwood and I would not dream of buying one without the other. Your family have a proud heritage, sir. It is my sincerest wish to preserve and honour that.'

'I must peruse the contract with my own attorney.'

'So shall you, Master Marwood.'

'And my wife still has her quibbles.'

'I thought my two hundred pounds took care of them.'

'It helped,' said the landlord with a laugh like a death rattle. 'It helped to soften her inclinations.'

'Work on her earnestly.'

'It has been my life's endeavour.'

Ashway pulled away from the window and walked back into the room. Watching the end of the rehearsal had only deepened his hatred of Westfield's Men. Their very existence was a reminder of the privilege and title from which he was excluded by birth. To oust them would be to promote worth in place of idleness. Theatre was nothing but a distraction from the working world of the city.

He fixed an eye on the squirming publican.

'You have given me your word, Master Marwood.'

'It is my bond, sir.'

'I expected no less.'

'We have always dealt honestly with each other.'

'And both of us have prospered,' noted Ashway. 'Bear that in mind in case your wife has further doubts. I will have the contract sent to you forthwith.'

'Give me time to study it at my leisure.'

'Keep me waiting and my interest will wane.'

'All will be well, I am sure.'

'Good,' said the alderman going back to the window to gaze down. 'I'll take possession of the Queen's Head and throw Westfield's Men back into the gutter where they belong, vile rabble that they are! Let their illustrious patron give them all begging bowls!' Something aroused his curiosity. 'Come here to me.'

'What is it, sir?'

'That man below there.'

'Which one?'

'The sturdy fellow with the boy.'

'I see him.'

'Who is he?'

Alexander Marwood watched the tall, muscular figure take his scrawny young companion across the yard to the stage and hoist him up with one fluent movement of his strong arms. The landlord knew him as the one member of the company whom he could respect and trust.

'Well, sir,' said Ashway. 'Who is he?'

'The book holder.'

'What is his name?'

'Nicholas Bracewell.'

Expectation put colour in her cheeks and rekindled the spark in her eyes. The day was rich with promise and she let it show in her face, her voice and her movements even though she collected some glances of disapproval from the household steward. Matilda Stanford had been stirred by the touch of true love and nothing could subdue her. The staid Simon Pendleton might expect her to share in the family sorrow over the murder of Michael Delahaye but she did not put on a false show of mourning for his benefit. All her thoughts were fixed on the afternoon ahead. *Love and Fortune* was more than just another performance by Westfield's Men. If she had the courage to respond to the message of the sonnet, it was a tryst with her beloved.

'Shall we be safe, Mistress?'

'Stay close to me, Prudence.'

'I do not know whether to be excited or afraid.'

'I confess I am a little of each.'

'Would that we had a gentleman to protect us!'

'We shall have. Be patient.'

Prudence Ling was far more than just a maidservant. Small, dark and spry, she was an attractive young woman with lively conversation and plenty of bounce. Most important of all, she was utterly trustworthy. Prudence had been in service with Matilda for some years now and their friendship had reached the point where they could exchange any confidences. The maidservant had no time for moral judge-

133

ment. If her mistress wished to deceive her husband while he was away, then Prudence was ready to help with all her considerable guile. It was she who had procured the hooded cloaks that the two of them now wore and it was she who had led the way out through the garden gate so that their exit was unobserved by the steward of Stanford Place. Hiding their faces behind masks, they joined the crowd that was converging on the Queen's Head.

'I have but one fear, Mistress.'

'Be still, child.'

'What if they mistake us for ladies of pleasure?'

'Think on goodness and ignore them.'

The two women paid their entrance fee and went up to the middle gallery to claim seats on the front bench. They were wedged in between a couple of leering gallants but their masks gave them concealment and the badinage soon died. Other ladies with more available charms were taking their places nearby to watch the entertainment and to ply their trade at the same time. Prudence sneaked a sideways look at them and giggled her amusement.

The wind had freshened now and the sky was overcast. A full and fractious audience needed a vigorous comedy to warm them up and that is what they were given. Inspired by the speech that Lawrence Firethorn delivered just before they began, Westfield's Men played *Love and Fortune* with a verve and commitment that was lacking from their previous offering. In place of tepid tragedy was a joyous comedy of romantic misunderstanding. Riotous laughter soon filled the makeshift auditorium and hearts were moved by the shifts and sufferings within the drama.

Matilda Stanford was entranced from the moment when Lawrence Firethorn stepped out in a magnificent costume of red and gold velvet to deliver the Prologue in tones of ringing sincerity. Her mask fell from her hand to reveal her in her true beauty and the actor spotted her immediately. Though heard by all, his words were clearly directed at her and she let herself be caressed by the language of pure love. Firethorn continued to woo her throughout in such a way that she was impervious to the presence of other spectators and believed herself to be the sole witness of a command performance. *Love and Fortune* was bursting at the seams with fun and frolic but her attention never wandered from Lawrence Firethorn. She did not notice the lovelorn swain with his clean-shaven naivety who was also dedicating his performance to her. Nor did she consider for a second that it was he who had written the new Prologue as well as the additional lines which were included for her benefit alone.

Suddenly, it was all over. Matilda was caught up in a torrent of applause that went on for several minutes as Firethorn led his company out on to the stage. His eyes sent further messages of desire to her but she could not fathom their meaning. When the cast vanished behind the curtain and the crowd began to leave, she was plunged into despair. During the play itself, Lawrence Firethorn had been so close to her in spirit that she felt she could reach out to touch him but now he was miles away. Had she taken all those risks to such little purpose? Did her blossoming romance amount simply to this? Was there nothing more?

'A word with you, Mistress!'

'Away, sir!' said Matilda.

'But I bring you a letter.'

'Do not trouble me further.'

'It is from Master Firethorn.'

Breathless and battered, George Dart had struggled through the press to get to her with his missive. She snatched it from him and rewarded him with a coin that turned his elfin misery into beaming delight. Matilda opened the letter and read its contents with rising elation. It was an invitation to join Lawrence Firethorn in a private room and share a cup of Canary wine. She accepted on impulse and waved George Dart on so that she and her maidservant might follow. During the journey along the gallery, she showed the letter to Prudence. The maidservant was at once intrigued and concerned.

'Is this wise, Mistress?'

'There is only one way to find out, Prudence.'

'What of danger?'

'I embrace it willingly.'

'He is certainly the handsomest of men.'

'Master Firethorn is a god whom I would worship.'

Their guide took them through a maze of corridors until he reached a stout oak door. He paused to knock with timid knuckles. His master's roar came from within. George Dart opened the door for the two ladies to enter then he closed it behind them as Lawrence Firethorn bent low to plant a first delicate kiss on the hand of Matilda Stanford. Having done his office, the stagekeeper was now superfluous and could return to the multifarious tasks that still awaited him below. He made for the stairs but his way was blocked by a looming figure with staring eyes and gaping jaw. Edmund Hoode was aghast.

'Who were those ladies?' he demanded.

'Guests of Master Firethorn, sir.'

'But that was *her*! And she is *mine*!'

'I was sent to bid them here. That is all I know.'

'This is torture indeed!'

'You look ill, sir. Shall I send for help?'

Hoode grabbed him. 'Who *was* she?'

'Which one, Master?'

'There *is* only one, George. That beauteous creature with the luminous skin. That angel from the gallery.' He shook his colleague hard. 'What is her name, man?'

'Matilda Stanford, sir.'

'Matilda, Matilda . . .' Hoode played with the name and smiled fondly. 'Yes, yes, it becomes her. Sweet Matilda. O, Matilda mine. Edmund and Matilda. Matilda and Edmund. How well they flow together!' Titters of amusement came from within the room to darken his face. 'Lawrence and Matilda. There's discord and damnation for you!'

'May I go now, Master Hoode?' whimpered Dart.

'What's that?'

'You are hurting me, sir.'

The poet released his quarry and let him scuttle away down the stairs. His own pain now preoccupied him. The cruel irony of it all lanced his very soul. Hoode's own verses had been used to deliver up his mistress into the steamy embrace of Lawrence Firethorn. Deprived of the chance to write to her himself, he had been doing so unwittingly on another's behalf. It was insupportable and the horror of it made him sway and moan. When he put his ear to the door, he heard flattery and laughter and the betrayal of his greatest hopes. Inside the room, mutual desire was flowering into something more purposive.

Edmund Hoode had murder in his heart.

Chapter Eight

DURING THE PERFORMANCE OF *LOVE AND FORTUNE*, Hans Kippel sat in a corner of the tiring-house and wondered at everything he saw. Actors came and went, changing their costumes, characters and sex with baffling speed. Scenic devices were carried on and off. Stage and hand props were in constant use. Everyone was involved in a hectic event that gained momentum all the time and it was left to the book holder to impose order and sanity on the proceedings. From the stage itself came heightened language and comic songs that were interspersed with waves of laughter and oceans of applause. Swordplay, music and dance added to the magic of it all. In its own way, it was even more thrilling than watching the whole play in rehearsal. Tucked away in the tiring-house, Hans Kippel was part of a strange, new, mad, marvellous world that set fire to his imagination. He believed he was in heaven.

'I am sorry to leave you alone so long, Hans.'

'Do not vex yourself about me, Master Bracewell.'

'There was much for me to do, as you saw.'

'I have never seen anyone work so hard,' said the boy with frank admiration. 'Not even Preben van Loew.'

'Did the others keep an eye on you?'

'Dick Honeydew spoke to me many times though his skirts

made him look so like a woman. Master Hoode was very kind and so was Master Gill. I also talked a lot with George Dart and even had a few words with Master Curtis, the carpenter, who helped us at the house this morning.' His face clouded. 'Who started that blaze?'

'I will find out, Hans.'

'But why was it done, sir?'

Nicholas shrugged evasively and brought the boy out into the yard. The experiment of bringing Hans Kippel to the Queen's Head had been an unqualified success but he was now in the way. Having supervised the dismantling of the stage, the book holder now took time off to shepherd the boy back down to the wharf where Abel Strudwick was waiting. Nicholas paid him in advance and charged him with the task of rowing the apprentice back to the Surrey side of the river and of accompanying him safely home. The boatman was delighted with his commission, not least because his passenger was so enthused by the play he had just seen and so willing to listen to more of Strudwick's plangent music. Ambition nudged again.

'What did Master Firethorn say about me?' he asked.

'I go back to raise the matter with him now.'

'Tell him I am at his disposal.'

'He may not have need of you directly, Abel.'

'Shall I bring my verses to him?'

'I will ask.'

Nicholas strode back through the coolness of the early evening to attend to his final duties. He was checking that everything had been securely locked away when a broad palm gave him a hearty slap on the back.

'Nick, my bawcock! A thousand thanks!'

'For what, sir?'

'A thousand acts of goodness,' said Firethorn grandly. 'But none more welcome than the service you performed for me of late.'

'You speak of the lady, I think.'

'And think of her as I speak. Oh, Nick, my friend, she is an empress to my imperial design. I have never met a creature of such flawless perfection and such peerless beauty.'

Another slap fell. 'And it was *you* who found out who she was. A thousand thousand thanks!'

Nicholas had grave reservations about his role as go-between and he was uneasy when he heard what had transpired. Matilda Stanford had come to the Queen's Head with no chaperone but a maidservant and the two of them had been greeted by Firethorn in a private room. It boded ill for the young lady herself and for the company.

'Conquest is assured,' said Firethorn dreamily.

'Beware of what might follow, sir.'

'I care nothing for that. The present is all to me.'

'Have concern for the future as well,' warned Nicholas. 'The lady is married and to a man of great wealth and influence. Think what hurt he might inflict if he ever found out about this dalliance.'

'I fear no man alive, sir!'

'It is the company I have in mind. Master Stanford will be Lord Mayor of London before long. He could take his anger out on Westfield's Men and expel us promptly.'

'Only if he is cognizant,' said Firethorn. 'And he will not be. We will pull the wool over his mayoral eyes and make a mockery of him. I am no lusty youth with his codpiece points about to pop. Waiting only enhances the prize and I will bide my time until Richmond.'

'Richmond, sir?'

'The Nine Giants.'

'You have made an assignation?'

'I have but put the sweet thought into her mind.'

'And until then?'

'We simply dote on the ecstasy that lies in store.'

Nicholas was relieved that he was not rushing into his entanglement. Advance notice gave the book holder the opportunity to extricate the young bride. Flushed with excitement, Lawrence Firethorn was in a mood to agree to almost anything and Nicholas plied him with a dozen or more requests concerning company business. When the actor-manager acceded to them all, his employee honoured a promise he had been forced to give.

'I have a friend who writes verses, sir.'

'Let me see them, let me see them.'

'He is but a humble waterman.'

'What of that, Nick?' said the actor proudly. 'I am the son of a common blacksmith yet I have risen to the pinnacle of my profession. Who is this fellow?'

'Abel Strudwick.'

'I will read his work and give my opinion.'

Firethorn waved his farewell and swept off down the corridor. Nicholas was glad that he had mentioned his friend but held out little hope for him. The actor would have forgotten all about the request by the next day. Abel Strudwick would be only one of countless dejected scribes who were spurned by the star of Westfield's Men.

The taproom was the next port of call for the book holder. His intention was to speak to Marwood's wife but someone else claimed his attention first. Edmund Hoode was almost suicidal. Seated alone at a table, he was pouring beer down his throat as if he were emptying a bucket of water into a sink. Nicholas intervened and put the huge tankard aside.

'Give it to me, Nick!' gasped Hoode.

'I think you have drunk enough, sir.'

'Fill it to the brim with poison and make me happy.'

'We love you too well for that, Edmund.'

'You might but *she* does not. I am betrayed.'

'Only by yourself,' said Nicholas gently, sitting beside him. 'You do the lady wrong to expect too much from her. She does not even know of your existence.'

'But she read my sonnet!'

'Sent by another.'

'Yes!' growled Hoode, trying to stand. 'Lawrence has used me cruelly in this matter. On my honour, I will not permit it! I will challenge him to a duel!'

He reached for an invisible sword at his side and fell back ridiculously on to his seat. Nicholas steadied his friend then found himself the object of attack.

'I blame you, sir!' said Hoode.

'For what?'

'Foul deception. Why did you not tell me the truth?'

'I thought to save you from pain.'

141

'But you have made it all the worse,' howled the poet. 'You *knew* that Lawrence was in pursuit of my fair mistress yet you did not even warn me.'

'I hoped to head him off, Edmund.'

'Head him off, sir? When he is at full gallop? It would be easier to head off a charging bull!'

'Nevertheless, it may still be done.'

Hoode clutched at straws. 'How, Nick? How? How? How?'

'I will bethink me.'

'Matilda Stanford.' Fantasy had returned. 'I could weave such pretty conceits around a name like Matilda. It is a description of a divinity. Matilda the Magnificent. I cannot stop saying it—Matilda, Matilda, Matilda . . .'

'Remember to add her surname,' said the other.

'What?'

'Stanford. Matilda Stanford.'

'She will always be plain Matilda to me.'

'But not to her husband.'

'Husband!' He choked. 'The child is married?'

'To Walter Stanford. Master of the Mercers.'

'I have heard of him.'

'So should you have. He is the Lord Mayor Elect.'

Edmund Hoode stared blankly at the ceiling as he tried to process this new information. It introduced many unforeseen difficulties but romance could overcome them. He fell in love indiscriminately and let nothing stand in the way of his surging passion. The presence of a husband was a problem but it was not insurmountable. Far more serious was the existence of a rival of the calibre of Lawrence Firethorn. He had all the advantages. Hoode shifted his ground dramatically.

'I believe in the sanctity of marriage,' he said.

'So should we all.'

'Matilda must be saved from damnation.'

'That is my wish, too, Edmund.'

'I will protect her from the prickly Firethorn.'

'Do it with cunning.'

'I'll move with stealth,' he said. 'If I cannot have her as mine, she will be returned safe and sound to her lawful husband. Lawrence will fail this time. Should he try to board her, I'll take her by the ankles and pull her out from under him. He will not prevail.'

'We two are agreed on that.'

'Yes, Nick. It will be my mission!'

Abel Strudwick rowed with undiminished gusto across the river and guided his boat around and between the endless bobbing obstacles. Hans Kippel urged him to pull harder and play more music. The waterman was overjoyed. He saw in the Dutch apprentice something of the son who had been snatched from him by the navy and his affection for the boy grew. With a captive audience who appreciated his work so much, he launched into some of his most ambitious poems, long, meandering narratives about life on the Thames and the perils that it presented. His music took them all the way to Bankside then out on to the wharf and up the stone steps. A friendship was being consolidated.

There was one peril that Strudwick did not mention. The man with the patch stood in the open window of a house on the Bridge and applied a telescope to his good eye. He watched the waterman and his young passenger until the two of them had vanished between the tenements then he put the telescope aside and turned to his thickset companion. His voice was slurred but cultured.

'We must make no mistakes next time, sir.'

'I will carve the boy to pieces myself.'

'Look to that friend of his.'

'What was his name again?'

'Bracewell.'

'That's the fellow.'

'Master Nicholas Bracewell.'

Sybil Marwood was proving to be even more unyielding than her husband. She was a stout, sour-faced woman of middle years for whom life was a continuing disappointment. She had little time for Westfield's Men and even less for the arguments that Nicholas Bracewell was now putting on their behalf in the taproom at the Queen's Head. Leaning on the counter with her bulging elbows, she cut him down ruthlessly in mid-sentence.

'Hold your peace, sir.'

'I beg leave to finish, Mistress.'

'There is no more to say. We sell the inn.'

'And forfeit your birthright?' he said. 'Once the premises are in the hands of Alderman Ashway, you will be at his mercy.'

'We will have security of tenure.'

'For how long?'

'In perpetuity.'

'Even Master Marwood cannot live for ever,' reasoned Nicholas. 'What will happen to you if he should die?'

'I would remain here in his place.'

'Is that in the terms of the contract?'

'It must be,' she insisted. 'Or Alexander will not be allowed to sign it. I know my rights, sir.'

'Nobody respects them more than us, Mistress.'

Nicholas was making no impact on her. Simple greed had mortgaged her finer feelings. Sybil Marwood was so dazzled by the amount of ready capital that she and her husband would receive that she had blocked out all other considerations. The theatre company was a disposable item in her codex. As long as actors were abroad, the virginity of her daughter was under threat. The skulking landlord did at least have some vestigial feelings of loyalty to the troupe that had brought so much custom to the inn over the years but his wife had none. Her cold heart was only warmed by the idea of a healthy profit.

'Can no words prevail with you?' asked Nicholas.

'None that you can utter, sir.'

'What if Alderman Ashway plays the tyrant?'

'Then he will have *me* to face.'

'The deed of sale is drawn up by him.'

'Women have ways to get their desires.'

It was a cynical observation made with the veiled hostility which seemed to encircle her but it also contained some advice on which Nicholas was determined to act. Direct approaches to Marwood and to his wife had borne only diseased fruit. The book holder had to work a different way and he suddenly realized how. There was an element of risk but it had to be discounted. It was the last course of action open to them.

Nicholas took his leave and sauntered across the taproom. Edmund Hoode was still plotting revenge at his table, Owen Elias was regaling colleagues with the story of how he first discovered his vocation as an actor, George Dart was sharing a drink with Thomas Skillen and Nathan Curtis, and the indefatigable Barnaby Gill, dressed in his finery, was half-trying to seduce a young ostler from the stables. All of the company had now learned of the grim fate that menaced them and an air of despondency filled the room. The book holder was given fresh incentive to put his new plan into action.

He went straight to Shoreditch and swore Margery Firethorn to secrecy. She was thrilled. Fond of Nicholas Bracewell, she let herself be persuaded by his charm and his reason. It was wonderful to feel that she might be the one person who could turn the tide and she saw at once the personal advantage she would gain at home. The domineering Lawrence Firethorn would no longer be able to crow over a wife if she rescued Westfield's Men by her timely intercession.

'I'll do it, Nicholas!' she said.

'Privily.'

'Lawrence will suspect nothing.'

'He would not understand this manoeuvre.'

'Teach me what I must say.'

'Appeal to Mistress Marwood as a woman.'

'But she is a dragon in skirts, from what I hear.'

'All the more reason to flatter and fondle her.'

Margery chortled. 'You are wicked, sir!'

'I will call you when the time is ripe.'

'You will find me ready.'

She planted a kiss of gratitude on his cheek then sent him on his way. Setting her on Sybil Marwood might just be the solution. They were two of a kind, sisters under the skin, powerful women with red blood in their veins and fire in their bellies. With even moderate luck, Margery might be able to get through to the landlord's wife in a way that no man—not even Marwood himself—could possibly manage. It was all down to the ladies in the case. They spoke the same language.

As Nicholas marched homewards, he reflected on the day and the crisis with which it had begun. Hans Kippel was in grave danger. Enemies who would resort to arson would stop at nothing. Evidently, the boy had witnessed something on the Bridge which he should not have and his life was forfeit as a result. The only way to save him was to unmask his attackers first and bring them to justice. These thoughts took the book holder all the way down Gracechurch Street and back on to the Bridge.

The shops were closed now but there were still plenty of people milling around. Nicholas stood aside as two horses cantered past him. He then walked up to the house which he had visited that morning and appraised it more carefully. It was a small, narrow, two-story property that consisted of a tiny drawing room, a dining room, two bedchambers, and a kitchen that jutted out over the river so that a supply of water could be hauled up in a bucket tied to the end of a long rope. The dwelling also had its own privy. There was a public convenience on the Bridge itself but most householders took advantage of the site to make their own arrangements. The Thames was its own form of sanitation.

Nicholas saw the light in the downstairs window but he did not immediately knock on the door. Instead, he turned sideways to go down the slender gap between the house and the shop next door so that he could reach the parapet. Directly below was one of the starlings into which the stone pillars which supported the Bridge were set. The swift current foamed the water as it sluiced its way under the arch. Nicholas leaned right over to get a better view and discovered that he could see right into the kitchen of the house. Its timber-framing had sagged dramatically and it looked as if it was hanging on to the rest of the building with the tips of its fingers. He bent right over the parapet to peer into the kitchen.

'May I help you, sir?'

The voice was polite but unfriendly. Nicholas swung round to see a short, neat, erect figure blocking the narrow passage. His apparel suggested service in a grand establishment. The man stroked his greying beard.

'You are trespassing here,' he said.

'Do you live in this house, sir?'

'No, I have just been visiting.'

'You know the tenants, then?'

'Why do you ask?' His suspicion was candid. 'Have you any business to be here?'

'I was looking for someone.'

'Indeed, sir?'

'He has a patch over one eye.'

Simon Pendleton stared at him with cool distaste and took some time before he spoke. His tone was offhand.

'That is Master Renfrew,' he said.

'May I speak with him?'

'He is not at home, sir.'

'Will he return soon?' asked Nicholas.

'I fear not,' said the steward dismissively. 'He has gone away for a long time. You will not be able to see Master Renfrew. He is not here in London.'

'Then where is he?'

'Far away, sir. Far, far away.'

The bed creaked and groaned noisily as they flailed around on top of it at the height of their passion. He was a considerate lover who aroused her patiently by degrees and made her yield herself completely to him. She loved the weight of his body with its firm muscles and its thrusting power. She shared his total lack of fear or inhibition. Here was no ordinary client who tumbled into her arms for five minutes of over-eager satisfaction or who rolled off her in a drunken stupor before he could complete the business of the night. Kate had found herself a real lover and she revelled in the discovery.

When it was all over, they lay side by side in a peaceful togetherness. His chest was heaving, her heart was pounding and both of their bodies were lathered with sweat. It was minutes before either could speak. He then propped himself up on his elbow to gaze down at her with his one eye. His smile had a rugged tenderness.

'Thank you, my love,' he said softly.

'Thank *you*, sir.'

'We'll meet again some night.'

'That is my hope.'

'And my intention.'

He leaned over to kiss her gently on the lips then he reached across to the chair on which he had tossed his clothes. Fumbling at his purse, he brought back some coins to slip into the palm on her hand. Kate knew their value by touch and was instantly grateful.

'Oh, sir, you are too kind!'

'I repay good service handsomely.'

'Be assured of it here at any time.'

'I will always ask for you in this house.'

Another kiss sealed their friendship. Kate was no common whore from the stews. She was a very beautiful and shapely young woman of seventeen who chose her clients at the Unicorn Tavern with some care. They were always true gentlemen even if they could not always hold their wine or complete their transactions between the sheets. Kate had standards and the latest guest to her perfumed little bedchamber was a prime example of those standards. She even liked the black patch of his one eye. It gave him a raffish charm that sorted well with his relaxed manner. This was a man who knew how to please a woman properly.

As he got up from the bed and began to dress, she reached out for the rapier that lay against the chair. It glinted in the light of the candles. Kate pulled it a little way from its scabbard before pushing it slowly back in again. Then she noticed the name that was inscribed in large italics on the handle of the weapon.

'James Renfrew,' she read.

'At your service, madam.'

'What do your friends call you, sir?'

'Jamie.'

'Then that shall be my name for you. Jamie.'

'I will come when you call it.'

'Then will you never leave this bed, sir.'

He laughed merrily and pulled her to him in a warm embrace. Kate was the finest company he had found in Eastcheap and he would not neglect her. Cupping her chin in his hand, he brushed his lips past hers then smiled.

'I will be back soon, Kate.'

'I will be waiting, Jamie.'

Only a small party of foreign visitors was dining at the Lord Mayor's house that evening but they were accorded the lavish hospitality for which Sir Lucas Pugsley was justly famed. He sat beside his wife at the head of the table, fielding compliments and savouring the deference of other nations. Exuding good humour, he made his guests feel thoroughly at home. As soon as they had all left, however, he was able to show his true feelings to Aubrey Kenyon.

'I hate these grinning Italians,' he said.

'You showed them great civility, sir.'

'What else could I do, Aubrey? I am bound by the duties of my office here. But private opinion is another matter and in private, I tell you, these greasy fellows are not to my liking. We have enough aliens of our own.'

'London is a melting-pot of nations.'

'And it does not stop here,' said Pugsley irritably. 'Bristol, Norwich and other towns besides have their own foreign quarters. The rot is slowly spreading.'

'I know it well,' said the Chamberlain. 'There are over five thousand registered aliens here and that does not include the many who conceal the origin and escape the census. We have French, German, Italian, Dutch . . .'

'Dutch! Those are the ones I hate most.'

'An industrious people, sir.'

'Then let them stay in their own country and be industrious, Aubrey. We do not want them here to compete with honest English traders and craftsmen.' He was so animated now that his chain jingled. 'London is fast becoming the sewer of Europe. What other nations spew out, we take in and suffer. It is not good, sir.'

'The city has never welcomed foreigners.'

'Can you blame it?'

Before the Lord Mayor could develop his theme, they were interrupted by the arrival of a friend. Alderman Rowland Ashway was perspiring freely from his exertions. He was conducted into the dining room and rested on the back of a chair while he recovered, letting an expert eye rove around the tempting remains of the banquet. Aubrey Kenyon gave his graceful bow then slid out through the door to leave them alone together.

'What means this haste?' said Pugsley.

'I bring news that may advantage you.'

'Then let me hear it.'

'Walter Stanford is much discomfited.'

'That is sweet music to my ear. How?'

'His nephew has been killed,' said Ashway. 'They pulled the dead body of Lieutenant Michael Delahaye from the Thames. He was cruelly murdered.'

'How has Stanford taken it?'

'Sorely. He had high hopes of the young man and made a place for him in his business. Coming after the death of his first wife, this blow is doubly painful.'

Pugsley smirked. 'This is good news indeed. But will it make the Master of the Mercers abandon his mayoralty?'

'It will make him think twice.'

'That is some consolation. Thank you, Rowland. You shower many favours on me, I know not how to repay them all. You did well to bring me this intelligence.'

'We must pray that further disasters befall him.'

'If that young wife of his should vanish,' said the Lord Mayor. 'Now that would really cut him to the quick.'

Ashway was thoughtful. 'Most certainly.'

'Lieutenant, you say? The nephew was in the army?'

'Recently discharged.'

'And what was his name?'

'Michael Delahaye.'

* * *

'Michael Delahaye, sir. A soldier lately returned from the Netherlands.'

'Where is he now?'

'The body was released an hour ago.'

'To whom?'

'His uncle. Alderman Stanford.'

'The Lord Mayor Elect?'

'Even he.'

Nicholas was surprised. Having called at the charnel house to see if the body had yet been identified, he found the old keeper replaced by a more respectful individual and the corpse from the river replaced by one that was hauled out of a ditch. He collected all the details he could then came back up into the living world again. The livid scar on the chest of the dead man could now be explained. It was patently a wound sustained in battle but its owner had been cut down before it had been allowed to heal. The connection with Walter Stanford intrigued him. It had been a bad week for the mercer. While he was learning of the murder of his nephew, his wife was being courted by Lawrence Firethorn. If the actor were not prevented, Stanford might well find a corpse on the slab of his marriage as well.

Nicholas turned towards Gracechurch Street and strolled on as quickly as he could through the morning crush. No play was being performed that day but he was summoned to a meeting about the planned visit to the Nine Giants in Richmond. Night had been quiet at the house and he had felt it safe to leave Hans Kippel there now. The boy's compatriots took their duties as bodyguards with the utmost seriousness. They had armed themselves with swords or staves in case of attack and Preben van Loew had found an antiquated pike. Under the command of Anne Hendrik, they were a motley but effective crew. Besides, there was no performance at the Queen's Head to amuse the boy this time and he would only be in the way.

The book holder let Abel Strudwick row him across the river from Bankside so that he could thank his friend for taking care of the apprentice on the previous day. The waterman was delighted to have been of help and got what he felt was a rich reward when he was told that his name had indeed been mentioned to Lawrence Firethorn. He could not wait to take his verses to the actor-manager before embracing the stardom that beckoned. Nicholas had tried to dampen his over-zealous reaction but to no avail. Strudwick had sensed recognition at last.

As he turned into Gracechurch Street, Nicholas had put all thought of the water poet out of his mind. His preoccupation was with a murdered soldier who had been stripped of his clothes and his dignity then hurled into the Thames without even a face to call his own. Service to his country should have earned Michael Delahaye some kinder treatment than that. Was the soldier killed by his own enemies or did his relationship with the Lord Mayor Elect have any bearing on the case?

So caught up was he in his rumination that he did not observe the thickset man who was trailing him through the crowded market. The first that Nicholas knew of it was when a hand grabbed his arm from behind and the point of a knife pricked his spine.

'Do as I bid,' hissed a voice. 'Or I kill you here.'

'Who are you?'

'One that is sent to bear a message.'

'With a dagger in my back.'

'Walk towards that alley or I finish you here.'

The book holder pretended to agree. In the heaving mass of a market day, he had no choice. His assailant had caught him off guard and was now easing him towards a narrow alley. Once he entered that, Nicholas knew, he would never come out again alive. He tried to distract the man.

'You are Master Renfrew, I think.'

'Then must you think again, sir.'

'There is no patch over your eye?'

'No, sir. I see well enough to stab you in the back.'

'Do you lodge at a house on the Bridge?'

'That is of no concern to you.'

'Did you play with fire the other night?'

'Keep moving,' grunted the man.

As Nicholas was prodded by the dagger again, he reacted

with sudden urgency. His free arm struck out at the canopy of a market stall while a heel was jabbed hard into the shin of his captor. Wrenching his other arm away at the same time, he lurched forward a few paces then swung around to confront the man who was now hopping on one leg and trying to disentangle himself from the canopy while being abused by the stallholder. Nicholas had only a few seconds to study the swarthy, bearded face before the bull-like frame came hurtling angrily at him. He caught the wrist that held the dagger and grappled with his attacker. Uproar now spread as the two men cannoned off the bodies all around them. The irate stallholder joined in the fight with a broom which he used to belabour both of them.

The assailant was strong but Nicholas was a match for him. Recognizing this, the man made a last desperate effort to seize the advantage, angling the dagger towards the other's body and thrusting home with all his might. The book holder took evasive action in the nick of time. He turned the man's wrist sharply and sent the blade towards the latter's stomach. The animal howl of pain was so loud and frightening that it silenced the crowd and even made the stallholder hold off with his broom. With a surge of strength, the man flung off Nicholas and ran off through the crowd with bullocking force. The book holder looked down at the front of his jerkin.

It was spattered with blood that was not his own.

Triumph was followed by setback. After his victory in the field on the previous afternoon, Lawrence Firethorn came off badly in skirmishes the next day. It began at home with a spectacular row over the household accounts. He fought hard but his wife was at her most vehement and sent him off with his ears ringing. No comfort awaited him at the Queen's Head. His first encounter was with Edmund Hoode who refused outright to provide any more verses for the actor-manager's romantic purposes and backed up that refusal with the threat of quitting the company. While Firethorn was still recovering from that shock, Barnaby Gill chose his moment to praise the fine performance given by Owen Elias in *Love and Fortune* and to let his colleague know that he was in danger of being eclipsed by one of the hired men. There was worse to come. Alexander Marwood sidled past with a hideous smile to announce that he had now decided to sign a contract with Rowland Ashway for the sale of the inn.

When he had received Matilda Stanford in a private room, he had felt like a king. That was yesterday. Today his subjects were in armed revolt and he could not put them down. He prowled the yard at the Queen's Head while he tried to compose himself. It was the worst possible time to accost him with a handful of poems.

'Good day, Master Firethorn.'

'Who are you?' snarled the other.

'Abel Strudwick. I believe that you know of me.'

'As much as I care to, sir. Away with you!'

'But Master Bracewell mentioned my name.'

'What care I for that?'

'I am a poet, sir. I would perform on the scaffold.'

'Then get yourself hanged for ugliness,' said the irate Firethorn. 'You may twitch on the gallows and provide good entertainment for the lower sort.'

Strudwick bristled. 'What say you, sir?'

'Avoid my sight, you thing of hair!'

'I am a water poet!'

'Then piss your verses up against a wall, sir.'

'I looked for more civility than this.'

'You have come to the wrong shop.'

'So I see,' said the waterman, casting aside his former reverence for the actor. 'But I'll not be put down by you, sir, you strutting peacock with a face like a dying donkey, you whoreson, glass-gazing, beard-trimming cozener!'

'Will you bandy words with me, sir!' roared Firethorn with teeth bared. 'Take that epileptic visage away from here before it frights the souls of honest folk. I'll not talk to you, you knave, you rascal, you rag-wearing son of Satan. Stand off, sir, and take that stink with you.'

'I am as wholesome a man as you, Master Firethorn, and will not give way to a brazen-faced lecher who opens his mouth but to fart out villainy.'

'You bawd, you beggar, you slave!'

'Thief, coward, rogue!'

'Dog's-head!'

'Trendle-tail!'

'Hedge-bird!'

'You walking quagmire!'

Abel Strudwick cackled at the insult and circled his man to attack again. Having come to offer poetry, he was instead trading invective. It was exhilarating.

'Your father was a pox-riddled pimp!' he yelled.

'Your mother, Mistress Slither, conceived you in a fathom of foul mud. She was mounted by a rutting boar and dropped you in her next litter, the old sow.'

'Snotty nose!'

'Pig face!'

'Pandar!'

'Mongrel!'

Strudwick grinned. 'Your wife, sir, under pretence of keeping a decent home, cuckolds you with every gamester in the city. Diseased she is, surely, and dragged through the cesspits of whoredom by the hour. Even as we speak, some lusty bachelor is riding her pell mell to damnation!'

Firethorn writhed at the insult and replied in kind. The volume and intensity of the argument had risen so much by now that a small crowd had formed to cheer and jibe and urge the combatants on. It was a fascinating contest with advantage swinging first one way and then the other. Firethorn had clear vocal superiority and used all the tricks of his art to subdue the waterman. Strudwick had greater experience on his side and vituperation gushed out of him in an endless, inventive stream. Actor met streetfighter in a war of words. It was at the point where they were about to exchange blows that Nicholas Bracewell came running across the yard and dived between them to hold them off.

'Peace, sirs!' he exclaimed. 'Stand apart.'

'I'll run this black devil through!' said Firethorn.

'I'll tear his liver out and eat it!' said Strudwick.

'Calm down and talk this over as friends.'

'Friends!' howled the waterman.

'Mortal enemies,' said Firethorn. 'I'd not befriend this whelp if he was the last man alive in creation.'

'Let me be judge of this quarrel,' said Nicholas.

But they were too inflamed for a reasoned discussion of their complaints. They eyed each other aggressively like two dogs bred for fighting. Since the book holder was still keeping them apart, they resolved on another form of attack. Abel Strudwick waved a sheaf of poems in the air and glared at Firethorn.

'I challenge you to a flyting contest, sir!' he said.

'Let it be in public,' retorted the other.

'Upon the stage in this yard.'

'Before a full audience.'

'Name the day and the time.'

'Next Monday,' said Firethorn. 'Be here at one. When the clock strikes the half-hour, we'll begin.'

'My waterman's wit will destroy you utterly.'

'Take care you do not drown yourself in it.'

'I will bring friends to support me.'

'All London knows my reputation.'

'Stop, sirs,' said Nicholas. 'This is madness.'

But his pleas went unheard. Pride dictated terms. Lawrence Firethorn and Abel Strudwick had gone too far to pull back now. They would continue their duel on the following Monday with sharper weapons.

It would be a fight to the death.

Chapter Nine

THE SKY OVER WINDSOR WAS DARK AND SWOLLEN AS the funeral cortège walked solemnly up the path to St John's Church. Only a select gathering of family and friends had been invited to watch Lieutenant Michael Delahaye lowered into his final resting place. The priest led the way in white surplice and black cassock with his prayer book open in his hands. Six bearers carried the elm coffin with its ornate brass handles and its small brass commemorative plate. The widowed mother led the procession, leaning for support on the arm of her brother, Walter Stanford, and weeping copiously. Next came her four daughters, each one stricken by the loss, each one helped along by a husband. Black was the predominant colour and Matilda Stanford, who came next, wore a taffeta dress trimmed with black lace and a matching hat with a black veil. Leaning on the arm of her stepson, she wept genuine tears of sorrow and her sympathy for the bereaved was clear to see. Behind her came more figures in black and more lamentation. Michael Delahaye was going out of the world on a tide of grief.

The service was accompanied throughout by sobs, cries and moans as suffering mourners tried to come to terms both with the death of the dear departed and with the brutal nature of that death. Walter Stanford had deemed it wise to keep back the worst details of the horror. His sister and the rest of the family had enough misery to accommodate as it was. They had all been fearful when Michael had announced his intention of joining the army that set out for the Netherlands. His safe return was a cause for celebration and they had planned a small banquet in his honour. Instead of a long table loaded with rich food and fine wine, they were marking his homecoming with funeral bakemeats.

Matilda Stanford went through it all in a daze. The church was filled with so much high emotion that she was overwhelmed and heard very little of the service that was being intoned by the vicar. Only when the coffin was taken out into the graveyard and interred in the family vault did she come out of her reverie and she felt a stab of shame that gave her a prickly sensation. She was not thinking about Michael Delahaye, nor yet about his poor mother, nor even about her husband's grievous pain. She was not listening to any of the muttered words of comfort that were heard all round her as they began to disperse. She was not succumbing to notions of death itself and how it might visit her when the hour drew near.

At a funeral, in a graveyard, close to her husband and in the midst of a family tragedy, she found herself toying with a vision of Lawrence Firethorn. Guilt made her weep the most bitter tears yet and an arm tightened on hers.

But her mind still belonged to the actor.

After a week of upheavals, it was good to get away from the pressures of the city and out into the freedom of the countryside. A fire at his lodging, an attempt on his life and a puzzling encounter at the house on the Bridge had made Nicholas Bracewell more cautious than ever and he kept glancing over his shoulder to make sure that they were not being followed. It was Sunday morning and he had been instructed by Lawrence Firethorn to ride down to Richmond to take stock of the Nine Giants where the company was due to perform in the near future. Nicholas took Hans Kippel with him so that he could guard the boy and—because she was born there—Anne Hendrik went beside him on the road to Richmond.

The book holder was mounted on a chestnut mare with the apprentice clinging on behind him. Anne rode a dapple grey with an easy gait.

It had every appearance of a family outing and this was one of its objects. They had not simply taken on a parental responsibility for Hans Kippel. His damaged mind responded to a sense of familial reassurance and it was only when he was at his most relaxed that his memory began to function properly again. In taking him away from London itself, Nicholas hoped to separate the boy from the wellspring of his malady. The country air of Richmond might do wonders for the lad's power of recall. At all events, they made a happy picture, moving along at a rising trot and urging the horses into a gentle canter when the terrain invited it.

The book holder was relieved to put the week behind him. Quite apart from personal crises, it had been an extremely taxing period. He had stage-managed four very different plays for Westfield's Men as well as coping with sundry other duties. Placating Edmund Hoode had proved to be a time-consuming pastime and the ambitious Owen Elias was another constant drain on his patience. Regular sessions with Alexander Marwood had been another burden and Lawrence Firethorn's demands were endless. Then there was the problem of the versifying waterman.

Hans Kippel raised the problem from the bobbing rump of the horse.

'May I go to the Queen's Head tomorrow?'

'I think not,' said Nicholas.

'But I wish to see Master Strudwick on the stage.'

'It is not for your young eyes,' decided Anne. 'And certainly not for your young ears. London watermen use the vilest language in Christendom.'

'But Master Strudwick makes music.'

Nicholas smiled. 'He has another kind of harmony in mind for tomorrow, Hans. I will report everything back to you, have no fear.'

'Who will win the flyting contest?'

'Neither, if I have my way. It will not take place.'

The boy was disappointed but a half-mile taken at a canter obliged him to hold on tight and suspend his questioning. It was not long before Richmond Palace came into sight to focus all their attention. Overlooking the Thames with regal condescension, it was a magnificent building in the Gothic style, constructed round a paved court and rising up with turreted splendour. Even on such a dull day, its gilded weather-vanes added a romantic sparkle and its superfluity of windows lent it an almost crystalline charm. Hans Kippel was awe-struck. Glimpsed over the shoulder of his friend, Richmond Palace had a fairytale quality that enchanted him.

The village itself had grown steadily throughout the century as more and more people moved out of the plague-ridden city to its healthier suburbs. Many of the local inhabitants gained their livelihood from the Palace itself and it dominated their existence in every way. Nicholas escorted Anne to a cottage on the far side of the village and stayed long enough to witness the tearful reunion with her parents. Hans Kippel was lifted off the sweating chestnut to share in the hospitality. Nicholas rode back across the wide expanse of village green to get to the inn he had come to visit.

One glance told him that the Nine Giants would be ideal for their purposes. It was larger and altogether more generous in its proportions than the Queen's Head. Erected around a paved courtyard, it had three galleries with thatched roofs. Its timber-framing gave it the magpie colouring of most London houses but it was vastly cleaner and more well-preserved than its equivalents in the city. Not for the first time, Nicholas reflected on how much filth and pollution a large population could generate. Richmond was truly picturesque. The smile had not been wiped off its face by the crude elbows of the urban multitude. A presenting feature of the inn was the cluster of oak trees which gave it its name. Rising high and wide out of the paddock at the rear, they formed a rough circle of timber that had an almost mystic quality. The nine giants were soon joined by a tenth.

'Good day to you, Master.'

'And to you, good sir.'

'Welcome to our hostelry.'

'It is a fine establishment you have here.'

'I'll be with you anon.'

Nicholas had come into the yard to see a huge barrel being carried aloft by a giant of a man in a leather apron. He was loading up a brewer's dray with empty casks from the cellar and the work was making him grunt. The book holder dismounted and tethered his horse to a post. At that moment, the man dropped his barrel on to the dray with a terrifying thud then wiped his hands on his apron. Nicholas saw his face properly for the first time and laughed with sheer astonishment.

'Leonard!'

'Is that you, Master Bracewell?'

'Come here, dear fellow!'

They embraced warmly then stood back to appraise each other. Nicholas could not believe what he saw.

His friend had come back from the grave.

The thickset man lay on the bed with heavy bandaging around his midriff. His self-inflicted wound had been serious but not fatal and he was recovering with the aid of regular flagons of bottle ale. James Renfrew looked down at him with mild disgust.

'Drink wine and cultivate some manners,' he said.

'I'll look to my own pleasures, Jamie.'

'How do you feel today, sir?'

'Better.'

'Can you stand?'

'Stand and walk and carry a weapon.'

'There'll be time enough for that.'

'He is *mine*,' hissed the other.

'Master Bracewell?'

'Look what he did to me. I want him.'

'The boy is our main concern. He is a witness.'

'I'll pluck his Dutch eyes out!' He glanced up at the black patch and blurted out a clumsy apology. 'I am . . . sorry, Jamie. I did . . . not mean to . . .'

'Enough of that!' said Renfrew sharply. 'Hold your peace and get some rest.'

161

'Has the time been set?'

'It is all in hand.'

'When is it?'

'You will be told, Firk.'

'Give me but a day or two and . . .'

'The plan is conceived, have no fear. We will not move without your help. It will be needed.'

'And Master Bracewell?'

'That will come, too. That will come, too.'

Renfrew crossed to the window of the bedchamber and surveyed the river below. It was a forest of rigging that rose and fell on the undulating surface. He watched a boat being rowed expertly across the Thames and followed it until it vanished from sight behind a larger vessel.

Renfrew threw a nonchalant question over his shoulder.

'Firk . . .'

'What?'

'Have you ever killed a waterman?'

Nicholas Bracewell was delighted to see the mountain of flesh again. Leonard had a natural gentleness to offset his immense bulk and his big, round, freckled face shone with hope. He was still in his twenties with receding hair that exposed a wide forehead and a full beard that was split with a snaggle-toothed grin. They had met in the most trying circumstances. Both had been incarcerated in the Counter in Wood Street, one of the city's worst and most repulsive prisons. Nicholas had been falsely accused of assault by enemies who had wanted him out of the way for a time but his connection with Lord Westfield had soon purchased his release. Even that brief period of custody had been enough to convince him that he must never be locked away in one of the city's hell-holes again.

Leonard's case had been far more serious. He faced a murder charge that would lead to certain execution. It was a sad tale of being at the mercy of his own muscles. The genial giant had the most easy temperament and no aggressive instincts. When his workmates took him to Hoxton Fair, however, they decided it was time to goad him into some kind of action. Leonard was cajoled into taking on the invincible wrestler, the Great Mario, a towering Italian with too much guile in combat for any of the challengers who came forward in his booth. Most were dispatched without any difficulty but the newcomer was a tougher proposition.

'I did not think to win the bout,' said Leonard as he recounted the story again. 'I only fought to please my fellows. But the Great Mario did not wrestle fair. He tripped and punched and kicked and bit me. I got angry. Ale had been drunk and the weather was hot. My fellows were shouting me on at the top of their voices.'

'I remember. You grappled with the Great Mario.'

'And broke his neck. It snapped in two.'

'He provoked you to it, Leonard.'

'No matter, sir. They arrested me for murder.'

'How then came you to escape?'

'By the grace of God.'

'Was a general release signed?'

London prisons were notoriously overcrowded and many died inside them from the cramped conditions. Every so often the number of inmates would swell so dramatically that the prisons were bursting at the seams. A general release was sometimes issued to thin out the population in the cells to make room for more malefactors. Leonard would not have been the first alleged murderer to have been granted his freedom in this way but his delivery occurred by a slightly different means.

'The Lord Mayor of London took up my case.'

'In person?'

'Yes, Master Bracewell. I was much honoured.'

'Were you brought to trial?'

'Sir Lucas Pugsley saved me from that.'

'But how, Leonard?'

'I know not but his power is without limit.' He gave a defensive smile. 'One minute, I was lying in the straw at the Counter and saying my prayers. Next minute, the sergeant is taking off my chains and letting me go free. If that is what a Lord Mayor can do, then I bow down to him in all humility.'

'Have you ever met Sir Lucas Pugsley?'

163

'Indeed, no.'

'Then why did he take an interest in you?'

'Out of the kindness of his heart.'

'There must be more to it than that.'

'My master says it was just good fortune.'

'Your master?'

'He it was who brought the release to the Counter.'

'But how was it obtained?'

'As I told you. From the Lord Mayor's hand.'

Nicholas was puzzled by the intercession from above.

'Who is your master, Leonard?'

'Alderman Ashway. I work for his brewery.'

Rowland Ashway arrived importantly at the Queen's Head early on Monday morning. He brought his lawyer with him who, in turn, brought the contract for the sale of the premises. Alexander Marwood had his own lawyer waiting and the four of them went through the document with painstaking care for a couple of hours. A few doubts were raised, a few objections stated, a few emendations made. When the quibbling was over, both lawyers claimed their fees then withdrew to the other side of the room to leave the others alone. Alderman Ashway loomed over the funereal publican with oily complacence.

'All is therefore settled, Master Marwood.'

'I would like my wife to see the contract.'

'When you have signed it, sir.'

'She may have anxieties.'

'Still them in the marriage bed.'

A retrospective wheeze. 'Times have changed.'

'Nothing now detains us,' said the alderman. 'Our attorneys have pronounced on the document and I have the money waiting for you to collect. Do but scrawl your name and the business is complete.'

'Must it be done today, sir?'

'I grow weary of your prevarication.'

'It shall be signed, it shall be signed,' gabbled the other. 'But I must have a moment to reflect. The Queen's Head was willed to me by my father. I must pray for his guidance and be reconciled with his soul.'

'Will you then reach out for your pen?'

'Most assuredly.'

Marwood bowed obsequiously and rubbed his hands together as if he were grating rotten cheese between them. He had bought another small delay but Rowland Ashway was determined that it would be the last.

'We will return later,' he announced.

'You are always welcome here.'

'To witness the signature.'

'Well, yes, but . . .'

'This is the day of decision, Master Marwood, and I will brook no more evasion. Append your name and your good will to that same document or I will tear it up and leave you to the mercy of Westfield's Men.'

He sailed out of the room with his lawyer in tow. Alexander Marwood trotted meekly after him and smoothed his acceptance of the ultimatum. When he came out into the yard, however, something stopped the landlord and he became prey to fleeting regret.

The actors were gathering for rehearsal.

Abel Strudwick was a creature of extremes. Once he was committed to a course of action, he went the whole way with no hint of holding back. He had been shocked and wounded by Lawrence Firethorn's cavalier treatment of him at the Queen's Head and felt the pangs of the discarded. As one dream crumbled, however, another came into being. In cutting the actor-manager down in a verbal duel, he would not only be gaining his revenge, he would be showing the world his true merit as a performer. When he had made the final thrust into Firethorn's black heart—he was confident of a swift victory—he intended to bestow the ultimate favour upon the audience by reading some of his poems. This was no mere flyting contest. It was the harbour from which his new career could be launched.

To this end, the visionary waterman had handbills printed to advertise his feat and distributed them freely to his passengers, around the taverns and among his fellows at the wharfside. Abel Strudwick was pitting his skills against a famous Thespian. It was an intriguing prospect and it drew scores of people who would not normally have visited a theatrical event. The large audience which had come to watch *The Queen of Carthage* was thus further enlarged by an influx of rowdy watermen who jockeyed for position near the apron stage. As a prelude to an inspiring tragedy, they were being offered a clash of naked steel.

Somebody was doing his best to spoil their fun.

'It is not too late to change your mind, Abel.'

'That would be cowardly!'

'I talk of a dignified withdrawal.'

'Talk of what you wish, Master Bracewell,' said the angry waterman. 'I have vowed to do battle this day.'

'Both of you will incur severe injury.'

'It matters not, sir.'

'But what if you should lose?' suggested Nicholas. 'This would do harm to your reputation.'

'Defeat is impossible. Rest your tongue.'

They were in the taproom at the Queen's Head not long before the contest was scheduled to take place. The book holder had made several attempts to talk his friend out of the whole thing but the latter was adamant. He had been slighted and sought recompense in the only way that would satisfy him. By way of preparation, he was sinking pints of Ashway's Beer to clear his mind for argument.

Nicholas left him alone and slipped off to the tiring-house to make a last appeal to the other half of the dispute. Like the waterman, Lawrence Firethorn had steadfastly refused to listen to reason so far and he would not be diverted from his purpose now. Before he gave his acclaimed performance as Aeneas in the play, he meant to visit destruction upon the hirsute head of Abel Strudwick. The book holder got short shrift.

'Speak not to me of retreat, Nick.'

'Think of the good name of the company, sir.'

'It is to defend that name that I measure swords with this unbarbered ruffian.'

'You should not descend to a vulgar brawl with him.'

'There will be no brawl,' said Firethorn grandly. 'I will disarm the rogue with my first speech and he will stand there helpless while I cut him to shreds.'

'A little diplomacy might save a lot of pain.'

'Begone, sir! I'll not be flouted out of my purpose.'

Nicholas Bracewell had foreseen the impasse and had evolved a contingency plan. It was time to activate it.

Meanwhile, in another part of the inn, another plan of his was being implemented. Margery Firethorn was paying a call on Sybil Marwood. They were in a private room that overlooked the courtyard and their interview was thus punctuated by the throbbing murmur of the crowd. Margery eschewed her usual over-assertive conversational style and opted for a softer and more confiding approach. She had been well-primed by the book holder with information that he had gleaned from his chat at the Nine Giants with his old friend from the Counter. The mighty Leonard had unwittingly provided valuable insights into the working methods of Rowland Ashway.

'I came to express my sympathy, Mistress Marwood.'

'On what account, pray?'

'Why, this betrayal that your husband is about.'

'Betrayal?'

'He intends to sell the inn to Alderman Ashway.'

'For a good price, Mistress Firethorn.'

'What do men know of price?' said Margery with cold scorn. 'When they have money in their hand, they cannot conceive its value. Only a woman can set a true price.'

'That is so,' conceded the other.

'Your husband sells the Queen's Head and gets a fair return for the inn, that is agreed. But, Mistress, how much does he get for the home he is also losing? For the good will he has built up here? For the years of sweat and toil that both of you have put into the establishment?' Margery heaved a sympathetic sigh. 'This is a place with historic value. It breathes tradition. Did your spouse exact payment for that?'

'I have not seen the terms of the contract.'

'No?' said the other, driving a wedge between husband and wife. 'That is not considerate. My own dear husband would never dare to sign away our property without my amen to the notion. Master Marwood abuses you. He writes his name on a document and your whole lives are at risk.'

'Risk?' The alarm bell was ringing.

'Surely, your husband has informed you.'

'*What* risk, madam? Speak it plain.'

'Eviction.'

'From our own home!'

'It will belong to Alderman Ashway.'

'The contract will protect us.'

'How do you know when you have not seen it?' Margery got up and headed for the door. 'Thank you for listening to me. I will not take up any more of your time.'

'Wait!' said Sybil Marwood. 'I desire more clarity.'

'It would only distress you further.'

'I wish to know, madam. Advise me in this matter and I will be deeply in your debt.'

Margery turned with queenly charm and smiled at her.

'I talk to you but as a woman.'

'Let me hear you.'

'And I do not take sides in this quarrel. But . . .'

'Well?' said the other impatiently. 'But, but, *but* . . .'

'The Queen's Head is not the only inn that the gluttonous alderman has gobbled up. The Antelope and the White Hart in Cheapside have both been swallowed and the Brazen Serpent is to be his next meal.'

'That is his pleasure. He is a wealthy man.'

'Whence comes this wealth, Mistress Marwood?'

'How do you mean?'

'Alderman Ashway seeks a good profit,' said Margery sweetly, 'but that cannot be obtained if he give too good a price for the property. Or if he pays too good a wage to his tenant publican. Do you follow me here?'

'I begin to, madam.'

'The landlord of the Antelope was driven out within six months of yielding up ownership. His successor works for longer hours and a lower wage.'

'Can this be so?' gasped the other.

'Look to the suburbs. The alderman bought both the Bull and Butcher in Shoreditch and the Carpenters Arms in Islington. Speak to the unhappy landlords. They are now mere slaves where before they were masters. Would you and your husband wear this humiliation?'

A rousing cheer from the yard below took Margery over to the window but she had done her work. Stung with rage and flustered with fear, Sybil Marwood raced out of the room in search of her husband. She felt that she had been kept wilfully in the dark by the menfolk and it was time to voice her complaint. As she stormed into the taproom, her husband greeted her with open arms.

'Come, Sybil! Our future joy is assured.'

'What say you, sir?'

'I have signed the contract with Alderman Ashway.'

'Tear it up at once!' she yelled.

'Too late, madam.'

'Why?'

'It has been sent back to him by messenger.'

The commotion which drew Margery Firethorn to the window was caused by the appearance onstage of Abel Strudwick. With the aid of his fellow-watermen, he scrambled up on to the scaffold and paraded around like a wrestler showing off his muscles. Good-natured jeers went up and there was a ripple of applause. It was only when Strudwick stopped to acknowledge his reception that he realized how much beer he had consumed. His head was muzzy and he had to splay his legs to prevent himself from swaying. There was another, more immediate problem. Viewed from the yard below, the work of the actors had looked as easy as it was stimulating. Now that he was actually up there himself as the cynosure, he became aware of what a test of nerve it was. A sea of heaving bodies lay below. Galleries of grinning faces stretched above. Shouts and cheers and wild advice came from hundreds of throats. His iron confidence began to melt in the fiery heat of all the attention.

It was not helped by the sonorous bell that chimed the

half-hour and made him jump with fright. Before he could recover, there was a fanfare of trumpets and then Lawrence Firethorn made a triumphal entry. Flanked by six resplendent soldiers, he wore golden armour, a golden helmet and golden greaves upon his shins. A glittering sword was held aloft in one hand while the other bore a golden shield. The contrast was startling. On one side of the stage was a dishevelled, bow-legged waterman with a round-shouldered stoop: on the other was a virile warrior who stood straight and proud. As the fanfare ended, the actor delivered his rebuke with imperious force.

> Avaunt! Begone, thou ragged pestilence!
> 'Tis Jupiter, thy god, who spurns thee hence.
> Heaven's king am I and lord of all the earth,
> I do not deal with curs of lowly birth.
> Miscreant wretch, avoid this sacred place,
> Do not offend it with thy loathsome face.
> I walk on high with pure, etheral tread,
> You row across the stinking Thames instead.
> By Saturn's soul and Neptune's majesty,
> Base trash art thou. I take my leave of thee.

With the words still echoing around the yard, the godlike presence turned on his sandalled heel and made his exit with dignified briskness. Lawrence Firethorn had been so impressive that he had robbed Strudwick of all power to reply. It was only when a burst of applause broke out for Jupiter that the boatman came out of his daze and tried to strike back. When he lurched after the actor, however, he found his way barred by the six soldiers in shining armour, each holding a pike whose blade had been dutifully polished that morning by George Dart. In the heat of the moment, Strudwick resorted to intemperate abuse.

'Come back, you hound! You snivelling, sneaking rat! Come here, you caitiff. Show your monkey's face again and I will knock off your knavish helmet and put a cuckold's horns upon your head. 'Twas I that rode your foul fiend of a wife and had such clamorous sport between her spindly legs.

Thy dame is pizzle-mad, sir, and her oily duckies are sucked by every gallant in the town!'

'WHAT!!!!!'

The scream of fury was so loud and penetrating that it silenced Strudwick and the whole audience at once. Margery Firethorn climbed out through the window like a tiger hurtling out of its lair in search of prey. She pushed her way through the seated spectators in the lower gallery and cocked a leg over the balustrade before jumping down on to the stage itself. Words came hissing out of her like poisonous steam.

'Who are you to speak, you pimp, you goose, you carrion crow! I am that same wife you talk so rudely of and I am as sound a Christian as any woman alive. Fie on your foul tongue, you varlet, on your sewer of a mouth, on that running sore of a mind that you scratch for argument to make it bleed villainy. Out, out, you clod, you tottering wretch, you drunken bawd, you scheming devil, you thrice-ugly beggar, you vile and noisome vapour. Draw off lest you infect us all with this leprous speech of yours!' She stood over him with such fearsome rage that he cowered before her. 'A foul fiend, am I, sir? I will haunt your haunches with my housewife's toe for that. I have spindly legs, you say. They hold me better than those poor, mean sticks of yours that cannot hold up the weight of a beer-filled belly without they bend like longbows at full draw. Pizzle-mad, you claim . . .'

Abel Strudwick's defeat was comprehensive and the audience howled and jeered at his expense. He yet had one card to play. Shrugging off Margery's attack, he ran to the front of the stage and tried to redeem himself by reciting his latest poem about a humble waterman who becomes a famous actor and who plays before the Queen. It was a disastrous remedy. The spectators were provoked to such cruel mirth and ribaldry that missiles soon began to be hurled at the stocky figure. Strudwick kept on, dodging the apple cores and rotten eggs as best he could, caught between death and damnation, between the still fulminating Margery behind him and the foaming torrent of abuse in front of him. *The Queen of Carthage* rescued him.

Seeing his friend in such a quandary, Nicholas gave the

signal to start the play early. The trumpet sounded and the Prologue stepped out in a black cloak. Margery and Strudwick went mute and backed away. When the first scene swirled on to the stage, the two of them nimbly dodged the Carthaginian soldiers to escape. Strudwick dived gratefully forward into the arms of his fellows who felt that he had been somewhat maltreated. Margery beat her retreat through the curtain and hurried into the tiring-house. She made straight for the gold-clad figure of Jupiter and kissed him on the cheek.

'Well-spoken, Lawrence! You mammocked him!'

'Thank you, Mistress,' said a Welsh voice.

She jumped back. 'You are not my husband!'

'No,' said Owen Elias. 'That honour is denied me.'

'But you were the very image of his Jupiter.'

'That was the intention,' said Nicholas, waving another four soldiers on to the stage. 'I sought to uphold Master Firethorn's reputation while keeping him from any real harm.'

She was bemused. 'He had Lawrence's own voice.'

'But not his luck in love,' said Elias with a touch of gallantry, placing a bearded kiss on her hand. 'Edmund Hoode wrote the words. I but learned them in the manner of our master.' Celestial music sounded. 'Excuse me, dear lady, Jupiter is needed elsewhere.'

With Ganymede beside him, he made his entry.

Margery began to see how the whole thing had been carefully arranged by the book holder. But for her spirited intervention, the flyting match would never have taken place. As it was, she had conquered a worthy foe in place of her husband. She pulled at Nicholas's sleeve.

'Where is Lawrence?' she whispered.

'He will be here even now.'

'How did you keep him away from that ruffian?'

'See there, Mistress.'

Lawrence Firethorn was brought into the tiring-house by four strong men who clung on to him for their lives. Costumed as Aeneas, he was palpitating with anger and spitting

172

out curses. On a nod from Nicholas, the actor was released by his terrified captors.

'Heads will roll for this!' warned Firethorn.

'Stand by, sir,' said Nicholas.

'I'll wreak havoc on the whole lot of you.' He saw his wife. 'Margery! You have no place here, woman.'

'I have acted my scene and bowed out.'

'What do you mean?'

'Your cue, sir,' said the book holder.

'Am I locked in a madhouse?' growled the actor.

'Enter Aeneas.'

Music played and personal suffering was put aside. Lawrence Firethorn went out into the cauldron of the action as the cunning Aeneas and dallied with the affections of Dido, Queen of Carthage, as portrayed with winsome charm by Richard Honeydew. Here was the actor as his admirers really wanted to see him, not trading verbal blows with a contentious waterman, but operating at the very height of his powers and thrilling minds and hearts with uncanny skill. Back in the tiringhouse, Margery raised an inquisitive eyebrow. Nicholas smiled.

'All will be explained in time,' he said quietly.

Sir Lucas Pugsley sat before a daunting pile of judicial documents and sifted slowly through them. Aubrey Kenyon was on hand to give any help and advice that was needed. The Lord Mayor had to preside at all meetings of the city's administrative courts. As chief magistrate, he had to act as judge, dealing with an enormous range of cases. Everything from petty law-breaking to complex commercial disputes came before him. It was also his avowed task to supervise the conduct of trade in the city and see that it was carried out in accordance with civic regulations. This function of his office often brought him up against the names of his friends.

He studied a new document and gave a wry smirk.

'Rowland Ashway is arraigned again.'

'For what, Lord Mayor?'

'Adulterating his beer. The charge will not stick.'

'His brewery has a good reputation.'

'There will always be those who seek to bring a conscientious man down,' said Pugsley. 'How can one trust the word of a landlord, I ask you? These fellows pour water into their beer then swear it was done at the brewery so that they may claim some recompense. The law here is nothing but a whip with which a guileful publican can beat an honest tradesman.'

'Will the case come to court?'

'Not while I sit in judgement, Aubrey.'

'That is the third time Alderman Ashway is indebted to your wisdom,' said the Chamberlain. 'He has aroused much resentment among jealous landlords.'

'They'll get no help from me.' He put the document aside, picked up another then cast that after the first. 'Enough legality for one day, sir. I sometimes think that London runs on the quibbles of attorneys.' He sat back in his chair. 'We have worked hard, Aubrey. I flatter myself that I do the labour of any three men.'

'At least.'

'Walter Stanford will not be able to keep my pace.'

'He may not wish to try, Lord Mayor.'

'Signs of hesitation?'

'This death in the family has preyed upon his mind. It has slowed down his steps towards the mayoralty.'

'That is the best news yet. What of this play?'

The Nine Giants?'

'Is the monstrous piece still promised?'

'By Gilbert Pike. He has written such plays before.'

'This will tax his imagination most,' said Pugsley sourly. 'Where will they find nine giants among the mercers? Where eight? Five? One?'

'Richard Whittington must be allowed, sir.'

'Even so. But do not mention his name to Rowland.'

'That story still smarts with Alderman Ashway.'

'And so it should,' noted the Lord Mayor. 'When the much-vaunted Whittington sat in my place, he made himself very unpopular with the brewers when he tried to enforce standard sizes for barrels.'

'He also attempted to regulate the price of beer.'

'The brewers got no mercy from a mercer!'

Aubrey Kenyon creased his face at the feeble joke and took the opportunity to work in a reminder of a subject that he took very seriously.

'The noble gentleman did sterling work during his terms of office. He kept the city busy and he kept its citizens well-subdued.' He crossed over to Pugsley. 'You have not forgot the public holiday?'

'This Thursday. Preparations are under way.'

'A strict hand is a sign of a sound mayoralty.'

'Then that is what you will get from me, sir. Let others talk of Dick Whittington. If you want discipline and good government, look no further than Sir Lucas Pugsley. On Thursday I will keep a very careful watch.'

It took an hour to pacify Lawrence Firethorn and only the presence of his wife held him back from reviling his whole company. In his opinion, he was the victim of a dreadful conspiracy that could never be forgotten or forgiven. A stoup of wine, a barrel of flattery and the gentle persuasiveness of Nicholas Bracewell finally made him see the true value of the stratagem. Abel Strudwick had been bested, Firethorn's reputation had been enhanced and the performance of *The Queen of Carthage* scaled peaks it had never before assayed. There could be no better advertisement for the work of Westfield's Men.

Warming to it all, Firethorn summoned George Dart to escort his wife back to Shoreditch then he touched on two important issues with the book holder.

'Has that death's-head of a landlord signed yet?'

'I have not spoken with Master Marwood yet.'

'Give him my compliments and bring him to heel.'

'Alderman Ashway has much influence.'

'See that you counteract it, Nick.' He became secretive. 'First, I have another errand for you. Deliver this letter to Stanford Place.'

'Is this sensible, Master?'

'Do as you are bid, sir. The letter is expected and you will present it at the garden gate upon the stroke of five. Someone shall be there to receive it.'

Nicholas was not happy to leave the Queen's Head when such a vital talk with the landlord was imminent but he could not refuse the commission. He hastened out into Grace-church Street and headed north towards Bishopsgate. Fine drizzle was now falling out of a pock-marked sky. When he reached Stanford Place, he went around to the garden and lurked beside the gate until the chimes of the clock were heard. Prudence Ling was a punctual gatekeeper and snatched the letter from him with a giggle before hiding it under the folds of her cloak. She also gave the visitor an admiring glance. Nicholas did not waste his advantage.

'There is sorrow in the house, we hear.'

'The master's nephew, sir. Most horribly killed.'

'Has the murderer been found?'

'Not yet.'

'Tell me the way of it, Mistress.'

Prudence needed no second invitation. She gabbled her way through the details and answered every question that he asked. Ten minutes at a garden gate turned out to be a rev-elation. Nicholas hated being a party to the projected betrayal of a loyal wife but there had been some consolation. Pru-dence was a mine of information. There was more value yet in his visit. As he made his way back to the front of the house, a coach was just drawing up and Walter Stanford him-self was getting out. He was weighted down with sadness and the spring had gone out of his step but it was not the Lord Mayor Elect who commanded attention. Nicholas was far more interested in the steward who opened the door to welcome his master and who bowed ingratiatingly before him. The book holder felt a thrill of recognition as connec-tions were made.

He had met Simon Pendleton on the Bridge.

Chapter Ten

DOMESTIC TRAGEDY INFLICTED DEEP WOUNDS ON Walter Stanford and he dragged himself around for days after the funeral. He brought his sister back to Stanford Place so that he could look after her properly and they spent much time together on their knees in the little chapel. His work was not entirely neglected and he burned large quantities of midnight oil in his countinghouse. He also resumed his regular visits to the Royal Exchange. His smiling face hid the pain of an anguished soul, his pleasantries concealed a profound sorrow. Though he had disapproved of much that Michael Delahaye did, he had loved him like a second son and felt that he would at last be able to exert a firm paternal influence on his wayward nephew. That fond hope now lay buried in the family vault at Windsor. *Requiescat in pace*.

The first floor of the Exchange—the pawn, as it was known—had been rented out to shopkeepers whose booths sold such luxury items as horn, porcelain, ivory, silver and watches. It was from one of these shops that Gilbert Pike looked down to espy his friend below and he hurried down to the courtyard as fast as his venerable legs would carry him. He waded out through the waves of bartering humanity until he reached Walter Stanford. Greetings were followed by the old man's condolences but the Lord Mayor Elect did not wish to dwell on sadness. He turned to a more uplifting subject.

'Now, sir, how does my play fare?'

'It is all but finished, Walter,' said the other with enthusiasm. 'I still have the trick of words and I vow that *The Nine Giants* will please you and your good lady mightily.'

'Does it beat the drum for the Mercers' Company?'

'Until every ear be deafened.'

'And humour, Gilbert? I asked for lightness.'

'It will set the table on a roar.'

'That will be welcome at this bleak time,' said the other. 'But tell me now, who are our nine giants?'

'Dick Whittington is first.'

'No man could question that.'

'Then come Geoffrey Boleyn and Hugh Clopton.'

'Both mercers and mayors of high repute.'

'Fine fellows,' agreed Pike. 'Except that Clopton does not lend itself to rhyme. John Allen is the next in line with Ralph Dodmer and Richard Gresham close behind.'

'All six of these are giants indeed.'

'Lionel Duckett, too, and with him Rowland Hill.'

'That brings the number up to eight.'

'My ninth giant is Walter Stanford.'

'I pale in such company, Gilbert.'

'You may yet stand taller than all the rest, sir.'

They fell into a discussion of the pageant and its simple structure. The doddering author could not resist quoting from his work. One of the nine giants brought special pleasure to Walter Stanford.

'I like the notion of Ralph Dodmer.'

'Lord Mayor of London in 1529,' said the old man. 'He was a brewer who rebelled against the dominance of the Great Twelve. He refused to translate to one of the dozen leading Guilds even though it was the only way to ensure his mayoralty. No mere brewer could get election.'

'Dodmer suffered for his principles.'

'Indeed, sir. A spell in prison and a heavy fine changed his mind for him. Our brewer saw common sense.'

'And became affiliated to the mercers.'

'Then did he take revenge on all his fellows,' said the chortling Pike. 'He kept the aleconners alert enough. Tavern keepers caught watering the beer or serving short measure were fined and jailed, and had their cheating measures burned in public. Brewers who tampered with their beer were hauled before the court. An alewife found using pitchers with naughty bottoms was sent to play Bo Peep through a pillory.'

'He swinged the whole profession.'

'*The Nine Giants* will tell it true.'

'Then harp on the brewers, Gilbert,' said his friend. 'That is where we may score against a certain alderman. Let Ralph Dodmer scourge his fellows soundly. I would make another brewer squirm in his seat.'

'Rowland Ashway, I think?'

'Turn those red cheeks to a deeper hue.'

'His blushes will light up the Guildhall!'

With his florid cheeks shining almost as brightly as his scarlet nose, Alderman Rowland Ashway stood in the window of a room that overlooked the inn yard. The White Hart in Cheapside had been chosen because of its size and its situation. Preparations were being made against the morrow. Extra benches and trestle-tables had been procured. Additional serving-men had been hired. Fresh barrels of Ashways Best Beer were even now being rolled across the pavestones. The brewer was pleased by what he saw. When there was a knock on the door, he swung round and welcomed the tall figure who entered with a grunt of almost porcine satisfaction.

'Is everything in order, sir?' said the newcomer.

'I have seen to it myself.'

'Then we have no cause for vexation.'

'Unless our plans go awry.'

'They will not,' said the other confidently. 'Errors cannot be tolerated. All will be done as discussed.'

'Good. Here's gold to help your purposes.'

Ashway tossed a bag of coins on to the table and his companion nodded his thanks before picking it up. The man was well-favoured and dressed with a lazy elegance that came in sharp contrast to the sartorial pomposity of the brewer. A feathered hat was angled on his head so that its brim came down over one eye that was shielded by a black patch. His chin was clean-shaven. They were not natural friends but mutual advantage had turned them into partners. Rowland Ashway spelled out the terms of that friendship.

'We are in this together, sir, remember that.'

'I do not doubt it.'

'Fail me and you fail yourself even worse.'

'Success attends my mission.'

'And Firk?'

'He is recovered enough to aid me.'

'I hope to hear good news from both of you.'

'And so you shall,' said James Renfrew with a grim smile. 'So you shall, sir.'

Public holidays did not please the city authorities. They were at best occasions for drunken excess and at worst an excuse for violence and destruction of property. Nobody charged with maintaining the peace could rest easy and the more suggestible of their number had nightmares about total loss of control. The main problems came from the apprentices, exuberant young men who chafed under the yoke of their masters and who seized every opportunity to assert their manhoods with unruly behaviour and passages of mob hysteria. Holidays gave law-abiding citizens a chance to rest from their labours and to celebrate a sacred or secular festival. Those same holidays also spilled a deal of blood, clogged up the prisons and led to a rash of unwanted pregnancies.

Shrovetide was carnival time, a final fling before the rigours of Lent. Mothering Sunday came next, a public holiday when those away from home—the rowdy apprentices in the workshops of London—could visit families with gifts and eat the simnel cakes baked for the occasion. Easter solemnity was offset by Hockside fairs and a variety of entertainments. May Day was the major source of concern. This most important spring festival had no Christian foundation at all for the ancient custom of going a-maying was unashamedly pagan. Londoners revelled in its spacious jollity and its sexual freedom. There was often rioting through the bawdy houses or affrays at playhouses or gratuitous attacks on shops and houses. Those who had to enforce order never lost sight of the spectre of Evil May Day in 1517 when a riot saw hundreds of frenzied youths on the rampage, terrorizing the city and showing open defiance to authority. Thirteen of the mob were later arrested and hanged in a savage gesture that imprinted the day for ever on the minds of London.

Whitsun and Midsummer Eve produced their potential dangers but none could rival May Day. October was a quieter month but even the occasional saint's day could be fraught with difficulty. Caution was advisable.

'Stay indoors with your mistress, Hans.'

'I would rather visit the play with you, sir.'

'The city is too turbulent a place today.'

'You will keep me safe, Master Bracewell.'

'Remain here at home.'

The apprentice was plainly disappointed. Though he had yet to recover his memory, his youthful instincts had returned intact. He wanted to be off in search of sport with his fellows or, at the very least, to be part of the audience which would come in high humour to the Queen's Head to watch a performance of *The Constant Lover* given by Westfield's Men. Anne Hendrik ruffled the boy's hair affectionately.

'Stay here and keep me company, Hans.'

A resigned nod. 'As you wish, Mistress.'

'Preben van Loew and I will dream up games for you.'

'Where is the holiday in that?'

Nicholas Bracewell took his leave of his young friend and was seen off at the front door by Anne. The outside of the house was still bruised and blackened from the fire and the very sight of it was warning enough. He gave her a kiss then set off through the streets. Wanting to visit the house on the Bridge again, he yet felt a strong obligation to cross the river by boat. It had given him no pleasure to see Abel Strudwick so totally outwitted at the flyting contest but he felt that it was a necessary hurt to ward off heavier blows for all of them. When he found the waterman at the wharf, he made an apology that was never completed. Strudwick interrupted with chuckling resilience.

'Nay, sir, do not bother about me. My back is broad though I would rather bend it in the service of these oars than let that harridan beat it with her scoldings. She gave good insults and they were justly deserved.'

'You take your punishment nobly, sir.'

'I spoke out of turn, Master Bracewell,' admitted the other. 'I'll face any man in the kingdom with my curses but I'll not offend a lady if I have a choice.'

'Mistress Firethorn is an honest woman.'

'She proved that on my pate.'

Abel Strudwick rowed between two other boats that all but collided with him. Ripe language hit both of them like a tidal wave. Replies were foul and fierce but he got the better of them with the virulence of his tongue. It put him into excellent humour again.

'Have you fresh music?' asked Nicholas.

'My Muse has left me awhile, good sir.'

'She will return again.'

'Then I will keep her here on the water with me,' said the other. 'My verses do not belong on the stage in front of baying clods and sneering gallants.' He looked all around. '*This* is my playhouse, sir. The gulls can hear my music and applaud with their wings. I am author and actor when I am out in midstream. No bawling woman can drag me down in my occupation, however well she swim. I am a true waterman, sir.'

Nicholas was delighted that his friend had bowed so humbly to the reality of the situation and he gave him an extra tip when he disembarked. Other passengers clambered into the boat at once. Holidays turned the Thames into a thousand moving bridges. Abel Strudwick would be kept busy until nightfall. He still found time for a farewell.

''Good fortune attend the play, sir!'

'Thank you, Abel.'

'It is a comedy that you stage, I think.'

'Tragedy is out of place on such a merry day.'

'Pray God some rabble do not spoil your offering.'
'No fear of that, I hope.'

Celebrations began early at the White Hart in Cheapside. Wine, beer and ale were plentiful and there was food enough to satisfy the most gluttonous appetites. As the day wore on, the tap room became so full with boisterous apprentices that they spilled out into the yard and passed the time in japes and jeers and being sick in the privies. Serving wenches were groped, ostlers were mocked and scapegoats had their breeches torn off. Small fights broke out to liven up the occasion and old scores were settled between youths from rival trades. Afternoon found the drunken rowdiness slowly changing into a brawling fever for which the area was famous.

Cheapside was the broadest and straightest of London's streets, a major artery that carried the life-blood of the city. Along the centre of the street, from St Paul's to the Carfax, was an open market for all manner of goods. Every important public procession passed through Cheapside and shoddily produced goods were traditionally burned there. It was another kind of procession that now staggered along, a ragged band of apprentices who had been gathered up from other inns and taverns along the street by the industrious Firk who had spread the word that beer was being sold at reduced prices in the White Hart and that a wild time was in store for all who came. As Firk led the way into the yard, the newcomers were given a hostile reception by those already packed in and there was much preliminary pushing and shoving. Abundant supplies of beer and ale were brought out to quench the thirst of all and incite them on to more destructive pleasures. Firk watched until a stew was bubbling furiously and he gave a signal to the man who was watching it all from a room in the upper gallery with his one good eye.

James Renfrew calmly finished his glass of wine and crossed to give the naked woman who lolled on the bed a last kiss. Then he pulled on his doublet and went off downstairs to take charge of the fire that his accomplice was so busily stoking up. With sword in hand, he ran into the yard and jumped up on to a table top so that he could stamp on it with his feet to gain attention. Even the swirling revelry was stilled for a second. Renfrew was a striking figure with a voice that knew how to command.

'Friends!' he yelled. 'There's villainy abroad!'

'Where, sir?' shouted Firk on cue.

'Close by this inn. I saw it with my own eyes. Five brawny Dutch apprentices set on one poor English lad and gave him such a drubbing that I fear for his life.'

'Shame!' roared Firk.

'Where are they?' howled a dozen voices.

'They are everywhere!' replied Renfrew, pointing his sword in different directions as he spoke. 'Aliens are taking over London. We have Genoese, we have Venetians, we have cheese-eating Swiss. You may find Germans in every street and Frenchmen in every bawdy house. There are Dutchmen in Billingsgate and Polish in Rotherhithe. We are beset by strangers!'

'Drive the aliens out!' bellowed Firk.

'Vengeance on the strangers!'

'Break their foreign heads!'

'Smash their houses!'

'Kill them! Kill them!'

'London belongs to Londoners!' urged Renfrew.

'Yes! Yes! Yes!'

'We defeated the Spanish Armada,' he said, 'yet those same swarthy gentlemen now swagger through our city and defile our womenfolk! Foreigners out, I say!'

'Foreigners out! Foreigners out!'

Renfrew whipped them up until their blood-lust was so strong it simply wanted direction in order to expend itself. He and Firk led the charge out of the yard. With a hundred or more berserk apprentices at their back, they ran along Eastcheap and into Lombard Street, knocking aside anyone who got in their way, smashing windows out of sheer malice and screaming obscenities. Constables came out to confront them but the ferocity of the mob swept the thin line of authority aside as if it had not been there, surging on into Gracechurch Street then swinging right towards the Bridge with gathering fury. In the space of a few minutes, aimless youths with too much beer in their bellies had been turned into a vicious machine of destruction. It rolled remorselessly on.

Hans Kippel was close to the wharf when he heard the rising tumult. Frustrated at being kept indoors on a public holiday, he had begged permission to go out into the little garden at the rear of the house and had wandered off down to the river when nobody was looking. The boy hoped to find Abel Strudwick so that he could listen to some more verses but the waterman was nowhere in sight. What he saw instead was a torrent of baying apprentices, leaving a trail of debris on the Bridge as they poured into the object of their hate. Southwark was a haven for immigrants from many lands. Swinging boards from shops advertised craftsmen from all over Europe.

Enraged beyond all control, the mob tore down the boards and kicked in doors and shattered windows. Any opposition was ruthlessly stamped on and innocent by-standers were knocked flying on every side. Hans Kippel was hypnotized by the horror of it all. As the angry crowd ran towards him, he stood there trembling for his young life. Out of the mass of faces that bore down on him, he picked out two that he had seen before and quailed even more. One of the men wore a patch over the eye and the other a stubby beard. A memory which had been trapped inside his brain for a long time was suddenly released and it made him cry out in agony.

He found the strength to run but his flight was in vain. They were too fast and too crazed and too numerous. Before he was gone twenty yards, he was knocked over in the stampede and trampled by a score of feet. Using the cover of the mob, Firk slipped a knife into the boy's back then staggered on after James Renfrew. They had done what they had planned without even having to storm Anne Hendrik's house to get at their prey. The apprentices were still carried along by their own senselessness as the two agitators who had started the riot now vanished quietly around a corner.

Hans Kippel lay motionless. His holiday was over.

* * *

185

In a house of sorrow there was still an avenue of escape. All that Matilda Stanford had to do was to read again the letter which Lawrence Firethorn had sent her. In flowery language and a beautiful hand, he had written to give her details of the performance at the Nine Giants in Richmond the following week. It never occurred to her that he had not actually penned the missive himself but had instead dictated it to Matthew Lipton, the scrivener who was used by Westfield's Men to copy out the sides from the one complete version of any play they staged. Lipton's fine calligraphy was also in evidence in the poem that accompanied the letter. Here again, Firethorn had relied on another to supply his inspiration. Unable to coax any new verses out of Edmund Hoode, the actor-manager had used a poem he had once commissioned from the resident poet while in pursuit of Lady Rosamund Varley at an earlier phase of his lustfulness.

Matilda Stanford knew nothing of this and swooned at his ardour as if it had been new-minted that second. As she sat in her bedchamber with the letter and poem on her knees, she thought only of her lover's irresistible charm and felt the touch of his lips on her hand. Married to a mature and preoccupied husband, she had never known true passion before and could only guess at its implications. Innocence protected her from understanding Firethorn's true intent. All that she knew was that she had been offered an assignation by a prince among men. Though it would be immensely difficult to contrive, she had to find a way to get to Richmond.

Prudence Ling knocked on the door and came tripping in on her toes. Obliged to be sombre elsewhere in the house, she could show her girlish spirits when alone with her mistress. She saw what Matilda was reading and gave a conspiratorial giggle.

'I think I know the way of it,' she said.

'Of what, Prudence?'

'Bringing you to your lover.'

'In Richmond?'

'Even there.'

'Teach me how and I'll adore thee for ever.'

'Then here is the manner of it . . .'

The Constant Lover had displayed the constancy of his love, a volatile audience had been held throughout and the stage was now being dismantled. Nicholas Bracewell was in the thick of the action when Preben van Loew arrived panting in the yard of the Queen's Head. With tears streaming, the Dutchman told his story and begged his friend to come at once. Hans Kippel was close to death and calling for Nicholas. The book holder did not pause for a second. Leaving Thomas Skillen in charge, he borrowed a horse from the stables and rode home as fast as the thick crowds would allow. All the way across the Bridge, he saw evidence of the furious passage of the apprentices. The noise up ahead was muted now as the riot spent its energy in a raid on some of the Bankside stews. Soldiers had been called out to back up the constables and the sight of organized authority was enough to disperse the remnants of the mob.

Nicholas reined in his horse outside the house and dismounted to race upstairs to the bedchamber. Hans Kippel was lying on the truckle bed with his head cradled lovingly by a distraught Anne Hendrik. The doctor in the background shook his head sadly. He had done what he could but the boy was beyond medical help. Nicholas came to kneel beside the bed and took the hand of his young friend. Weak and fading, Hans Kippel rallied briefly at the sight of the book holder and there was a brave flicker of a smile. Words dribbled out of his mouth with painful slowness.

'I . . . saw them . . . again.'

'Who?' whispered Nicholas.

'The . . . two . . . men.'

'From that house on the Bridge?'

'Yes . . .'

'Did one have an eye-patch?'

A faint nod. 'My . . . cap . . .'

'What about your cap, Hans?'

'They . . . took . . . it.'

'The two men?'

'No . . . some . . . boys . . .'

'And what did they do with it?'

'Threw . . . river. . . .'

The apprentice was near to expiry. Nicholas tried to fill in some of the gaps to squeeze the last precious bits of information out of him.

'Some boys took your cap. They ran off. You chased them. They threw your cap over the Bridge. Was it by that house? In that narrow passage?' Flickering eyelids confirmed his guess. 'Did your cap land on the starling below?'

'I . . . climbed . . .'

'You climbed down to retrieve it. Then you came up again past the window at the rear of the house. You saw something, Hans. What was it?' Nicholas squeezed his hand to encourage him. 'Try to tell us. Try.'

'They . . . killed . . .'

'The two men murdered someone? With a dagger?'

'Throat . . .'

Hans Kippel let out a deep sigh. The effort of dragging the words out of himself and of confronting the memory that lay behind them had drained the last of his resistance. He slipped gently away and his head flopped to one side. Anne Hendrik sobbed and Nicholas comforted her with his own eyes moist. Then he laid the boy's head gently on the pillow and covered it with a sheet. The doctor stole quietly away to let them share their grief. Racked with remorse, they looked down at the prone figure in the little bed and hugged each other tight. The loss of a child of their own could not have been more painful or poignant because that was what Hans Kippel had become in the last sad days of his doomed life. He had turned lovers into a family and taught them a new kind of love.

The Dutch boy had witnessed an horrific murder and been chased by the killers. He had scrambled to safety for a while but had taken refuge in the dark recesses of his young and impressionable mind. They had caught up with him eventually and the nightmare was relived. The irony of it all was not lost on Nicholas. Mocking youths had snatched off the apprentice's cap and hurled it over the edge of the Bridge. In retrieving it, he had seen something which was to have fatal consequences. If Hans Kippel had not bothered about his cap, he would still be alive and happy. But the pride of a craftsman worked against him. The fledgling hatmaker could not leave his cap to the rising waters of the Thames. It simply had to be rescued somehow.

He had made it himself.

Threat of ejection from the Queen's Head had bonded the company together and lent their performance that holiday afternoon a freshness and defiance that transformed a good play into an enthralling experience. *The Constant Lover* was a form of a reply to a landlord who was neither constant nor loving and who had now sold the home of Westfield's Men from under them. Word had leaked out that the contract with Rowland Ashway had actually been signed and it was only a question of time before the alderman expelled them from his premises. Adversity may have drawn them together onstage. When they came off, it only served to heighten their differences. Edmund Hoode and Lawrence Firethorn chose the empty tiring-house as the venue for their argument. Deep insecurity gave them both an edge of wildness.

'I oppose it with every bone in my body, sir!'

'Take your skeleton away from me.'

'Have you no scruples at all?'

'Come, sir. None of that. You lusted after the lady yourself. You longed to lie in her enchanted garden.'

'I am not married,' said Hoode. 'You are.'

'So is Mistress Stanford. Where are *your* scruples?'

'I intend the lady no harm.'

'It matters not,' said Firethorn airily. 'I am the fitter man for her in every way. Both of us are wed and that gives our love some balance. We take equal risks in this business. One fire consumes us both.'

'It will burn up the whole company!'

'Conquer your jealousy, Edmund, and take your defeat like a man. Think not of yourself in this.'

'Nor do I,' said Hoode forcefully. 'It is the sweet lady herself who occupies my mind. I would save her from the disgrace that beckons.'

'Disgrace!' bawled the other.

'She must only suffer in this enterprise.'

'I offer her my true love.'

'Give her your breeches instead, sir, for that is where it is lodged.'

'Take care, Edmund. I have a temper.'

'Save it for the stage, sir.'

'My devotion to Mistress Stanford comes from a pure heart. I have sent her poems of love.'

'Written by *me*!'

'I have kissed her fair hand.'

'Rape upon rape!'

'She has been shown the utmost respect, sir.'

'Then prove it now by releasing her entirely,' said Hoode with vehemence. 'You have a loyal wife to warm your bed and if her loyalty will not suffice, there are others who clamour for your favours. Take one of them, sir, take two or take them all. But spare this gentle creature.'

'So that *you* may take my place?'

'No! I renounce her here and now.'

'Then stand aside for I do not.'

'Lawrence, this is plain idiocy!'

'Love makes a fool of all of us.'

'She is married to the Lord Mayor Elect,' said the other. 'Nick counselled well. Too much peril follows. The beery alderman may only put us out of the Queen's Head. Walter Stanford may put us out of our profession.'

'*He* is the cause I cannot now pull back.'

'Our new Lord Mayor?'

'Do you know how he intends to enter his mayoralty?' said Firethorn with rolling contempt. 'With a play. His wife requested a drama such as Westfield's Men present and he has replied with some rambling pageant.'

'I do not follow.'

'*We* are the finest company in London. We—and only we—should be summoned to make this occasion memorable. Westfield's Men have performed before the Queen and all her Court. Yet this mercer, this man of no taste, this money-grubbing merchant of a Lord Mayor spurns our talents and turns to amateurs! It is an insult.'

'It is also his prerogative.'

'I do not give a fig for that!' barked Firethorn. 'If he will betray our eminence, then I will gladly betray his. His wife has told me of this pageant that he has arranged. Do you know its subject? Nine worthies of his Guild. What drama lies in that? Was ever such a stale subject foisted upon an audience? And *that* is what has put us in the shade here.'

'You take it as a personal affront.'

'I do, sir. Matilda alone can recompense me.'

'Yet you spoke just now of love.'

'Love of her and love of my profession.'

'You would take revenge on Walter Stanford?'

'Indeed, I will,' said Firethorn heartily. 'Let him have *his* nine giants. In Richmond, I will have *mine*.'

The Bull and Butcher was a small tavern in Shoreditch that offered them an excellent meal in a private room. Rowland Ashway sat on one side of the table and ate with noisy gusto. Seated opposite him, James Renfrew was more interested in the Canary wine than the food. The table was loaded. They started with a dish of boiled carp then had been served with a boiled pudding. Chines of veal and of mutton came next with a calf's-head pie to follow. A leg of beef roasted whole then made its appearance. Capons were then set before them. A dish of tarts helped to sweeten the taste of all the meat and the rich sauces.

Ashway raised a cup to announce a toast.

'To our success, my friend!'

'It is not achieved as yet.'

'We have not far to go,' said the other. 'The boy has been killed and with him goes the fear of discovery. Now we may turn back to the main business of our little partnership. Walter Stanford must be stopped.'

'I thought to have done that already.'

'We have maimed him but not yet cut him down.'

'Do we proceed against him now?'

'With all haste, sir. He cannot and must not be Lord Mayor or all our hopes will founder.' Ashway reached for another tart. 'Luke Pugsley has served my purposes so well that I

191

would keep him there in perpetuity, but the law will not allow it. That is why I chose a successor of like temperament and soft intelligence.'

'Who was that?'

'Henry Drewry, the salter.'

'But you could not secure his election.'

'Stanford won the contest by a single vote. The case was altered cruelly. Instead of a pliant salter, I have to contend with a shrewd mercer and that's not good.'

'What of yourself?' said Renfrew. 'Does your own ambition rise as high as the office?'

Ashway grunted. 'As high and much higher. But the Brewers come fourteenth in the order of precedence. That puts me two places away from the Great Twelve and it is from them that the mayor is chosen.'

'You could translate to another Guild.'

'That is in hand, sir. Why do you think I have been at such pains to woo this fool of a fishmonger? Luke Pugsley has sworn to take me into his Guild and promote me to the mayoralty.' He scowled darkly. 'All that will vanish if this mercer takes the chain.'

'I hate the man,' said Renfrew flatly.

'Enough?'

'More than enough.'

The younger man picked up a capon and tore at it with his teeth. There was a violence in him which had not been appeased by the murder of a Dutch apprentice. He was ready to add more deaths to the list in pursuit of his ends. As he emptied another cup of wine, he looked across at the gross figure on whom his future depended.

'What of Master Bracewell?'

'His turn will surely come.'

'Let it be soon. Firk is promised.'

'We may bide our time a little.'

'But this book holder pursues us hotly.'

'He will find nothing,' said Ashway smugly. 'What he may know, he cannot prove. The boy was the witness and his voice has been silenced. Do not concern yourself about this Nicholas Bracewell. He is no threat to us now.'

There was much to do in the aftermath of Hans Kippel's death. The body had to be cleaned and laid out. A report on the circumstances of his death had to be given to the relevant authorities. In the wake of the riot, the city magistrates would be busy the next day but a murder was a more serious matter than assault or damage to property. Nicholas Bracewell was realistic. The chances of the killers being tracked down by official means was very slim indeed since the crime had been committed behind a shield. An outbreak of holiday anarchy had been provoked by guileful men. Nicholas recognized stage-management.

It took him a long time to calm Anne Hendrik down and to convince her that it was not her fault. Even if she had kept the boy locked up at home, he would still have been taken. Men who could set fire to a house could just as easily smash down its front door. He left her with Preben van Loew and set out on what was to be a long journey around the taverns of London. The riot was his starting-place and it was not difficult to trace it back to the White Hart. Frightened witnesses from Eastcheap all the way down to Southwark had marked its seering trajectory. The inn was still very busy and the drink was still flowing freely. Nicholas was not surprised to learn how the apprentices were first aroused and he knew at once who had supplied the strong beer.

But he was not in search of unruly youths who had been turned into a marauding pack. His quarry was a man who might be anywhere in the teeming city on that raucous night. With strong legs and a full purse, Nicholas was determined to find him. The first soldiers were in the Antelope, carousing with whores and far too inebriated to give him anything more than the names of their taverns which they frequented. The book holder trailed around them all and bought his information bit by bit with drinks for already drunken men. It was like trying to piece together a jigsaw out of wisps of smoke. Discharged soldiers did not wish to talk about their soldiery. On a public holiday such as this, they simply wanted to submit themselves wholly to the pleasures of the city. Nicholas was therefore sent on what seemed like one long and circuitous tour of every inn, ale-house, stew, ordinary and gambling den within the city walls.

One man half-remembered Michael Delahaye, another had gone whoring with him, a third knew him better but was too sodden to recall any useful details. It was painstaking but each new fact took Nicholas one step closer to the person who could really help him. He got the name at the Royal Oak, the address of his lodgings from the Smithfield Arms then found the man himself after midnight in the taproom of the Falcon Inn. Though he was fatigued by a whole day of celebration, the reveller responded warmly to the offer of a pint of sack and a plate of anchovies and made room for Nicholas on his settle.

Geoffrey Mallard was a small, stooping and rather dishevelled individual with a habit of scratching at his ginger beard. He had been an army surgeon with the English expeditionary force to the Netherlands and his memory was not entirely addled by over-indulgence.

'Michael Delahaye? I knew him well.'

'Tell me all you can, sir.'

'Do you ask as a friend?'

'I pulled his dead body from the Thames.'

When Nicholas told his tale, the surgeon was sobered enough by the news to supply all manner of new details. Lieutenant Michael Delahaye had not taken to soldiering at all. The glamour which had attracted him proved to be illusory and the muddy reality of service abroad was a trial to his free spirit. He writhed under the discipline and cursed the privations. There was worse friction.

'He made an enemy of his captain,' said Mallard.

'Why?'

'They loathed each other on sight, sir. Two worthy fellows in their own right who could never lie straight in the same bed together. They were warned and they were threatened but their enmity continued to the point where a gentleman must defend his honour.'

'A duel?'

'A bloody event it was,' said Mallard. 'Had they come to any surgeon but me, they would have been reported and hauled up for court martial. They were there to fight against our foes not against each other.'

'You say it was bloody . . .'

'Both of them were injured.'

'Was there a wound that ran across the chest?' He indicated the direction of the gash. 'Like this, sir?'

'There was indeed. I dressed that wound myself.'

'Then was the body that of Michael Delahaye.'

'How say you?'

'He was dropped into the Thames from the Bridge.'

'It could not have been Michael, sir.'

'No?'

'His wound was on his face,' said Mallard. 'The point of a rapier took the fellow's eye out. He is condemned to wear a patch for the rest of his life.'

'Who, then, was his opponent in the duel?'

'The captain whose chest was sliced open.'

'What was his name?'

'James Renfrew.'

Chapter Eleven

BEL STRUDWICK SAT AGAINST A WALL IN BISHOPS-
gate Street and mused on the vagaries of human
existence. When he had tried to be a performer upon
the stage, he had been cowed by the haughty Jupiter, flayed
by the furious Margery Firethorn and stung by the derision
of the audience. It had made him abandon all ambition in
that direction. Yet here he was, in the person of a beggar,
sitting on the ground at the behest of Nicholas Bracewell and
actually getting paid for it. The waterman grinned as he reflected on his promotion. What he was doing was acting of
a kind and it was professional in nature. It certainly saved
him from spending the day on the river with aching sinews.
There were handicaps. He was rained on for an hour, spat
upon now and again and—if the dog had not been smacked
firmly away—there would have been another soaking for his
tattered jerkin. Against all this he could see an unlooked for
bonus. Because he sat with one leg tucked under him in a
tortured posture, the occasional coin was tossed his way to
confirm the success of his portrayal.

His job was to keep an eye on Stanford Place so that he
could watch the comings and goings. A few visitors called
but all had left by the time that Walter Stanford himself came
out to make his way to the Royal Exchange. Strudwick caught

a glimpse of Matilda Stanford in an upstairs room but that was all. Various tradesmen called to make deliveries but none stayed more than a few minutes. It was late afternoon before the waterman felt that he was able to earn his money. Out of the house came the man whom Nicholas had described to him so exactly. There was a furtive air about Simon Pendleton and his normal measured gait became an undignified scurry as he weaved his way through the back streets towards the Guildhall.

Strudwick dogged him every inch of the way and hid behind a post when the steward stopped and looked around to make sure that he was not seen. Pendleton then opened a door and stepped smartly into a house. It had nothing like the grandeur of the mansion he had left, but it was a sizeable dwelling that conveyed a degree of prosperity. The waterman made a mental note of the address and then shambled past the front of the house so that he could sneak a glance in through the latticed window. The picture he saw was very expressive.

Simon Pendleton was talking in an agitated manner to a tall, stately individual in dark attire. The steward was pointing back in the direction from which he came as if reporting some disturbing news. His companion reacted with some alarm and reached into a desk to take out a roll of parchment. His quill soon scratched out a letter. Strudwick moved away from the window but remained close to the house. When a man wearing the livery of the Lord Mayor's Household came to the front door, the beggar trotted over to accost him.

'Away, you wretch!' said the man.

'It is not money I want, sir, just a kind word.'

'The kind word will come with a hard blow if you stay. Stand off, sir. Your stink will infect me.'

'I seek but instruction.'

'Then I instruct you to leave.'

'Does Abel Strudwick live in this house?'

'Who?'

'Strudwick, sir. A noble family of some repute.'

'This is the home of the Chamberlain, sir.'

'What name would that be?'

'Master Aubrey Kenyon.'

The man brushed him aside and went into the house. The waterman danced on his toes and clapped his hands together with glee. He was certain that he had just found out a significant piece of information and he had done so by the skill of his performance as an actor. It deserved some recognition. Abel Strudwick turned to an invisible audience and gave a deep bow.

In the busy street, only he could hear the applause.

They met him at the brewhouse and he took them down to the cellar where the barrels of Ashway Beer were kept to await delivery. The familiar aroma made Firk feel very thirsty but James Renfrew had more refined tastes. They found a quiet corner where they could not be overheard. Rowland Ashway had new orders to issue.

'Gentlemen, you travel to Richmond tomorrow.'

'Why there?' said Firk.

'Because I tell you,' said the alderman. 'A play is being staged at an inn called the Nine Giants.'

'By Westfield's Men?' guessed Renfrew.

'The very same.'

Firk was pleased. 'Then I'll go gladly, sir. I have an account to settle with a certain book holder.'

'That is not the main reason I send you, man. Someone else will be in Richmond tomorrow night.'

'Who, sir?'

'Mistress Stanford.'

'The new young bride?' said Renfrew with interest.

'Without her husband.'

'This is good fortune indeed, sir. But what brings the lady to the Nine Giants?'

'My informer does not provide that intelligence. When you listen at doors, you do not hear all but what he has gleaned is enough in itself.' He chortled aloud. 'I know more about what happens at Stanford Place than Stanford himself. It pays to have friends in the right position.'

'What must we do?' asked Renfrew.

'Seize on this accident that heaven provides.'

'Kill the lady?' said Firk hopefully.

'Kidnap her. That will cause panic enough. With his wife under lock and key, not even Walter Stanford will have the stomach to become Lord Mayor. We strike a blow where it will damage him the most.'

'Where will she be taken?' said Renfrew.

'That I will decide.'

Firk leered. 'And may she be tampered with?'

'No!' snapped Ashway. 'Mend your manners, sir.' He pulled a letter from his belt. 'And while you are in Richmond, you may do me another favour, sirs. Do you see this letter?' He waved it angrily. 'Shall I tell you who sent it? Shall I tell you who favours me with his royal command? None but Lord Westfield himself.'

'The patron of the players,' said Renfrew.

'He takes up their case as if he is judge and jury. The noble lord has heard of my purchase of the Queen's Head and orders me—orders, mark you, no hint of request here, sirs—he orders me to let Westfield's Men remain. And he does so in such round terms that I am treated less like an owner and more like the meanest lackey.' He tore the letter up and threw the pieces away. 'This is an insult that must be answered forthwith.'

'How?' said Firk.

'I'll put his company out of sorts for good!'

'Chase them out from the Queen's Head?'

'No, sir. Kill their king. Lawrence Firethorn.'

The prospect of an additional murder brought a low cackle from Firk. He had his own grudge against the company and this would help to assuage it. Before they could discuss the matter further, they were interrupted by heavy footsteps as a vast drayman came down the steps to collect a barrel. Ashway glanced across and relaxed.

'Ignore him, sirs. Too stupid to listen and too senseless to remember anything he hears.' He put an arm on each of their shoulders. 'All roads lead to Richmond. In one bold strike, we may finish off Stanford and get revenge on Westfield's Men.'

'Do not forget Master Bracewell,' said Firk.

Ashway smiled. 'Deal with him as you will. Firethorn first then this troublesome book holder.'

'The second will please me most.'

'How will you do it, Firk?'

'Strangling, sir. A very quiet death.'

He gave a macabre laugh and Ashway joined in but their companion remained silent and withdrawn. James Renfrew was staring angrily ahead of him as if viewing an object of extreme hatred with his single eye. His lip curled.

'There is an easier way yet, I think,' he said.

'What is that?' asked the brewer.

'Murder the man himself.'

'Walter Stanford?'

'Cut him down without mercy!'

'No,' said Ashway. 'We can disable his mayoralty by another means. It is far too dangerous to attack him directly. That must only be done as a last resort.'

'By *me*,' insisted Renfrew.

'Why?'

'It is my right and I claim it now. The worthy mercer is all mine and nobody else must touch him. I have waited a long time to settle my score with him.'

'Do you detest your uncle so much?'

'Beyond all imagining,' said the other. 'He ruined my life. I was young, I was free, I was happy. I spread joy among the ladies of the city and they could not get enough of me. Good Uncle Walter called me to order. He told me that my days in the sun were over. Henceforward, I had to work for him in some dingy room and learn responsibility.'

'Is that why you went in the army?'

Renfrew nodded. 'It was my only escape. My only way of prolonging my freedom—or so I fondly thought. The army was a living hell! Thanks to Walter Stanford, I went through two years of complete misery and ended up looking like this.' He lifted the eye patch to show an ugly, red, raw socket. 'Do you see, sirs? I went into the army as a handsome man with his whole life in front of him. I came out disfigured!' He put the patch back in position. 'My uncle killed the real Michael Delahaye. He deserves to die himself.'

'This wound is deep indeed,' said Ashway.

'He talks of nothing else,' added Firk.

'I share his loathing of Walter Stanford.'

'Nobody could despise him as I do,' said the vengeful nephew. 'I denounce all that he is and all that he stands for and will do anything to maim his chances as Lord Mayor. He has condemned me to a half-life under a stolen name. Two short years ago, ladies flocked to me and showered me with their favours. Now I have to buy their bodies and fornicate in darkness where they cannot see my face. That is what I owe to this monster of goodness, Walter Stanford!'

Rowland Ashway and Firk were mesmerized by the intensity of his anger. None of them saw the drayman lift a barrel on to his shoulder and struggle off upstairs with it. He moved ponderously and took care not to drop his cargo. It was a long and troublesome climb.

Leonard was carrying onerous news.

Walter Stanford made no objection at all when his wife asked permission to visit her cousin near Wimbledon. Acting on her maidservant's advice, Matilda claimed to have been invited to call on her sick relative at the earliest opportunity. Her husband did not even ask the nature of the putative illness because he was too overwhelmed with work and with worry. He simply put his coach at her disposal and told her that he would see her on her return. Grief had aged him visibly and put more distance between him and his wife. Matilda took sad note of it.

'I feel that I no longer know him,' she confided.

'That is often the way in marriage.'

'We seem to be growing apart.'

'Fill your life another way.'

'My husband's work always comes first.'

'That is hardly a compliment to you.'

They were being driven along a bumpy road on a dull afternoon by a coachman who was there only to obey orders. Matilda travelled with Prudence Ling and both were thrilled to get away from the confinements of London life. The verdant acres all around them gave promise of a freedom that neither had enjoyed for some time. On the command of his mistress, the coachman drove on to Richmond and stopped at the Nine Giants. While the ladies went inside to dine, he shared a drink with the ostlers and listened amiably to their country gossip. Matilda and her maidservant, meanwhile, had been shown upstairs to the room that had already been reserved by Lawrence Firethorn. Candles were lit and the table was set but the room was dominated by a large four-poster. Prudence giggled.

'It is big enough for you and him and me besides.'

'For shame, girl!'

'You cannot think this room an accident.'

'Master Firethorn is a gentleman.'

'Then he will say a proper thank you afterwards.'

'Prudence!'

'Why else have we come all this way, Mistress?'

'To dine with my love.'

'Meat before supper. You are that supper.'

'I will not hear this vulgarity!'

But Matilda Stanford had heard it in a way that had not impinged upon her consciousness before. Infatuation had made her deceive a kind husband and drive miles to her as-signation. What had sustained her all this while was the thought of being alone with the man she loved and admired so that she could feel once again those wonderful sensations that he elicited from her. To dine alone with Lawrence Fire-thorn was an end in itself to her and she was distressed by the idea that it might only be a means for him. It was a long wait in the upstairs room and the bed seemed to get larger all the time.

Westfield's Men journeyed to Richmond at a slower pace than the coach. Lawrence Firethorn, Barnaby Gill, Edmund Hoode and the other sharers rode their own horses but most of the company travelled on the waggon that was carrying their costumes, properties and scenic devices. George Dart and some of the other menials trotted at the cart's tail and dodged any messages left up ahead by the two carthorses. The imminent departure from the Queen's Head had lowered them all and Nicholas Bracewell tried to lighten the mood of dejection by ordering the musicians to play. Country air and lively ditties soon dispelled the city gloom.

Nicholas drove the cart with Owen Elias beside him.

'You have strange friends, sir,' said the Welshman.

'I would not call you *that* strange, Owen.'

'Not me, man. That mountain who accosted you as we left Gracechurch Street. Diu! I thought that you would harness him and let him pull the waggon alone.'

'And so he might. That was Leonard.'

'What did he want?'

'To show his friendship in the kindest way.'

'One giant sends us off to find the other nine.'

'He did more than that,' said Nicholas, recalling the warning that Leonard had given about the plot against his life. 'We met in peculiar lodgings, he and I. Imprisonment binds two such men together.'

'Do not speak of imprisonment!' moaned Elias. 'I am chained hand and foot in this company.'

'Master Firethorn would release you.'

' 'Tis he who keeps me in bondage. He takes all the leading roles and I serve my sentence as a galley-slave.'

'*The Wise Woman of Dunstable* offers you a hope.'

'In some small way,' said Elias. 'I have a part in which I may briefly shine but it is not enough, Nick. I would be in the centre of the stage. Look at my Jupiter, sir. I was taken for Master Firethorn himself.'

'No man is great by imitation.'

'I have skills that are all my own but they wither on the vine. Give me the role I covet above all others and I will prove my worth!'

'What role is that, Owen?'

'A Welsh one, sir.'

'Henry the Fifth?'

'Aye, man—Harry of Monmouth!'

Lawrence Firethorn had to mix desire with diplomacy in a way that irked him. The company reached the Nine Giants a mere half an hour after the two ladies and his first impulse was to bound up to his room to claim the favours of his mistress. But Edmund Hoode's sensibilities had to be borne in mind. If he were to learn of Matilda's presence at the inn— let alone of her tryst with Firethorn—he would be uncontrollable. It was important, therefore, to settle him and the rest of the company down before its leading man could slip away to enjoy the spoils of war.

What he did do—while the others were being shown to their accommodation—was to make contact with his beloved to reassure her that all was well.

Matilda Stanford jumped up with a mixture of joy and alarm when he let himself into the room. He showered her hand with kisses and told her that he would return within the hour to dine alone with her, making it very clear that Prudence was expected to withdraw tactfully to the next chamber. He was at once inspiring and frightening, a noble knight with high ideals of chivalry and a lecher in search of a lay. Matilda was thrown into confusion. He swung open the door and paused for effect.

'When I come back, my love,' he said softly. 'I will tap on the door like this.' He knocked three times. 'That is my password to paradise. Do you understand?'

'Yes, sir.'

'How many times?'

'Three.'

'At least!' he said under his breath. 'Admit no other to this chamber until I knock thrice.' He blew her a kiss and withdrew. 'Out, then, into the night.'

The door closed and Matilda clutched at her breast to stop her heart pounding. She wanted him more than ever but not in the way that he had implied. Her plan had been to dine with him alone before being driven on to spend the night near Wimbledon with her cousin, who had been advised by letter in advance of the visit. Firethorn evidently had ideas for her sleeping arrangements and the anxious Matilda did not know how to cope with them. Part of her wanted to flee, another part urged her to stay. A wild suggestion sprang from Prudence.

'To save your honour, I will change places with you.'

'How so?'

'Lend me that dress,' she said, 'and blow out some of the candles. If the room be dark enough, I'll make him think I am you, Mistress.' She giggled again. 'And when we lie abed together, he will not know the difference.'

'Prudence!'

'I do it but as an act of sacrifice.'

'Leave off these jests.'

'This way, all three get satisfaction.'

'I will not hear another word,' said Matilda firmly. 'Both of us will stay here. Your presence will shield me from any danger.'

'I beg leave to doubt that.'

Before they could debate it further, they heard footsteps outside the door and craned their necks to listen. There were three loud knocks on the door. They exchanged an astonished look. Firethorn had talked about a delay before his return. Obviously, he had dealt with his business much faster than expected. The three knocks were repeated. Matilda gave a signal and Prudence rushed to throw the door wide open.

'Welcome again, good sir!'

The man with the black eye-patch smiled slyly.

'Thank you.'

Westfield's Men were given excellent hospitality by mine host and found another treat in store. Staying at the inn with them were several who were due to be guests at the wedding on the morrow. It was as part of the nuptials that the company were to present their play. Hearing of this, the wedding guests called for some entertainment in advance and were quickly answered. Peter Digby and his musicians played for them, Richard Honeydew sang sweet madrigals, Barnaby Gill made them guffaw with his comic dances and Firethorn obliged with a speech or two off the cuff from his extensive repertoire. Westfield's Men were not only given free cakes and ale. The wedding guests each tossed in a few coins to make their gratitude more substantial. With one exception, the company was thrilled.

That exception was Owen Elias, an eager talent who was

proud of abilities that were just never given an opportunity to display themselves. It was others who won the plaudits from the guests. He lurked somnolently on the fringes and drank too much beer. When Gill was asked to perform his jig for a fourth time, Elias could take no more and slunk quietly out into the yard in search of his own audience.

Nicholas was pleased by the turn of events but he had not forgotten Leonard's warning and kept his wits about him. He was much exercised, too, by the information that Abel Strudwick had supplied. If there was a form of conspiracy afoot and the Chamberlain were part of it, then it must reach to the very highest levels of municipal administration. Alderman Rowland Ashway was deeply involved in it and his agents were totally ruthless. If a defenceless young apprentice like Hans Kippel could be murdered, then the killers would stoop to anything—even to an attack on Lawrence Firethorn. The book holder started as he recalled the warning. Leonard had told him that both he and the actor-manager were marked men. In the middle of a large gathering in the taproom, Nicholas was quite safe but there was no sign of Firethorn. Concern flared up.

A quick search of the ground floor of the premises yielded nothing. Nicholas was about to go upstairs when he heard a distant sound that stilled him somewhat. Out in the darkness was a voice so quintessentially that of Lawrence Firethorn that he relaxed at once. The great man was merely rehearsing under the stars and giving the angels themselves some nocturnal entertainment. Letting himself out in the yard, the book holder realized at once from where the speech was coming. The paddock was a ghostly silhouette in the moonlight. Nine giant oak trees stood in a circle to form a natural amphitheatre. Sublime verse was declaimed with such feeling and ferocity that it sailed upwards into the branches of the trees and came back in weird echoes.

Lawrence Firethorn was truly supreme. Only he could make a speech crackle with such intensity and only he would steal off into the night to rehearse alone and to perfect his art. Nicholas walked towards the paddock so that he might enjoy the treat to the full. It was only when he recognized the play that his panic returned. Henry the Fifth was haranguing his troops before battle in the lilting cadences of a true Celt. Once again, the imitation had been uncanny but this was not the actor-manager in conference with the giant oak trees. It was Owen Elias.

The moment Nicholas realized this, the speech was cut dead to be replaced by a loud gurgling. He ran towards the paddock as fast as he could but the foliage was so dense and widespread that it shadowed the whole area. Only the terrible noise guided him, the final, fading cries of an actor on the verge of the ultimate exit. Nicholas sprinted all round the circle until he collided with a pair of dangling legs and was knocked to the ground. High above him, swaying to and fro, was the twitching Owen Elias who grasped feverishly at the rope around his neck. For a man whose voice was his own greatest joy, it was a cruel way to die.

The Welshman was an unintended victim. Taken for Lawrence Firethorn, he was at least quitting his life in a leading role. The rope was slung over a branch then secured around the trunk of a tree. Nicholas drew his dagger and hacked through the hemp to bring his friend crashing to the ground.

There was no time to attend to him because Firk leapt out from his hiding place with a sword in his hand. He circled his prey menacingly. Nicholas had only the dagger with which to defend himself. Firk rushed in and slashed the air viciously with his blade, catching the other a glancing blow on the left arm. The stinging pain and the gouting blood made Nicholas change his tactics at once. At their last encounter, his attacker had been stabbed in the stomach and must still be suffering from that injury. The book holder put pressure on the wound. He dodged behind a tree then skipped on to another so that Firk had to waddle after him. Nicholas broke into a run and weaved in and out of the nine giants with the sword whistling at his heels all the way. The further he went, the more he tired his pursuer. Firk was panting violently and threshing the air with increasing fury. Leaves fell at each stroke and whole branches were lopped off. Fatigue eventually slowed him and he leaned against a tree to catch his breath, one hand holding the sword while the other grabbed at his wounded stomach.

Nicholas switched from defence to attack, moving in to circle his man with the dagger at the ready. Firk responded with a few murderous swipes but his strength was clearly diminished. He made a sudden lunge at his foe but Nicholas parried the sword with his dagger, stepped back a few yards, flicked the blade into his hand then threw the weapon hard at the advancing Firk. It hit him in the shoulder and spun him round. The rapier dropped to the ground and Firk staggered after it. Nicholas was on to him like a shot, grappling madly and rolling in the grass until both were muddied all over. Even in his weakened state, Firk was still strong but he was up against someone who had more than strength on his side.

New power surged through Nicholas. As well as fighting for his own life, he was avenging the deaths of his friends. He was pitted against the man who had cut down Hans Kippel with callous violence in the street. He was wrestling with the creature who had hanged a poor actor intent on improving his craft. They rolled again and Nicholas finished on top, pinning his opponent to the ground and managing to get both hands to his neck. His first squeeze drew a roar of protest from Firk but that did not halt him. The book holder ignored the punches that rained on his chest and the grasping fingers that tried to pluck out his eyes.

He tightened his grip as hard as he could. The spirit of Hans Kippel lent his puny strength and Owen Elias groaned his encouragement from the ground. Between the three of them, they throttled every semblance of breath out of Firk and left him prone on the ground in an attitude of complete submission. The weary Nicholas hauled himself up and went over to the purple-faced Welshman who was slowly recovering from his brush with death. Loosening the knot around his friend's neck, the book holder pulled the noose off and tossed it over to the corpse.

Owen Elias croaked his gratitude and raised a weak arm in salute. There would be no part for him in the play but at least he would live to act another day.

Lawrence Firethorn, meanwhile, was loping along the passage to the private room where his treasure was stored away. Having spoken to the landlord and ordered that food and wine be sent up, he could now begin the soft preliminaries of love and prepare her for the joyful consummation that was to follow. He paused outside the door to adjust his doublet, smooth his beard and lick his lips then he knocked boldly three times and sailed through the door to claim his prize.

'I have come to you, my love!' he sighed.

But Matilda Stanford was not there to receive him. Most of the candles had been extinguished and the room looked empty in the half-dark. Fierce disappointment then gave way to rekindled lust as her inviting noises came from the four-poster. He crossed to the bed to see her body writhing under the bedclothes to allure and excite. Evidently, she could not wait for the leisurely meal and the long seduction. Her ardour brooked no delay and it produced a like passion in him. Running to the door, he slammed home the bolt so that they would not be disturbed then he began to tear at the hooks on his doublet and pull down his breeches. The sounds from the bed grew more desperate every second and he amplified them with his own grunting and groaning.

Firethorn was half-naked by the time he launched himself on to the four-poster, landing beside his love and pulling back the sheets to behold the beauty of her face. His first kiss was to have ignited her passion to the utmost limit but his lips instead met with cold response. He soon saw why. Instead of holding Matilda Stanford, he had his arms around a squirming maidservant whose mouth was covered with a thick rag.

Prudence Ling had been bound and gagged.

Nicholas Bracewell was hurrying back towards the Nine Giants when the actor-manager came tumbling out in search of him to announce the kidnap. The coachman had now been alerted as well and discovered that his coach had been stolen. Others came pouring out of the inn to see what the commotion was all about. The book holder gave his grisly news then raced off to the stables to find a horse and lead the posse in pursuit of the coach. He had instantly worked out who the driver must be and wanted to take him to task about Hans Kippel as well. A dozen armed men were soon in the saddle. Nicholas split them into two groups so that they could scour the road in both directions. The horses were soon spurred into a mad gallop as the chase began.

It was only twenty minutes before they caught sight of the coach. Nicholas was at the head of the group which rode furiously along the London Road and sent up clods of earth in their wake. When he saw the coach cresting a rise up ahead so that its profile was seen momentarily against the sky, he called for even more speed and commitment from his mount. Though the vehicle was being driven hard, it could never outrun the chasing pack and they closed steadily on it. The driver put his own survival first. Heaving on the reins, he pulled the two horses to a juddering halt then leapt from the box into the saddle of the animal who had been tethered to the coach and pulled along with it. To create a diversion, he yelled at the top of his voice and slapped one of the coach horses on the rump. Both of them bolted at once and the vehicle was taken on a mad, swinging, bumping journey across the grass.

Nicholas's immediate concern was the safety of the passenger inside the coach and he set off after it. With a wave of his hand, he sent his fellows off after the lone rider who was moving at a full gallop towards the shelter of a small wood. The coach was now completely out of control and swayed dangerously from side to side. It lurched high in the air as one of its wheels struck a large stone then it veered over at a crazy angle as it was pulled across a slope. Nicholas knew that it was only a matter of time before the vehicle overturned or smashed into a tree. He used his heels to demand even more from his mount and slowly caught up with the coach, keeping well clear of the whirring wheels as they swung towards him. Above the din, he could hear the screams of the terrified occupant as she was thrown wildly around.

Pulling level with the bolting horses, he timed his moment then dived sideways on to the back of the nearest animal and held on grimly to the harness. When he had hauled himself up and sat astride the horse, he gathered up the reins and applied steady pressure until the headlong flight became a measured canter then eventually diminished to a merciful trot. When he finally pulled them to a stop, he jumped down and ran to open the coach door. Tied hand and foot, Matilda Stanford fell into his arms.

An evening of happiness and light ended in a darker vein. The body of Firk was taken away to the local undertaker and a statement about his death given to the county coroner. Matilda Stanford and Prudence Ling were driven on to Wimbledon by the coachman to pass a restorative night with the cousin. Along with the rest of the company, Lawrence Firethorn was shocked by the attempted hanging of Owen Elias. He took Nicholas Bracewell up to his room so that the full details could emerge in private.

The book holder was explicit and unfolded the tale without any trimmings. Murder, arson, riot, kidnap and municipal corruption were revealed in their true light. Firethorn heard it all with immense interest, feeling for the plight of Owen Elias and coming to see how his own wilful involvement with Matilda Stanford had indirectly led to it. If she had not been enticed to the Nine Giants to satisfy him, then the Welshman would still be able to contribute his skills to the company instead of languishing in bed with a bandaged neck. The actor-manager was ashamed and shaken but his priorities remained unchanged. When Rowland Ashway was named as the architect of all the villainy, Firethorn saw it entirely in personal terms and actually grinned.

'If the alderman be arrested,' he said jauntily, 'then will his contract with Marwood be null and void. Westfield's Men will stay at the Queen's Head. Some good may yet come of all the upset I have borne!'

Nicholas had to exhibit supreme self-control.

Next day found Lawrence Firethorn at his best. He assembled the company early on and delivered a moving speech about the importance of overcoming all the setbacks they had endured. Concern for Owen Elias was understandable but the best way to speed his recovery was to put on the finest performance they could manage. In the space of ten minutes, Firethorn transformed a jaded group of men into an alert and determined theatre company. Nicholas had returned from his earlier visit to the Nine Giants with sketches and measurements of the acting area. It did not take long to erect a stage to begin rehearsal.

They heard the bells from the wedding nearby and gave a rousing welcome to the bride and groom when they arrived at the inn to begin the celebrations. Fine weather enabled the banquet to be served in the yard itself and the whole gathering was in excellent spirits by the time the play was due. Lord Westfield himself was the guest of honour, sitting beside the bride in his flamboyant attire and telling her that he would now give his wedding present. Westfield's Men took over.

The Wise Woman of Dunstable could not have been a more appropriate choice. It was a pastoral comedy about the virtues of true love and fidelity. Three suitors vied for the hand of a rich and beautiful widow who wanted nothing more than to live quietly in happy contemplation of her departed husband. All sorts of stratagems were employed to get her to the altar, the most ludicrous by Lord Merrymouth, an egregious old fop with a game leg. Firethorn showed brilliant comic invention in this role and equipped the posturing peer with all sorts of humorous ailments. The widow herself finally agreed to make a choice and everyone thought it would be between the two young, handsome suitors. But the ghost of her former husband—Edmund Hoode at his best—came back to give her sage advice. She chose Lord Merrymouth.

This not only put the other over-amorous gentlemen to flight, it ensured her widowhood for the old aristocrat was so overwhelmed with pleasure that he drank himself to a stupor then fell into a pond and drowned. Firethorn even made the death scene unbearably comic. In the title role itself, Richard Honeydew was a wise woman of great charm and lightness of heart. The play ended with a dance then the audience pounded their tables in appreciation. Westfield's Men bowed in acknowledgement of their rapturous reception then went into their closing dance once more by way of an encore. Led by Firethorn, they directed their final bow at the window through which Owen Elias had watched their performance. Still in pain from his ordeal, he applauded with gusto and the tears ran down his cheeks. Westfield's Men had given him the most exhilarating tonic. He belonged.

Walter Stanford's face was designed for mirth and good humour but it was furrowed by anger and disillusion now. At the suggestion of Nicholas Bracewell, his wife had set up an interview between the two men in a private room at the Royal Exchange so that the household steward at Stanford Place would not be aware of the net that was now closing in on him. The Lord Mayor Elect first thanked the book holder profusely for saving the life of his young bride by stopping the runaway horses, though her reason for being at the Nine Giants in the first place was tactfully concealed from her husband. No intimacy had occurred between her and Firethorn. She would not go astray again.

Nicholas had been right in his instincts. Once the connection between Rowland Ashway and Aubrey Kenyon was made, much was explained. With a sudden increase in wealth, the brewer was able to buy up the inns and taverns to whom he supplied his beer. Stanford suspected a whole network of corruption in the conduct of municipal affairs with the Chamberlain at the centre. Only he would be in a position to mastermind such financial chicanery. With a willing but credulous man like Sir Lucas Pugsley as Lord Mayor, the two men had been able to feather their own nests without the slightest suspicion falling on them. Ashway worked on the fishmonger as a friend while Kenyon used his expertise as an administrator to pull the wool over the latter's eyes. They were a potent combination.

Their reign was threatened by the election of Walter Stanford to office. Whatever his weaknesses, the mercer had tremendous acumen and a nose for any mismanagement. Under his surveillance, the corruption would not only have to cease but its extent during the previous mayoralty would have been uncovered. Ashway and Kenyon were left with only one option. Stanford had to be stopped.

'And so they killed Michael,' he said. 'Because so much of me was invested in my nephew, they hoped that my grief would rob me of the urge to go on.' He looked at Nicholas. 'How was it done, Master Bracewell?'

'The murder was committed in that house on the Bridge,' said the other. 'I was deceived for a while when I learned that it was owned by Sir Lucas Pugsley. It was borrowed from him by Alderman Ashway for the purpose. Though the murder happened by daylight, the body was not disposed of until night. Under the cover of darkness, it was dropped out of the window but it struck the starling on its way to the water.'

'The smashed leg!' said Stanford.

'Yes, sir. It must have been caught in the eddies then buoyed up by a piece of driftwood that carried it downstream. By complete chance, we encountered it.'

'You and your waterman.'

'Abel Strudwick. A sound man with all his faults.'

'One question, sir. Why was my nephew's face so mangled and bloody? We could scarce recognize him.'

'That was the intention.'

'What say you?'

'It was not your nephew, sir.'

'*Not?* But William and I saw him.'

'You saw only what looked like him,' explained the other. 'Michael Delahaye is still alive.'

'But that does not make sense.'

When Nicholas enlarged on his claim, Walter Stanford was forced to accept that it was all too logical. The army surgeon had told the book holder everything. Michael Delahaye was not just another grumbling soldier, he was a complete dissolute who resented his uncle for cutting short his strenuous overindulgence. Joining the army in order to prolong his wasteful ways, the soldier had found it so intolerable and depressing that it had turned a merry gentleman into a malevolent one. Walter Stanford became the target for that malevolence. When Michael Delahaye was offered a chance to strike back at his uncle, he seized it because it gave him the opportunity to escape for ever from the oppression of respectability and start a new life of debauchery under a new name. It also gave him the supreme satisfaction of killing off the mortal enemy he had made in the army.

Cold silence had fallen on Stanford as he listened. To lose a loving nephew was one form of misery. To learn that he was the object of that same person's hate was far worse. The one saving grace was that the whole plot had been exposed by a man of such evident discretion.

'What must I do, Master Bracewell?'

'Nothing, sir.'

'But they will flee the approach of justice.'

'Only if you frighten them away,' said Nicholas. 'We must tempt your nephew out of hiding or this will never be settled. Be ruled by me, sir. Prepare yourself for action but take none yet. Wait but a little while and they will surely strike again. Be patient.'

Stanford thought it over and nodded his agreement. He was deeply disturbed by what he had heard and he needed time to assimilate it all. What really cut him to the quick was the news about Michael Delahaye and he did not try to shuffle off his responsibility in the matter. His intentions had been good but he had applied intense pressure to his nephew to get him to conform and to abandon his wilder ways. He had helped to turn an idle but relatively harmless young man into a monster and it preyed on him. Having been through one grim ordeal, he now faced an even more punitive one.

'What am I to tell my sister?' he asked.

'What she needs to know.'

'She believes her son was hauled out of the river.'

'Then that is what happened, sir,' said Nicholas levelly. 'There is no need for her to learn the full truth. The son whom she loved and knew died in the Netherlands. Do not bring him back to torment her.'

Once again, Stanford accepted sage advice and looked across at the other with increased respect. Nicholas clearly had to be given some freedom where the stage-management of everything was concerned. He would know how to flush the villains out of their holes.

'When will they strike?' said Stanford.

'Soon.'

'How soon?'

'At the Lord Mayor's Show.'

Chapter Twelve

RIDINGS WERE AN INTEGRAL PART OF LIFE IN THE capital. The processions were not merely a source of entertainment and wonder for the commonalty but a means of impressing upon them the dignity and power of their rulers. In medieval times, the most splendid processions were those on royal occasions, especially a coronation or a wedding. By the later years of the reign of Queen Elizabeth, however, the Lord Mayor's Show had come to rival even these, taking the whole city as its stage and encompassing traditions that went back to the very origin of old London town. The Show had now completely taken over from the Midsummer Marching Watch as the main civic annual parade and nobody dared to miss it. Ridings meant public holidays when people could enjoy a dazzling spectacle then go off to celebrate what they had seen in general merrymaking.

Extra soldiers and constables were on duty as a result of the recent riot but nobody expected that there would be any real troubles. A Lord Mayor's Show did not stir up apprentices to attack the immigrant craftsmen of Southwark. It was an attestation of civil power in a city that was nominally ruled by a sovereign, a shared belief that London was the most eminent place in Europe, a time when the whole populace was bathed in feelings of pride and identity and well-being. Walter Stanford was known to be exceptionally keen on civic tradition. The Show which carried him into office promised to be an outstanding one.

Some wanted to make it more memorable still.

'Everything turns on today,' said Rowland Ashway.

Aubrey Kenyon nodded. 'We must not lose our nerves.'

'Indeed, sir, or we are like to lose our heads.'

'Hopefully, that might be Stanford's fate.'

'It *has* to be, Aubrey, or we are undone.'

They were talking in Kenyon's house before going out to take up their places in the procession. The aldermanic robes made Ashway look fatter and more florid than ever whereas the Chamberlain's stateliness was enhanced by his regalia. They looked an ill-matched pair but they were yoked together in crime now and depended critically upon each other. There was someone else upon whom they relied.

'Can he be trusted to do his office?' said Kenyon.

'Nobody is more eager to perform it.'

'He let us down at Richmond.'

'That was the fault of Firk,' sneered Ashway. 'He hanged the wrong man and fell foul of that book holder. Did he but know it, Master Bracewell did us a favour. He killed off Firk and saved us the trouble of doing it ourselves. Delahaye is another kind of man again.'

'Renfrew,' said the other. 'He likes to be called James Renfrew. Lieutenant Delahaye is dead.'

'So will this Captain James Renfrew be in time,' said Ashway quietly. 'When he has done what we have paid him for, we must finish him off as well. He knows too much, Aubrey. It is the only way.'

'And today?'

'We must put our faith in his madness.'

'He hates Stanford even more than we do.'

Ashway smirked. 'I love him for that.'

Since 1453, when Sir John Norman was rowed up the river in a fine barge with silver oars, the Lord Mayor's Show had taken place on both land and water. Both banks of the Thames were thus lined with ranks of spectators who waited expectantly to see a floating marvel. Everyone knew the itinerary. Walter Stanford, Lord Mayor of London, would first tour his ward—that of Cornhill in which the Royal Exchange symbolically stood—then proceed to the nearest stairs where he would embark and be rowed up to Westminster to take his oath in the Exchequer before the judge. After that, he would return by barge to Blackfriars and process to St Paul's for a service of thanksgiving before going on to the Guildhall for his Banquet. Veteran onlookers knew how to move around the city to get several perspectives on the Show. Newcomers with staring country eyes stayed rooted to the same spot for hours in order to catch a mere glimpse of the pomp and circumstance that marked the occasion.

Walter Stanford himself took it all with the utmost seriousness. Dressed in the traditional robes and wearing the famous tricorne hat, he was for that day alone the father of the whole city but it was his position as an uncle that worried him. Somewhere along the way was a crazed nephew with a grudge against him and a need to nip his mayoralty in the bud. Behind his smiles and his waves and his apparent delight, therefore, was an anxiety that would not leave him. His faith had been placed in a man who was nothing more than a book holder in a theatrical company. Was his trust well-founded?

Leaving his ward, he followed the procession along a cheering avenue that led to the river. At the front of the parade were two men who bore the arms of the Mercers' Company. They were followed by a drummer, a flute-player and a man with a fife. Behind them, in blue gowns and caps and hose and blue silk sleeves, were sixteen trumpeters blowing their instruments in strident unison. Horse-drawn floats came next, each one elaborately mounted by an individual Guild and competing with each other in colour and spectacle. The Fishmongers' Ship was among the finest on display, a huge galleon that seemed to sail above the craned heads of the populace as it passed by. Another favoured contender was the Goldsmith's Castle, a quite magnificent structure that was first produced for the coronation of Richard II.

And there were many others to keep the fingers pointing and the jaws dropping.

Fittingly, it was the Mercer's Maiden Chariot which outshone them all. This pageant was a Roman chariot, some twenty feet or more high, with sides of embossed silver and surmounted by a golden canopy above which sat Fame blowing her trumpet. In the chariot sat the Mercer's Maiden. This was customarily a young and beautiful gentlewoman with a gold and jewelled coronet on her head. At the Lord Mayor's feast, she dined royally at a separate table. This year, however, there was a significant break with tradition. Instead of choosing some long-haired young lady from one of the mercers' families, Walter Stanford selected his own wife as the Maiden and she was overjoyed. Seated high above the long ribbons of yelling people, Matilda Stanford felt the thrill of being a performer and the extraordinary honour of being wife to the Lord Mayor. The journey in the chariot helped her to forget all about Lawrence Firethorn and find her husband instead.

At the rear of it all came the Lord Mayor himself. He was preceded by the Sword Bearer in his immense fur hat and by the Sergeant-at-Arms who bore the mace. Other ceremonial officers walked close by with the Chamberlain among them but Stanford paid him no attention. It was important not to arouse the suspicions of Aubrey Kenyon or of any of the others until they could all be safely apprehended. When the Lord Mayor was not bestowing a genial wave on the crowd, he was keeping one eye on the soldier who marched just ahead of him. Dressed in an armoured breastplate and wearing a steel helmet, the man trailed his pike in the same manner as his fellows but he was no ordinary member of the guard. Nicholas Bracewell had a duty that went well beyond the ceremonial.

Abel Strudwick had rowed his boat out into the middle of the river to be part of the huge armada that accompanied the procession up to Westminster. All around him were other craft with eager spectators and it gave him a feeling of superiority to think that they had simply come to gawp and goggle. Poetry had put the waterman on the Thames that day. He was there to find inspiration for some new verses, to immortalize a great event with the creative fire of his imagination. From where he sat and bobbed, he had a fine view of the parade as it moved from land to water.

First to set off was the Mercers' Barge with its coat of arms proudly displayed aloft. Behind it came the Bachelors' Barge which was followed in turn by the vessels of the other companies, strictly in order of precedence. Strudwick saw the arms of the Grocers, the Drapers, the Fishmongers—with Sir Lucas Pugsley aboard—the Goldsmiths, the Skinners, the Merchant Taylors, the Haberdashers, the Salters, the Ironmongers, the Vintners and the Clothworkers. No place for Rowland Ashway there. The alderman had to wait upon the Dyers before his Guild could step forward for attention. It was an imposing sight that was made even more vivid by the fact that the companies wore their distinctive liveries.

The waterman felt no verse stirring as yet but he remained confident. What drew his gaze now was a sight that never failed to impress and even frighten a little at a Lord Mayor's Show. Two huge and grotesque creatures were in the prow of the last barge, pretending to draw a model of Britain's Mount. Strudwick recognized them as Corinaeus and Gogmagog, fabled inhabitants of the city in ancient days.

They were giants.

Walter Stanford was vastly more confident now that he was afloat with his guard all around him. Out in the open street, he felt he was a target for a knife, an arrow, even for a sword if its owner could get close enough. He began to enjoy the procession as it sailed slowly down river between the echoing banks of applause. Nicholas was close enough to him for a brief conversation.

'Your fears were groundless, sir,' said Stanford.

'The day is yet young.'

'What harm could touch us here?'

'None, I hope,' said Nicholas.

But his instincts told him otherwise. The Lord Mayor and his retinue were standing on the upper deck of the barge so that they could be seen more clearly. Corinaeus and Gogmagog were several yards in front of them. The book holder took a professional interest in how the giants had been fashioned. They were about twelve feet high and made out of carved and gilded limewood. Skilful painters had given them hideous leering faces. Corinaeus was dressed like a barbarian warrior and sported a morning star on a chain. Gogmagog wore the costume of a Roman centurion and carried a spear and a shield that was decorated with a symbolic phoenix. Nicholas admired the strength of the men inside each of the models. They were even able to manipulate levers that made their weapons lift and fall in the air.

It was when Walter Stanford stepped forward to take a closer look at the giants that the danger came. Corinaeus made no move but Gogmagog responded at once. Through the slit in the bodywork, the man inside saw his chance and acted. Raising his spear, he tried to jab it hard at Walter Stanford but a soldier was there to parry the blow with his pike. What came next caused even more panic in the barge. Gogmagog rose feet in the air and then hurled himself directly at the Lord Mayor with a force that would have killed him had the giant made contact. But the pike of Nicholas Bracewell again did sterling duty and guided the huge wooden object over the side of the barge and into the water. The splash drenched people for twenty yards around and caused some of the smaller boats nearby to capsize.

Michael Delahaye had failed. He glared at his hated uncle with his one malignant eye then hurled a rope at the advancing guards to beat them back. Before they could get him, he had dived over the side of the barge into the river. It all happened with such speed that everyone was totally confused but Nicholas had his wits about him. Throwing off his helmet and divesting himself of his breastplate, he ran to the side of the barge and flung himself after the would-be assassin. Delahaye was strong and cleaved his way through the water but his pursuer was the better swimmer and clawed back the distance between them. Bewildered spectators on boat and bank watched in silence at the two pinheads that seemed to be floating on the waves. None of them understood the significance of what they were witnessing.

Abel Strudwick was well-placed to view the final struggle. When Nicholas caught the kicking legs of his man, the latter turned to fight, pulling a dagger from his belt and hacking madly at his assailant. But the latter got his wrist in a grip of steel that would not slacken. They struggled and splashed with frenetic energy then both disappeared beneath the dark waters. Strudwick rowed in closer and peered down but he could see nothing. Long minutes passed when nothing happened and then blood came up to the surface of the water to brighten its scum. A head soon followed, surging up with desperation so that lungfuls of air could be inhaled. The swimmer then lay on his back to recover from the fatigue of a death-grapple. The waterman rowed in close and helped Nicholas Bracewell into his boat so that he could enjoy some of the cheers of congratulation that were ringing out.

Michael Delahaye did not surface.

The atmosphere at the Queen's Head was vastly lighter now that the threat of eviction had disappeared. With the arrest of Rowland Ashway, the contract to buy the inn was effectively rescinded. The alderman would never be able to take possession of his intended purchase now. Relief was so great and comprehensive that a smile dared to flit across the face of Alexander Marwood. He had not only been reprieved from a deal which turned out to be more disadvantageous than he had thought. The landlord was also reunited with a termagant wife who had badgered him incessantly about the idiocy of his action in signing. Nocturnal reconciliation let Marwood recall happier days.

Edmund Hoode was in a generous mood. He bought pints of sack for himself and his friend then sat at the table opposite him. A week had passed since the Lord Mayor's Show but it still vibrated in the memory.

'You were the hero of the hour, Nick,' said Hoode.

'I thought but of poor Hans Kippel.'

'His death is well-revenged now. And all those other villains are locked secure away, including the Chamberlain himself. Who would have thought a man in such a place would have stooped to such crimes?'

'Temptation got the better of him, Edmund.'

'Yes,' said the other harshly. 'The same may be said of Lawrence. But for you again, that dalliance might have led us into further disaster. What an actor, Nick! But what a dreadful lecher, too! Margery has much to endure.'

'She is made of stern stuff.'

They sipped their drinks and enjoyed the comfort of being in their own home again. The Queen's Head might not be as well-appointed as some inns but it was their chosen base and its landlord was anxious to renew his dealings with them. Nicholas had negotiated a new contract that favoured the company and he contracted an important concession from Marwood. A job had to be found at the inn for a man who had been an immense help to the book holder and whose occupation was now at risk. Leonard would henceforth be working at the Queen's Head and it would be good to see his friendly face around the establishment.

Nicholas thought of another friend and smiled.

'What do you make of Abel Strudwick?' he said.

'His verse is an abomination,' snapped Hoode.

'Yet he has finally found a market. His ballad on the Lord Mayor's Show is the talk of the town. He describes my fight below the water in more detail than I could myself.'

'The fellow is a bungling wordsmith.'

'Let him have his hour, Edmund.'

'He uses rhyme, like a sword, to hack.'

'There are worse things a man may do.'

Hoode agreed and took a kinder view of the waterman. He felt a vestigial sympathy for him because of the way that he was routed at the flyting contest. It had been a fight between the world of the amateur and that of the professional. Abel Strudwick had no chance. He was entitled to his brief moment of glory as a ballad-maker. Such thoughts led Hoode on to consider the merits of the raw amateur whose passions were not inhibited by too great a knowledge of the technicalities of poetry. He recalled the Lord Mayor's banquet to which Nicholas had been bidden as an honoured guest.

'Tell me, Nick. What was it like?'

'What?'

'This play of theirs—*The Nine Giants*.'

'Do I detect jealousy here?'

'No, no, of course not,' said Hoode quickly. 'I am above such things, as you well know. My plays have held the stage for years and I fear no rival. I just wish you to tell me what this pageant of the nine worthy mercers was like.' He fished gently. 'Tedious, perhaps? Over-long and under-written? Basely put together?'

'It was very well-received,' said Nicholas.

'By Mistress Stanford?'

'By her especially.'

Hoode drooped. 'Then is my cause truly lost.'

'I liked the piece myself. It had quality.'

'What sort of quality, man?'

'Height and hardness.'

'You lose me here.'

'*The Nine Giants* resembled our own at Richmond.'

'They stood in a circle?'

'They were tall, straight and monstrously wooden.'

Edmund Hoode laughed for an hour.

THE END

*Lord Westfield's Men return
in an all new mystery . . .*

THE MAD
COURTESAN

by Edward Marston

Now in bookstores.
Published in hardcover by
St. Martin's Press.

*And now,
Chapter One of*
THE MAD COURTESAN . . .

Chapter One

NICHOLAS BRACEWELL DUCKED IN THE NICK OF TIME and the rapier whistled above his head to describe a vicious semi-circle of thwarted rage. Backing away and drawing his own weapon, he had to repulse a violent attack as his adversary closed on him at once and scythed away with murder in his heart. Here was no occasion for the finer points of swordplay. It was a wild, undisciplined tavern brawl that called for strength of arm and speed of brain. Nicholas demonstrated both in equal measure as he parried further blows, flicked his wrist to expose his target then went down on one knee as he thrust his blade straight and true into his enemy's side. There was a howl of fury mingled with disbelief as the man staggered backwards, then, dropping his sword, clasping his fatal wound with both hands and emitting one last roar of anger, he fell to the ground in a writhing heap.

The applause was paltry but well-earned and Nicholas acknowledged it with a modest smile. Though he was only the book holder with Westfield's Men, he was an expert in the mounting of stage fights and he had proved that expertise once again. The watching actors and apprentices gave him due reward with their eager palms while Nicholas helped up the now grinning corpse of Sebastian Carrick and dusted him off with a few considerate smacks. The two men were standing on the makeshift stage in the yard of the Queen's Head in Gracechurch Street, the inn where the company performed most of its work and attested its claim to be considered the leading theatrical troupe in London. One of the main reasons for its pre-eminence was the crucial influence of Nicholas Bracewell behind the scenes. He was the sheet anchor to a vessel that sailed through an almost permanent tempest and he had saved untold mariners from a gruesome death below the mountainous waves.

Sebastian Carrick was the first to offer compliments.

'You excel yourself, Nick,' he said.

'It is easy when you have the trick of it.'

'But a devilish task to learn that trick. You can instruct us all in the art of fencing, seasoned though we be. I have never before encountered such a shrewd teacher as Master Nicholas Bracewell.'

'You are an apt pupil, Sebastian.'

'Aye,' said the actor with a grin. 'A grateful one, too. I had rather be killed by you than by any man in London!'

General laughter broke out among the spectators. Sword fights were an integral part of theatre and they had to be choreographed with sufficient verve and realism to convince an audience that would press very close to the stage. The death of Sebastian Carrick had been so well-rehearsed that even those who had witnessed the sequence many times were momentarily fearful that they had indeed lost a friend and colleague. When Nicholas thrust home his blade, however, it simply passed between the side and the arm of his quarry but with a timing and accuracy born of years of experience.

Carrick gave the book holder a confiding nudge.

'I doubt that Owen will fight as fairly as you, Nick.'

'He is an able swordsman.'

'Able enough to cut me down for good and all.'

'You do him wrong, Sebastian.'

'Marry, that's *his* complaint.'

'Then must you settle your account with him.'

'I would be rid of this turbulent Welshman.'

'Soothe his turbulence.'

Owen Elias, the subject of their exchange, stood no more than a dozen yards away and glowered at his fellow-actor. He was a stock man in his thirties with broad shoulders above a barrel chest. His face was striking rather than handsome with smouldering eyes that were ignited by some dark, Celtic passion. He had good reason to resent Sebastian Carrick. Not only had the latter borrowed money from him which he was refusing to repay, he had committed what was, in the Welshman's view, the cardinal sin. He was preferred as an actor. By virtue of his grace, charm, and poise, Carrick was repeatedly cast in better roles than those offered to Elias and it rankled. Turbulence ensued.

It was time for the rehearsal to begin properly and Nicholas Bracewell took control with accustomed firmness. The stage was set for the first scene, the actors withdrew to the tiring-house, the musicians took up their positions in the gallery above. Westfield's Men steadied themselves for yet another performance of *Vincentio's Revenge*, one of the stock plays in their extensive repertoire, a brooding tragedy that was shot through with violence. Early in Act Three, the lascivious courtier, Lodovico—as played by Sebastian Carrick—would be killed in a tavern brawl by Owen Elias in a role that was not even dignified by a name. Lodovico might appear to die but it was The Stranger who suffered the more serious professional wound.

Even amid the happy turmoil of preparation, Nicholas spared a thought for the tribulations of Owen Elias. As an actor, the Welshman was incomparably better than Sebastian Carrick but the latter had physical attributes which made him more appealing and personal qualities that made him more acceptable. Tall, slim and dashing, he had the lazy confidence of a philanderer allied to an air of almost aristocratic refinement. Owen Elias was too ebullient and wilful. He was altogether too combative in urging his right to promotion within the company and he thus reviled the easy tact and plausibility which gained advantage for his rival. Nor could he forget or forgive the effortless skill with which Carrick had persuaded him to open his purse and part with money that he could ill afford to lose. *Vincentio's Revenge* was nothing beside the dire retribution that Owen Elias contemplated.

'Stand by!'

The command from Nicholas Bracewell stilled the murmur and put every man on the alert. On a signal from the book holder, Peter Digby and his musicians coaxed solemn sounds from their instruments as The Prologue entered in a black cloak to introduce the play. For the next two hours, the company reacquainted themselves with *Vincentio's Revenge* and—even though their audience consisted of no more than some curious horses and some gaping ostlers—they gave the work their full concentration. No matter how many times they had performed a piece, they never took it for granted. A play was like a sword. It needed to be polished and sharpened each time before use. Audiences detested the sight of rust and the feel of a blunt edge. Westfield's Men always kept their weaponry in good order.

When the rehearsal was over, the actors drifted off into the inn itself to take refreshment before the paying public began to arrive. Nicholas had much to do before he could join them, supervising the stagekeepers as they struck the set for Act Five prior to sweeping the boards and strewing them with rushes, making sure that costumes and properties were in their appointed places, chiding the musicians for being noticeably late with their dirge in Act Four and attending to the ever-widening responsibilities of his job. Because it had been, for the most part, a good rehearsal, he went about his work with the quiet satisfaction of one who had made a substantial contribution to the successes of the morning. He was especially pleased with the tavern brawl. Owen Elias and Sebastian Carrick had never fought with such controlled venom. It had been a highlight of the drama.

Ensconced in the taproom, The Stranger was keen to reenact the scene with his smiling Lodovico.

'Give me the money, you viper!'

'Would that I could, dear friend!' sighed Carrick.

'Friend, am I not: dear was I never!'

'I count you among my closest fellows.'

'Count out some coins instead, Sebastian.'

'You will be paid in good time.'

'I urge the reckoning now.'

'You do so in vain, Owen,' said the other with a shrug. 'Truly, I have no money, sir. I have borrowed afresh to buy myself food and drink.'

'To borrow and not repay is to steal.'

'Be patient but a little longer.'

'Give me my money, Sebastian.'

'As soon as I may.'

'Now!' yelled the fiery Welshman, grabbing him with both hands. 'Pay me forthwith or—by St David!—I'll tear you limb from limb and feed you to the innyard dogs.'

Sebastian Carrick tried to defuse the situation with an amiable laugh but it only enraged his attacker even more. Rising to his feet, Owen Elias hauled him up from his bench and flung him across the room with sudden power. Fury and envy surged up and conjoined in the Welshman's breast to send him hurtling after his honey-tongued colleague in order to belabour him unmercifully. Before he could even land the first punch, however, he was drenched from head to toe by a few gallons of cold, brackish water from one of the wooden fire buckets. Nicholas Bracewell had arrived in time to see the quarrel and to dampen it down before it got out of hand. Sebastian Carrick grinned with relief but Owen Elias only glowered as the whole taproom filled with derisive laughter. Chafed but chastened, he did not resist when the book holder hurried both him and his fellow out into the yard. Nicholas did not mince his words and his soft West Country vowels were hardened into a curt threat.

'Do you seek dismissal from the company, sirs?'

'Indeed not,' said Elias.

'Nothing would grieve us more,' said Carrick.

'Brawling will not be tolerated,' emphasized Nicholas with a warning finger. 'We are only here at the Queen's Head on sufferance and we must give our nagging landlord no more excuse to send us hence. Save your argument for some private place or, better still, resolve it here and part as friends. Would you have Westfield's Men evicted over some petty difference between you?'

'It is not petty,' said Elias, still dripping wet. 'It is a very serious matter and I will be answered.'

Carrick smiled. 'That bucket was an eloquent reply.'

'You owe me six shillings, sir!'

'First, do but loan me a further five.'

'Scurvy rogue!'

'Peace, peace!' ordered Nicholas. 'Raised voices solve nothing. Let's hear this out calmly.' He turned to Carrick. 'Tell your tale first, Sebastian.'

'But *I* am the injured party!' wailed Elias.

'Your turn will come,' said Nicholas, quelling him with a glance. 'Your temper needs more time to cool.'

The Welshman knew better than to argue with the book holder. A big, broad-shouldered man with a muscular strength beneath his affable manner, Nicholas could assert himself if the need arose. His fair hair and full beard danced gently in the wind but his stern eyes kept Owen Elias subdued as the facts of the case were laid out. Sebastian Carrick made light of the whole business, promising that the debt would soon be paid and apologizing for any harm he had unwittingly inflicted on his fellow. Elias took several deep breaths before he trusted himself to words again but they came out in a remarkably measured and reasonable way. When both pleas had been voiced, the actors waited on Nicholas Bracewell to pronounce judgement.

'You are both in the wrong,' he said. 'Sebastian, you should have repaid this money long since. Owen, you should not have provoked a brawl to gain your purpose. Is that much agreed between us?' The actors nodded. 'Then let us find a way out of this dilemma. A creditor wants something that a debtor does not possess.'

'You have hit on the problem, Nick,' said Carrick with a nonchalant shrug. 'My purse is quite empty.'

'It is *always* empty!' challenged Elias.

'A man must live, sweet sir.'

'Live, yes, but not prey upon his fellows!'

'Pleasure comes at a price.'

'Then have it at your own expense and not mine.'

Nicholas interceded. 'Hear my device. It may suit the both

of you in equal parts. Sebastian has no money until I pay his wage at the end of the week. Master your pain and indignation until then, Owen, and I will save one shilling of that wage for you.'

'It is not enough,' said Elias.

'It is far too much!' exclaimed Carrick.

But Nicholas stuck by his decision and—though neither man was pleased—both came to accept the compromise. Owen Elias realized that payment by instalments was better than nothing at all and he took comfort from the fact that it was Sebastian Carrick who had protested most. Evasion of his creditors was an article of faith with the latter. The only thing he ever willingly repaid was a debt of honour incurred at the gaming table. Money that was charmed from the purses of colleagues was his to keep. Friends were fair game.

He sighed. 'It is a grisly resolution, Nick, but I will abide by it. Here is my hand on it.' Owen Elias shook the proferred hand. 'Well, now that matter is done, I must away to borrow afresh or I will dwindle into complete poverty!'

Sebastian Carrick gave a mock bow then sauntered back into the taproom with an amused resignation. His attitude produced more sparks from Owen Elias.

'Look at him, Nick! Do but look at the saucy knave!'

'The dispute is settled, Owen. Be content.'

'He is a vile robber!'

'Your money will be restored.'

'It is my reputation that he is stealing,' protested the other. 'I am the finer actor yet *he* filches the finer parts. *I* have laboured to establish myself with Westfield's Men yet this upstart displaces me within a few months. It is not just, it is not kind, it is not bearable.' He extended his arms wide in supplication. 'What am I to do, Nick?'

'Endure these slights with dignity.'

'Never!'

'Make friends with Sebastian. It is the only way.'

'I would sooner consort with a leper.'

'Do not come to blows with him again,' warned Nicholas.

'I dare not,' said Elias with lilting menace. 'For next time, nobody would be able to stop me. I would kill him.'

Cornelius Gant pointed the musket at the horse's head and callously pulled the trigger. There was a loud report and a cloud of smoke went up from the weapon. The animal staggered bravely for a few seconds then sank to the ground in a sorry heap and began to twitch violently as the last ounces of life poured out of its noble carcass. It was a grotesque and sickening sight. When its death throes were finally over and its frenzy mercifully abated, it lay cold and silent on the cobblestones, its black coat gilded by the sun and its body twisted into such an unnatural shape that it drew groans of horror from all who had witnessed the summary slaughter. A happy crowd became hostile in a flash. They cursed the cruel owner and formed a ring of gathering fury around him. Cornelius Gant was defiant. As they closed in, baying for retribution, he held the musket like a club and threatened to strike. The tension was heightened until it was on the verge of an explosion.

Then the horse neighed. As if waking from an afternoon sleep in a verdant meadow, it sat up, whinnied mischievously and gazed around its dumbstruck audience. Gant's ugly old face was split by a toothless grin as he saw the incredulity on every side. After entertaining the throng with all manner of clever tricks, horse and man had reached the climax of their act in the most dramatic way. Cornelius Gant had shot Nimbus dead and the animal had expired to such convincing effect that all present were completely taken in. Many were so relieved to see the horse alive again that they burst into tears. Relief gave way to joy and expressed itself in a riot of applause. Gant chose his moment well. He clicked his fingers and Nimbus got up from the ground to shake itself all over before knocking its owner playfully sideways with its rump. As fresh mirth greeted this latest trick, the horse rounded on Gant, took the brim of his hat in its teeth then lifted it off with another whinny. The hat was dropped into the middle of the yard and the crowd responded generously. A waterfall of coins gushed into the receptacle. Horse and owner took a bow in unison.

Cornelius Gant was a wiry man of middle height, shrunk

by age and battered by experience. His apparel was that of a discharged soldier but his piggy eyes and distorted features suggested less honourable employment. Only when he grinned did he look even remotely personable. In gratitude for his handsome performance, however, the crowd ignored his defects of nature and showered him with congratulation. The whole inn buzzed with excited comment. Gant was glad that they had stopped at Coventry. Its welcoming hostelries had given him rich pickings for three days but it was now time to take his horse and its wondrous feats on the next stage of their journey to the capital. It was there in London, in the finest city in Europe, that true fame and fortune lay and nothing less would suffice his vaulting ambition.

Well-wishers sent them off with ringing cheers.

'Nimbus is the greatest horse alive!'

'And even greater when he is dead!'

'It is the most amazing sight that ever I saw.'

'No heart can resist them.'

'They will spread merriment wherever they go.'

'That animal is a gift from God.'

It was left to the waddling publican of the Shepherd and Shepherdess to sum up the feelings of his customers. Gant and Nimbus had not only astounded the onlookers, they had been good for business. Wiping podgy hands on his beer-stained apron, the publican beamed gratefully after the departing guests and gave a knowing chuckle.

'They will conquer London within the week!'

Lawrence Firethorn was in excellent spirits as he sat back in his chair and savoured the last of the Canary wine in his goblet. Flushed with success after another performance in the title role of *Vincentio's Revenge*, he was celebrating his triumph in a private room at the Queen's Head with Barnaby Gill and Edmund Hoode. All three of them were sharers with the company, ranked players who were named in the royal patent for Westfield's Men and who were thus entitled to a portion of any income. Apprentices were given their keep and a valuable training, hired men—like Sebastian Carrick and Owen Elias—earned a weekly wage but it was the sharers who were the real beneficiaries. Not only did they get their slice of any profits, they also had first claim on the leading parts in any play. Their status was paramount. In the eyes of the law and the regulatory agencies, they *were* the company and other members of the troupe were merely their employees. Westfield's Men had ten sharers but its operational decisions were invariably taken by its three senior figures. Lawrence Firethorn dominated that trio.

'I was in good voice this afternoon,' he boasted.

'Too good a voice,' said Gill testily. 'You roared the lines like a wounded lion. Speak the speeches as they are written, Lawrence. Do not deafen your fellows with ranting.'

'The audience worshipped my Vincentio.'

'So might the rest of London for they must all have heard it. Why must you bellow so much? Even your silence is beset by too much noise.'

'Tragedy calls for sound!'

'Your sound was certainly tragic, sir.'

Firethorn bristled. 'At least I did not whisper my words like an old man muttering into his beard.'

'I conveyed meaning with every subtle gesture.'

'It is as well you did not rely on your voice, Barnaby. You sounded like a male varlet plying his foul trade in the stews of Southwark!'

'I'll brook no more of this!' exclaimed Gill, using a quivering fist to pound the table around which they sat. 'I demand an abject apology.'

'Demand what you wish. You will get nothing.'

'Gentlemen, gentlemen,' said Edmund Hoode wearily as he interrupted yet another of the all-too-frequent arguments between the two men. 'Both of you gave of your best in *Vincentio's Revenge*. I could not fault either performance. Each was soft enough, each was loud enough. Enough of this vain disputation. We have business in hand.'

Gill stood on his dignity. 'I have been insulted.'

'And so you will be again, sir,' said Firethorn. 'You invite ridicule. If you will hiss like a serpent on stage, we will find you a place in the menagerie at the Tower.'

'They will lock *you* in the neighbouring cage for they surely have need of a trumpeting elephant!'

'Desist, sirs!' said Hoode, throwing himself between them once again to prevent the elephant from trampling on the serpent and to stop the serpent from wriggling its way up the elephant's trunk to spit its venom into the brain. 'This will not serve our cause at all.'

He poured more wine for both of them then gave them even more liberal doses of flattery. They slowly allowed themselves to be soothed and to forget their latest verbal duel. Lawrence Firethorn was the acknowledged leader of the company, a striking man in every way, hugely talented and hugely ambitious, blessed with genius but cursed with the vanity of his profession. Alert, handsome and muscular, he dressed like a gallant in the latest fashion. Barnaby Gill was shorter, older and less well-favoured. The established clown, he had an uncanny ability to reduce any audience to hysterical laughter with his comic songs, gestures, dances and facial expressions. Offstage, he was a lurking melancholic with a weakness for the society of pretty boys that had made the gibe about a male varlet particularly painful. He chose his apparel with great care but erred on the side of ostentation. Firethorn and Gill might wrestle incessantly in private but they worked in perfect harmony on stage.

One of Edmund Hoode's primary duties was to sustain that harmony by writing parts in which each man could display his undoubted brilliance. As an actor-playwright, he was required to produce a regular stream of new plays for Westfield's Men as well as to polish and adapt his earlier work for revival. Unlike the others, Hoode was not ensnared by pride or obsessed with the need to impress. Tall, slim and clean-shaven, he was a gentler soul, a dreamer and a romantic. His pale, round, wide-eyed moon of a face had been shaped to hang in the sky of unrequited love and he had no taste for the strident confrontations beloved by his companions.

Lawrence Firethorn addressed the issue before them.

'Gentlemen, we seek another sharer,' he said solemnly. 'Old Cuthbert is to retire and he must be replaced.'

239

'I do not agree,' said Gill.

'Wisdom never commended itself to you.'

'If we lose one of our number, we have a larger slice of the receipts. Old Cuthbert served the company well but he serves it better still by letting us divide up his share.'

'Put need before greed, Barnaby,' said Firethorn. 'Ten is a good, round number and we will hold fast to it. So, sirs. Who is to be brought into the fold?'

Hoode was unequivocal. 'If it were left to me, I would choose Nick Bracewell without a qualm. He is the rock on which Westfield's Men build their entertainments. Take but him away and we would all be sucked into the quagmire.'

'Master Bracewell is a mere book holder,' said Gill petulantly. 'We must not even consider bestowing such an honour upon him.'

'If worth held any sway, the honour is his already.'

'Indeed, Edmund,' said Firethorn. 'Nick is pure gold and nobody loves him more or values him higher than I. But he is not, alas, our new sharer. We must look elsewhere.'

'Outside the company?' said Gill.

'Inside,' said Hoode. 'It rewards loyalty.'

Firethorn nodded. 'We promote from within. It breeds good will and ensues us a known friend. I think there are but two men in the company whom we should weigh in the balance here. Sebastian Carrick and Owen Elias.'

'Then it must be Sebastian,' decided Hoode.

'The Welshman for me,' said Gill, puffing at his pipe. 'He has been with us longer and learned more eagerly. Owen has a temper, I know, but this elevation might curtail it and turn him into a gentleman.'

'Sebastian already *is* a gentleman,' said Hoode. 'He can grace the stage where Owen can only occupy it. I do not deny that Wales has given us the finer actor here. Owen Elias has qualities that Sebastian could never match. He has a voice and presence to rival Lawrence himself but he also has a wayward streak that goes ill with responsibility. As a hired man, he is an asset to the company: as a share, he might turn out to be a liability.'

'I side with you, Edmund,' said Firethorn. 'Sebastian has the better disposition. Sebastian Carrick it is.'

'Owen Elias,' insisted Gill.

'Carrick.'

'He gets my vote, too,' said Hoode. 'He is our sharer.'

'Then where will he find his proportion?' Gill puffed hard then exhaled a cloud of smoke. 'Sebastian has to *buy* his share. He is reckless with his own money and even more reckless with borrowed coin. Owen Elias is conscientious and frugal. Sebastian is too fond of his pleasures.'

'No man can be blamed for that,' said Firethorn easily, 'or none of us would escape whipping. But you raise a fair question, Barnaby, and it must be answered. How will Sebastian furnish us with his investment?'

'He has many rich friend,' said Hoode.

Gill grimaced. 'They are poorer for his acquaintance.'

'He will find the money somehow. He longs to be a true member of the company. Stay with him, Lawrence.'

'A doubt begins to form,' admitted Firethorn.

'We have the means to still it,' said Hoode. 'Let us not commit ourselves too soon. We will put Sebastian to the test by offering him a half-share in the company. Should he come through that trial, he takes up Old Cuthbert's place. Is this not the best way?'

Lawrence Firethorn stroked his dark, pointed beard as he pondered. Barnaby Gill tapped out his pipe on the edge of the table and sniffed noisily. After long consideration, both men nodded their agreement. Sebastian Carrick would be put on probation. It remained only to determine the length of that probation and the scale of his financial contribution.

Gill foresaw a possible difficulty.

'How can we persuade him that a half-share is a form of distinction rather than a humiliation?'

'I'll make light of that task,' said Firethorn airily.

'Sebastian will see it as one step towards full glory,' said Hoode. 'He will understand our caution.'

Gill snorted. 'It is more than caution in my case.'

'Throw aside all objection,' urged the playwright.

'Yes,' reinforced Firethorn. 'To win his confidence, we

241

must show him ours. Have no fears about Sebastian Carrick. He will prove a fortunate choice. I'd stake my life on it.'

Turnmill Street was the most notorious thoroughfare in the whole of Clerkenwell, a long, dark, dangerous, disease-ridden strip of sin that ran parallel with the River Fleet before bending round to thrust itself into Cow Cross with bestial familiarity. In its fetid lanes and alleys, in its narrow courts and yards, in its filthy taverns and tenements, all manner of lewd delight was bought and sold. Turnmill punks were the wildest and most willing in London and they made nightly assignations with courtiers and commoners, soldiers and sailors, merchants and men of law, gapers from the country and gallants from the town. At the Sign of the Cock, the Fleur de Lys, the Blue Axe, the Red Lattice, the Rose and other bold outrages against decency, a lustful client could send his soul to eternal damnation and purchase the pox in exchange. Turnmill Street was a warren of infamy. Stews and gambling dens, inns and ordinaries, courtesans and cata-mites knew but one landlord. He dwelt in Hell itself.

Of all the houses of resort, none was more popular than the Pickt-hatch, so-called because its upper half-door was surrounded with spikes for security. The pickt-hatch was a common name and sign for brothels but the establishment in Turnmill Street outstretched its rivals in venery. It was run by a wobbling mound of flesh named Bess Bidgood and its reputation brought in ample custom for the large stable of whores whom the motherly hostess kept beneath her wicked roof. Quality and quantity were on tap at the Pickt-hatch.

The young man who lay naked on the bed in a state of joyous near-exhaustion had opted for quality and he had not been disappointed. When Bess Bidgood had lined up her ladies for him to choose at his own discretion, his practised eye had picked out the leanest of them. Frances was not the plump and eager wench in red taffeta that most men coveted but a thin, watchful, feline creature with a carnal charm that was all her own. He wanted an angry lover and none could have been more feral than this wildcat. She bit and fought him every inch of the way and left her own special trademark

242

on his back as she raked it from shoulder to buttock with searing fingernails, pain and pleasure intermingling so closely that they became one. He was in ecstasy.

Frances was content. Here was no sweating husband who talked of his wife, no crude swaggerer who pumped mindlessly into her, no drunken fool whose manhood failed them both and who snored on top of her. She had found a real lover for once, a handsome swain who sensed her needs and matched them with his own. As she ran a hand down the vivid red furrows on his back, she admired the sleek muscularity of his body and relished the feel of his soft beard between her breasts. In a squalid room whose dank walls were covered in painted cloth, they shared a mild sensation of love. It was soon over, however. He rose and dressed while she waited for payment, combing her long black hair with languid movements and resigning herself to more brutish passion from her next client.

His smile was warm and grateful. Dropping some crowns into the goblet on the floor, he slipped an arm around her to give her one last, long kiss then he opened the door and went swiftly out. Frances reached instinctively for the goblet and found it empty. His farewell embrace had been a cruel trick to recover his money and she was left with nothing but a sour memory. Grabbing the knife beneath her pillow, she raced out into the murky passageway but he was already vanishing down the steps. She went quickly back to her bedroom window and flung it open, waiting until her deceitful lover came out into the street before giving a signal with the knife. She then turned back into the room and flung the weapon with such force at the door that it sunk two inches into the wood and vibrated almost as angrily as she did.

The young man, meanwhile, ambled happily along and told himself that the gift of his body was reward enough for any woman and that—by rights—Frances should have paid him. He laughed aloud as he imagined her horror at finding the goblet raided by his sly hand and congratulated himself on getting so much out of the Pickt-hatch for so little. It had been a most pleasant night.

'Stay, sir!' called a voice behind him.

'Why so?'

He turned to ask the last question of his life and got the answer in the shape of a hand-axe that came out of the darkness with vengeful power to cleave his head open and put an extra inch between his staring eyes. Blood drenched him in an instant and the open mouth filled with gore. Before he hit the ground and lay in the offal, he was dead.

Sebastian Carrick had paid for his pleasure after all.

The theatrical world of Elizabethan England has never been so deadly. These novels of history and intrigue by

EDWARD MARSTON

are published by Fawcett Books.

THE MERRY DEVILS

All was in an uproar backstage with Lord Westfield's Men when a mysterious third demon appeared onstage with the two that had been written into the script. The next time the play was given, only *one* devil appeared while another lay murdered behind the curtain. This Elizabethan acting troupe must confront the terror of a London madhouse and the sermons of a Puritan fanatic if they are to solve this mystery.

THE QUEEN'S HEAD

An actor in the esteemed theatrical company called Lord Westfield's Men is murdered in a barroom brawl. The company is sworn to avenge his death, but a command performance for Queen Elizabeth I makes life very complicated indeed.

THE TRIP TO JERUSALEM

Lord Westfield's Men take to the highroad in search of fresh audiences untouched by the horrors of the Black Plague. Wherever they go, they are thwarted by misfortune, and the last act of a bloody drama is about to begin.

EDWARD
MARSTON

Available in bookstores everywhere.